TRUE
BLUE

A POLICEMAN'S STORY

By Jonathan Nerlinger

ISBN: 0-75965-983-4

This book is printed on acid free paper.

1stBooks - rev. 9/17/01

Dedication

This novel is dedicated to all of the men and women who wear a badge in this country. Their badges are symbols of Pride, Honor, Integrity, Courage and Righteousness.

In different parts of this great land, they are known by different names. But whether they are called Police Officers, Deputy Sheriffs, Highway Patrol Officers, Troopers, Federal or State Agents, their mission is the same.

They protect our communities and make us feel safe and secure in our homes, and in our daily lives. They are a special breed of people, deserving of our respect and thanks. They are truly "Society's Protectors."

This book is also dedicated to Sandra, without whose inspiration, encouragement and support, it would never have been written.

To Raphael; A GREAT MAN
AND A GREAT FRIEND.

Chapter One

The First Years

John Nolan spent the first part of his childhood in a relatively small town back east. His parents, David and Rebecca, were decent, hardworking people of European descent. They had immigrated to the United States of America a few years before John was born. John has an older sister named Rita. She was born the month his parents arrived. John has many fond memories of his childhood. He remembers the closeness of his family. The warmth and tenderness of his mother, the strength and righteousness of his father and the support and love of his sister.

Although poor when it came to material possessions, John's family was rich in love and devotion. John remembers that his parents both worked and had to struggle to make ends meet. But, even though his parents worked long, hard hours, they always found a way to spend quality time with their children. John's core values are very strong. He attributes this to his parents and their teachings.

The learning process began early in his life. John's parents taught him to believe in God and family. He learned to respect others and to treat them as he would want to be treated. He learned to appreciate cultural and ethnic diversity. John learned that being honest is the only way to live one's life. He learned that honor, integrity, high standards and high moral values should never be compromised. He understood about responsibility and trustworthiness as a youngster.

The family lived in the poor section of town. Unfortunately, in most towns and cities across this great nation, the poor section of town usually means the rough part of town as well. In order to survive, John had to learn to defend himself at an early age. Notwithstanding the fact that he was a gentleman's gentleman, John's father was an incredibly strong and naturally tough man. He was also an experienced fighter and a decorated World War II soldier. He instructed his son in the art of self-defense. Of equal importance was the fact he taught John to fight only as a last resort. John learned it is better to walk away whenever possible and to always endeavor to use brain power instead of muscle power.

John's parents lived by their own teachings. They conducted their lives exactly as they taught their children; do the right thing, live a clean life and help others, particularly those less fortunate than you. John has many memories in which his parents helped others. Even though his family didn't have much, his parents always found a way to help those less fortunate. From feeding the hungry, to donating warm clothes in the winter, they always helped others as best they could. John never forgot…

In the early sixties, John's parents moved the family to sunny California where they settled in the suburbs of Los Angeles. John finished high school there but, in his senior year alone, he had the dubious distinction of being the only student in his class to come very close to being expelled not once, but twice, for fighting. There had been two separate incidents in less than a month.

John simply could not allow himself to stand by and watch as one of the school bullies picked on an obviously smaller, weaker student. The idea of watching a scared student being pushed around by a teasing, taunting bully did not sit well with him. Whenever John witnessed one of these incidents, he felt compelled to intervene on behalf of the "victim." That usually meant fighting the bully along with the certainty of winding up in the principal's office. Hence, the near expulsions.

As the reward for his efforts, John was kicked off of the varsity football team. That really hurt him. He was an excellent athlete who loved his football. But, on the other hand, he had no regrets for his actions. He believed he had done the right thing. John's father went to the school to try to convince the principal John had done the right thing and that he was a fine boy. The football coach also spoke up on his behalf. The principal concurred John was a good student and a fine athlete. He even agreed there were mitigating circumstances, however, he would not condone John's actions and he would not reconsider his decision to kick John off the football team.

It was because of incidents such as these that John started thinking about becoming a policeman. After high school, he chose administration of justice as his college major. He had nothing but respect and admiration for police officers. After all, the teachings of his parents were exemplified in the life and behavior of a police officer. Honesty, honor, integrity, courage and respect were just a few of the key words they lived by. Policemen had always been heroes in John's eyes. They made the streets safe for women and children and they protected the meek from the evil predators of our society. Besides, the uniforms looked absolutely great and the badges were strong symbols of pride, honor and courage. John had made up his mind. He would become a police officer.

While still attending college and working part time in a grocery store, John applied for the police department. He had a somewhat steady girlfriend named Debbie. She and John had been together on and off since their high school days. However, when she found out John had actually applied to become a police officer, she told him she could not envision herself dealing with that type of life—always wondering if her loved one would come home. It was obvious that John cared for Debbie, however, nothing was going to stop him from his chosen path. The two had numerous discussions on the subject, however they never reached any definitive resolution. Ultimately, John and Debbie decided it was time to go their separate ways.

After a very lengthy testing and hiring process, John received his notification in the mail. He'd made it! He was hired and given a reporting date for the academy. He immediately called his parents to tell them the news. When they found out, they felt both pride and concern. They were pleased that their son had chosen such a noble and respectable profession, however, they were also quite concerned for his safety.

John and his parents spent several hours sitting around the kitchen table that night, drinking coffee, reminiscing, and eating the pastries Mom always baked and had on hand. John acknowledged the fact that his parents were very concerned for his safety. He reassured them he would be fine and, at the ripe old age of twenty-two, John Nolan found himself preparing to report for his first day at the police academy.

Chapter Two

The Academy

Sixteen weeks of hell coming up, Nolan thought as he drove his aging sedan towards the academy that early morning in the fall of 1971. Nolan had heard all of the horror stories of the academy. He knew it would be full stress every day. He knew he would be evaluated constantly. Drill Instructors, or D.I.'s as they are commonly called, would be looking for any sign of physical or psychological weakness.

He was told that if any of the D.I.'s determined a cadet was even questionable, that cadet would be terminated and bounced out of the academy so fast, it would make the cadet's head spin. Couple that pressure with the constant stress of keeping academic grades up and doing well on the physical training portion of the curriculum, it was no wonder there were so many cadets who quit in just the first week of training.

Nolan entered the academy grounds and drove slowly to the parking area. He was thirty minutes early. Although he was nervous, Nolan felt confident, determined and very happy. He thought he looked pretty sharp too. As instructed, he wore a suit and carried an attaché case for his first day. As he entered the cadet parking area, Nolan encountered a police officer who looked as though he had just stepped out of a recruiting brochure. He was obviously in great shape, and he wore a meticulously tailored uniform complete with soft hat. He glared at Nolan and yelled, "What are you looking at, you idiot? Park your car and get over here!"

Nolan quickly parked his car, exited with briefcase in hand and ran over to the officer. "Are you here to become a policeman?" the officer asked in an obviously sarcastic tone. Nolan replied, "Yes sir!" "Then double-time it over there and line up in alphabetical order with the rest of the idiots." The officer pointed to a group of men and women standing in line about 50 yards away. "Sir, yes sir," he replied. As Nolan was running towards the others, he thought, "What the hell did I get myself into?" Nolan found his position in line and then watched, as the same scenario he had encountered with the officer in the parking lot, played out over and over again as other cadets arrived.

At precisely 0800 hours, one sergeant and four officers, including the one Nolan had encountered in the parking lot, introduced themselves to the group numbering eighty-six cadets. "Look around at the faces of the people next to you, in front of you and behind you," the sergeant said. "I can guarantee you that by the end of this week, at least twenty of those faces will be gone." The sergeant went on to announce that by midpoint in the training, another twenty cadets would be history. "If you have what it takes to make it, you'll graduate in a class of forty or less."

After those inspiring words, Nolan and the others were oriented to the facility. At the noon lunch break, one of the D.I.'s announced that ordinarily, lunch consisted of thirty minutes. However, because the class was in dire need of marching practice, until further notice, the lunch period would consist of five minutes for eating and twenty-five minutes for marching practice. The mind games have begun, Nolan mused as he gobbled down his sandwiches.

As advertised, after exactly five minutes had elapsed, one of the D.I.'s lined the class up and the next twenty-five minutes were spent practicing marching maneuvers. Immediately following marching drill, cadets were assigned their lockers, their equipment and their classroom seating assignments. In addition, each cadet was loaded down with reams of paperwork for study and review.

Nolan looked at his watch at about 4:15 p.m. that long first day. Almost over, he thought as he sighed. Just then, one of the D.I.'s clad in shorts, a T-shirt and running shoes, announced to the class they would be going on a run in their street clothes. That made Nolan angry because he didn't have a lot of money and he had bought this, his one and only suit, to wear during all of the phases of the testing procedure, and as ordered, for this very first day of training at the academy.

Off they went on a seemingly endless two-mile run. Many of the cadets did not keep up. They simply could not make it. Other cadets ran off to the side and could be heard vomiting. The D.I.'s really seemed to get a lot of enjoyment out of watching people hurl their lunch. As sickened cadets were in the process of vomiting, one of the D.I.'s would run up and ask, "Did your lunch taste better the first time, maggot?" The remainder of the D.I.'s would then all laugh heartily, almost in unison. It was quite obvious this was not the first time they had performed this routine.

Because of running that distance in street shoes, Nolan's feet were killing him by the time the run was completed. The cadets were lined up once again in the now familiar training and marching area. Nolan was all sweated through and felt demoralized. As he looked around at his fellow cadets, Nolan could see by their body language that most of them were disgusted and demoralized as well. The class was called to attention, and prior to dismissing the cadets, the D.I. ordered them back at 0630 hours the following morning.

Nolan hung his head and walked back to his car slowly and quietly that first day. He was having second thoughts about his career selection. Nolan remembered his father's words at the kitchen table the night he told his parents of his acceptance into the academy. "They're going to mess with your mind—first they'll tear you down as a group. They'll tear through you and eliminate the weak. Then, they'll test you one by one to see what you're made of. Finally, by the end of your training period, they will have shaped those who remained into a cohesive and capable unit. All for one, and one for all. Standard military ops."

On the drive home, Nolan did some soul searching to determine if police work was what he really wanted. In his own mind, he methodically validated all of his reasons for deciding on a career in law enforcement. The answer came to him very quickly and with great certainty. He was determined to become a police officer, and neither mind games, nor a difficult academic curriculum, nor a heavy-duty physical training regimen would keep him from reaching his goal. Nolan resolved to go forward every day of the academy with vigor and tenacity. He would never again doubt his career choice.

By the start of the third week of training, Nolan noticed that trends had already begun to emerge. What the sergeant had told the class on the very first day was accurate. They had lost about twenty-five people by that point in the training. The academic leaders in the class had already established themselves. So too, had the physical training leaders. Cadets were tested weekly in each area and the results posted for all to see. Nolan felt fortunate. He was working hard and was in the upper portion of his class in both academic and physical training scores. The D.I.'s kept up the pressure and stress on all of the cadets, constantly looking for those who showed any sign of weakness.

During the seventh week of training, Nolan came down with the flu. Fearing the wrath of his D.I.'s if he dared to call in sick, he reported for duty as usual. During physical training that first day he had the flu, the class went on a four-mile run and completed a series of wind sprints thereafter. Following the wind sprints, they practiced weaponless defense techniques and one-on-one fighting.

Towards the end of that training segment, Nolan's flu-weakened body began to show signs of fatigue. He was having a tough day. One of the D.I.'s noticed that Nolan was having a bad day and that he was sick. He called Nolan off to the side and asked him if he was going to give up and quit. Before Nolan could answer, the D.I. taunted him further by telling him that if he quit, he could go home, drink hot tea and, "have mommy take care of you." Nolan responded by telling the D.I. he would never quit. The D.I. in turn demanded, "In that case, drop down and give me fifty." Out of sheer determination, Nolan quickly pumped out fifty push-ups and stood up to face the D.I. The D.I. did not utter another word. He simply turned and walked away. Nolan made it through the rest of that day and the balance of the week.

The next couple of weeks came and went without too much fan-fare. In the tenth week, there was a morning when the criminal law instructor could not make it to lecture the class because he had been subpoenaed to court. Having been notified too late, the D.I.'s had no replacement lecturer, and no class syllabus from which to teach the cadets. And, the next lecturer was not scheduled to arrive for another hour. In an obvious effort to kill some time and have some fun at the cadets' expense, the D.I.'s decided to pick cadets at random and have them go up to the front of the class. There, they were given a topic and had to immediately begin lecturing their fellow cadets on that particular topic. Hooray, another mind game.

It was readily apparent the D.I.'s just wanted to see if the chosen cadet had the wherewithal to get up in front of the class and give an impromptu lecture or speech. The D.I.'s made no attempt to hide the fact that they were having a great time, and they gave some very bizarre topics to the succession of cadets ordered to the podium. Nolan hoped time would pass quickly and the D.I.'s would grow weary of their game. No such luck. The seventh cadet chosen to address the class was none other than Nolan. He stepped briskly to the podium and turned to face his classmates and his D.I's, whose desks were positioned behind those of the cadets.

One of the D.I.'s bellowed, "Okay Nolan, give us a five-minute speech on the love life of a Tibetan Yak and an African Tse Tse Fly." For just a very brief moment, Nolan stared at the D.I. and thought he was insane.

However, realizing this was a test, and being quick on his feet, Nolan said, "Well, this just happens to be a topic with which I'm very familiar. You see, when I was a young child, my family and I lived in Tibet and I had a pet yak. I really liked my yak. Every day, I would brush my yak and take my yak for a walk. I frequently watched as this one particular Tse Tse fly would approach my yak. Interestingly enough..." "That's enough, Nolan, sit down," the D.I. hollered, as he laughed out loud. Eight additional cadets would become "podium victims" before the next lecturer mercifully arrived.

By the twelfth week of academy training, only a few cadets considered borderline remained in the class. The D.I.'s, like a swarming brood of vultures awaiting the death of an injured animal, stayed on them all the time to see if they would break, or in a couple of cases, bring up their test scores. Lecturers who had taught the cadets with regularity since the very first week would arrive to teach their respective classes, and they would look in amazement at the dwindling number of cadets.

Several of the "regular" instructors made comments such as, "Pretty soon, we'll be conducting this class in a phone booth," and, "Your D.I.'s have really torn through this class." In fact, that was the case. The D.I.'s had never let up. It was hardcore full stress from the very first day of training and that discipline had continued right into the twelfth week.

The twelfth week also brought about the time for yet another mind game. One morning, cadets were bused to a private swimming club. Academy staff had made arrangements for the class to spend the morning at the facility because the swim club was closed for the "off-season." No members of the public or the club would be present. However, there was another reason this particular location had been selected. It had a thirty-eight foot diving platform. Cadets would be ordered to jump off of the platform, swim several laps and then, when they had little or no energy left, they would be required to effect a mock rescue of a 165 pound dummy.

Nolan remembered that winter morning at the pool had been a particularly cold one. Cadets, clad only in swimming gear, did whatever they could to stay warm until it was their turn. One by one, the cadets were summoned, ordered to climb the platform, and proceed with the exercise. Many of the cadets, including Nolan, had never dived off of such a high platform or diving board. But, no one dared to complain or utter any words of protest or concern. No one wanted to be singled out and ridiculed by the D.I.'s.

Nolan and several of his classmates noticed that one of their fellow cadets, Dave Brown, seemed especially nervous. Brown was normally very cool, calm and collected. He was near the top of the class academically and had scored the maximum number of points on every physical training test since week one. When it was his turn, Brown climbed the platform. When he was given the signal, he hesitated momentarily and then made his jump. As Brown was falling from the platform there was a look of horror on his face as he screamed, "I can't swim!" Brown hit the water and promptly sank to the bottom.

It took a few seconds for peoples' brains to register what Brown had said just before he hit the water. Then suddenly, as if by prearranged timing, ten to fifteen cadets and all of the D.I.'s dove into the water after Brown. Ultimately, Brown was rescued and dragged to the shallow end. His body was limp. His skin color was turning pale and his lips already had a bluish hue. One of the D.I's began C.P.R. in an attempt to bring Brown back. Fortunately, after just a few breaths, Brown began coughing and vomiting a lot of water. He would be okay.

None of Brown's fellow classmates had a chance to talk to him that day. A paramedic unit and an ambulance arrived at the pool almost immediately following the incident. Even though he protested vehemently, Brown was transported to a local hospital for observation. The next morning, back at the academy, Nolan, his classmates and all of the D.I.'s were glad to see Brown report for duty. When fellow cadets asked Brown why he hadn't told the D.I.'s he couldn't swim, he replied, "I didn't want them to think I was chicken. I didn't want to be singled out because I was afraid they would fire me."

Driving home that evening after hearing Brown's reason for jumping in the water without knowing how to swim, Nolan thought, "Imagine how bad that guy wants this job. He was willing to risk his life to avoid incurring ridicule and possible termination because of a weakness. Not knowing how to swim is not a weakness. Why didn't he just tell them?" Admittedly, Nolan had a little trouble dealing with that one. He wondered if he and the other cadets were determined, or simply brainwashed. His thoughts lingered on this topic for the better part of the evening. However, after a reality check, he dismissed the issue and focused on the work he had to do to prepare for the following day.

By Monday of the fourteenth week, the cadets, including Nolan, were beginning to display an increased air of confidence about them. Collectively, their academic scores were well above par. They were one of the highest scoring classes ever in the physical training and weaponless defense category and, as mandated by their D.I.'s, each and every cadet had achieved the minimum rank of "expert" at the shooting range. This was one squared-away outfit. Graduation day was now within their reach. The metamorphosis from civilian to rookie cop was almost complete.

That week, the class was scheduled for three days of driver training and pursuit training. The entire class had looked forward to this training. Nolan was excited too. He had not told anyone about his amateur car racing experience, or that he had won several trophies for slalom racing. After their arrival at the training site, the class was split into small groups. There were several instructors for each group. Because the class was so small, the teacher to student ratio was almost one to one. It was going to be a great three days.

Nolan's first task was the skid pad. Assigned to an instructor and driving a beat-up, old jalopy, Nolan was ordered out onto the freshly prepared skid pad. After a few minutes of near professional quality execution on the skid pad, the instructor asked Nolan if he had a skid pad in his back yard. Nolan explained that he'd had the opportunity to race at the amateur level and that he had lots of "skid" experience. The instructor told Nolan he would continue to put his skill to the test. The balance of that day was taken up with three-point turnarounds, backing and other driving maneuvers frequently used by police officers. Nolan's instructor was pleased with his driving ability.

Day two of driver training primarily consisted of driver training films and classroom instruction on hitting the apex, braking, power slides, "power U's," etc. When day three arrived, Nolan was ready. Each cadet was required to go in pursuit of his or her "suspect." An instructor would ride shotgun with each cadet to talk the cadet through any rough spots. The pursued vehicle was driven by one of the other instructors. A specific track had been set aside for this test.

When Nolan's turn came, the pursuit started off as had the previous ones. Communicating car to car via two-way radio, the driver of the pursued vehicle spoke to the instructor riding shotgun in Nolan's vehicle. The two had decided Nolan was too good for the regular track. "Follow him onto the other track," Nolan's instructor ordered.

Nolan complied and when the two vehicles reached the "other" track, the instructor shouted, "Okay, chase is on!" With that, the driver of the "suspect" vehicle smoothly accelerated and tossed his car into the first turn. To his pleasure, Nolan kept up, using all of the safety driving tactics he had learned, and then some. Faster and faster they went until finally, Nolan was advised to shut it down. "Nice driving, kid," his instructor told him. "Thank you, sir," he replied.

At the end of the day, the senior instructor approached Nolan, who snapped to attention. The instructor told Nolan to relax and advised him he appreciated his driving skills. He also told him that after he completed probation and a couple of years in patrol, he ought to consider putting in for an assignment as a driving instructor. Nolan humbly thanked the man. He felt as though he was walking on a cloud. It had been a great three days.

During the fifteenth week, lecturers finalized their classroom instruction to the cadets, while the D.I.'s began preparations for the graduation ceremony at the end of the following week. A total of thirty-eight cadets would graduate as police officers. The D.I.'s actually started treating the cadets with dignity and respect. This was an unexpected treat. Guess they figured the class had persevered and had earned their respect.

The sixteenth and final week began with the last physical training test of the curriculum. There seemed to be an almost relaxed attitude amongst the D.I.'s as well as the cadets as they were put through their final tests. As usual, the class as a whole did extremely well. The next couple of days would be spent practicing specific marching drills and maneuvers. As part of the traditional graduation ceremony protocol, the graduating class would put on a brief, but technically difficult marching drill display for the guests in attendance.

Additionally, the Chief and his designee would conduct the formal inspection prior to the inevitable speeches. Then, each new officer would be called up to accept his or her graduation certificate from the Chief. A handshake, a momentary pause for a few quick photos, and finally, the hat toss after the last dismissal. The cadets would rehearse every aspect of the graduation ceremony until the D.I.'s were satisfied. Each cadet was encouraged to have as many of his or her family members and friends attend this once-in-a-lifetime event.

Well, that Friday came soon enough. Officer Nolan watched from his position in class formation as the multitude of spectators arrived and found seating. Since he was now a "trained observer," he was able to quickly scan the growing crowd and locate his parents. The class was required to stay seated and not make contact with their guests until after the ceremony had been completed. Nolan saw that his dad was dressed in a suit and that he had his camera at the ready position. His mom had on a beautiful dress, and she was holding a small package of tissues, just in case.

He made eye contact with each of his parents, his dad giving him a big grin and a discreet "thumbs up," while his mom burst into tears. Good thing Mom brought her tissues, Nolan thought. He settled back into his chair. It would be another twenty minutes or so before the festivities got started.

Nolan reflected on several issues while awaiting the start of the ceremony. He thought about all of the hard work he and his classmates had accomplished by making it through the academy. He thought about those who did not make it and wondered what they were doing with their lives. He thought about the fact that he did not have a sweetheart in the crowd. That was when he scanned the crowd once again, and he noticed just how many beautiful women were in attendance. They were the wives and girlfriends of his fellow classmates. Lucky bastards, he thought.

Nolan was a handsome young man. On those few occasions during the previous four months when he and a few of his fellow cadets allowed themselves a Saturday night out, someone always arranged to have a female companion for him. She was either the friend of a girlfriend, a sister of a classmate, or some other acquaintance. He had no trouble finding temporary companionship with the opposite sex, but alas, he had no one he could call his very own special someone. Maybe now that he was done with the academy he could have a social life and find a sweetheart to call his own.

Just then one of the D.I.'s called the class to attention. The ceremony was about to begin. But first, all of the spectators and all of the graduating police officers would be subjected to a variety of guest speakers, culminating with traditional best wishes and political rhetoric, courtesy of the Chief himself.

After a flawless ceremony, it was finally all over, as signified by the final dismissal of Nolan's class and the hat toss. Nolan retrieved his hat and then raced over to see his parents. They were beaming with pride. His dad grabbed him and hugged him tightly. He told him he was very proud of him. Nolan's mom wept openly. She too hugged and kissed her only son. Together, the three of them walked toward the parking lot as Nolan escorted them to their car. Mom and Dad would hurry home and prepare for their son's arrival. They had planned a small celebration for him.

Nolan went to the men's locker room where he expeditiously changed into his "civies," grabbed the rest of his gear and walked to his car. He thought, "Wow, I did it! I'm really a police officer." He fired up his old car, cranked up the stereo and drove to his parents' house as happy as he could be. When he arrived and walked through the front door, a small gathering of family and friends sang, "For he's a jolly good fellow."

Naturally, he was embarrassed by all of the attention bestowed upon him, but it sure felt great. He was a happy young man.

Later that evening, the graduating class had their own celebration party at a local nightclub. Everyone behaved, had a great time and promised to stay in touch. Nolan was ready to go to work and catch bad guys.

Chapter Three

The First Night

On the Monday following his police academy graduation, Officer John Nolan reported for duty as instructed. He was scheduled to work the P.M. shift, also known as swing shift. He had all his shiny new gear with him, stuffed into a huge duffel bag. His uniforms, fresh out of the cleaners, were draped over his shoulder. He walked into the station and presented himself to the officer working the front desk. The officer made him wait a few minutes while he tended to some paperwork, but then he delivered Nolan to the on-duty sergeant, a crusty, older gentleman smoking a pipe.

Upon entering the sergeant's office, he snapped to attention and said, "Officer John Nolan reporting for duty." The sergeant looked up from behind his glasses and replied, "You don't have to do that crap anymore, son." "Thank you, sir" came Nolan's immediate answer. The sergeant grinned, got up from behind his desk and began to acquaint the rookie officer to his new surroundings. He was issued keys, a locker and all of the other necessities he needed to be a working police officer.

"Your watch starts in less than one hour," the sergeant said when he was through with Nolan. "Get into uniform and report to the briefing room. Your training officer is Dennis Winters. He's a fine policeman." Nolan changed into uniform, checking himself in the mirror repeatedly, to make sure everything was just right.

As he was about ready to pick up his bag and walk to the briefing room, the door to the locker room swung open and a tall, lanky, well groomed fellow, obviously a police officer, walked in. He looked directly at Nolan and asked, "You Nolan?" "Yes sir," he replied, and snapped to attention. "My name is Winters. I'm your training officer. Grab your gear and wait for me in the briefing room."

Nolan entered the briefing room, set his bag down, and started looking around. He was the only officer in the room at that time. There were several clipboards, containing wanted persons information, hung on evenly spaced hooks on the wall. Tables and chairs were neatly arranged and the blackboard had some writing on it that obviously pertained to some type of warrant service.

After a few minutes, Nolan heard the sound of laughter and loud voices approaching. The briefing room door opened and several officers, including Winters walked in, set their bags down and sat at the tables. Nolan smiled and nodded to the officers, however no one paid any attention to him. It was as if he wasn't there. Not even Winters gave him a second look.

Nolan got the hint and found a seat in the back of the room, away from the others. More mind game bullshit, he thought. A young looking sergeant entered the briefing room carrying a clipboard. He walked confidently to the podium, and as he began to speak, the room got very quiet. The sergeant paused, looked at Nolan and said, "You must be Nolan." Nolan jumped to his feet, stood at attention and said, "Yes Sergeant." "I'm Sergeant Carter. Sit down and pay attention."

Sergeant Carter went on to give briefing information about a 211 purse snatch suspect plaguing the area. Nolan feverishly wrote down all of the pertinent information in his field officer's notebook. The sarge continued with briefing information for several more minutes. Then, he served subpoenas to a few of the officers and gave out the evening assignments. When he was all done, he said, "Okay, let's hit the streets." With that, the officers got up and moved towards the armory to pick up shotguns.

Winters didn't get up when the others did. He was writing something in his notebook. Nolan stood at the back of the room waiting for his training officer. Finally, after all the other officers had left, Winters got up and told Nolan to get a shotgun and meet him on the parking lot. Nolan complied with Winters' command. Winters had the driver's door open to an almost new black and white. What a gorgeous looking car, Nolan thought. Winters took the shotgun from him. He showed him how he wanted the shotgun checked before loading and securing it in the unit.

Nolan removed the gear he needed from his bag and placed the bag in the trunk next to Winter's. He opened the passenger door and started to get in. "Not so fast," Winters said. "We need to check the unit." Winters began a walk around inspection of the police car looking for damage and checking the condition of the tires and other equipment. Nolan followed, studying his training officer's actions.

Exterior inspection completed, both officers entered the unit. Seated in the driver's scat, Winters checked the operation of the two-way radio, the lights, the horn and finally, the siren. Nolan couldn't help but smile when Winters hit the siren. Winters saw the grin on the new kid's face. "I did the same thing you just did almost seven years ago," Winters said as he looked at Nolan. Nolan realized he was smiling and immediately wiped the smile from his face. He could feel his face flush. He got embarrassed.

Nolan noted it was a cool, cloudy afternoon as they drove out of the parking lot. Winters took the microphone from its holder, keyed the mike and advised communications they were clear. Winters handed Nolan a map of the district and told him to get to know it quickly. He also told him that since this was his first night, he wouldn't require anything of him. "Just watch, listen and learn. Do exactly what I tell you, when I tell you. Is that clear?" "Yes sir," he answered. Then, "Sir, do you want me to write anything?" Nolan asked. "No, and stop calling me sir in every sentence. Put all the academy crap behind you. You're in the real world now." "Yes sir," Nolan replied.

Winters drove the borders of the district and showed Nolan the larger thoroughfares. He pointed out major landmarks and trouble spots. In between, he asked Nolan specific questions about himself. "Are you married?" "No," was the reply. "I don't even have a girlfriend at the moment." "Let me guess," Winters said. "When she found out you were becoming a cop, she dumped you, right?" "Yes, how'd you know?" Nolan asked. "I went through something very similar when I came on the department. Don't worry. You'll find someone soon enough." Winters assured his young trainee.

The sun began to set as they patrolled and talked. Then, over the radio, breaking the normal chatter, Nolan heard a "hot shot," signifying a priority call was about to be broadcast. "Beep, beep, beep…" "Any unit in the vicinity, unknown trouble at the liquor store, 4352 San Pedro. Anonymous informant reports he saw the store clerk behind the counter with his hands up as he walked by. N.F.D." (No Further Description). Winters grabbed the mike, keyed up and said, "302's responding in less than one."

Nolan held on as Winters executed a quick U-turn. He heard the deep, throaty, roaring sound of the four-barrel carburetor opening up and coming to life as Winters floored it. "We'll be there in fifteen seconds. It's probably a "good" 211. We rarely have any calls to this liquor store. Go ahead and pop the shotgun out of the rack and give it to me when I open my door. Then, I want you to follow me. Stay behind me. Do what I do." "Okay," Nolan said eagerly. Winters announced their arrival at the scene to communications.

Winters stopped the unit about fifty or sixty feet from the front of the store. He opened his door to exit just as Nolan handed him the shotgun. "Let's go," he said. "Keep your eyes open for a lookout or a layoff car." Nolan nodded, exited the unit, and walked behind Winters, who pumped a round into the chamber of the 12 gauge.

As they got closer to the store, Nolan could see that two additional officers were making a similar approach from the other side of the store. Approaching the front of the store, Winters began slinking against the wall while moving forward in a crouched position. Nolan copied his every move, as instructed. When they reached the far wall of the store, Winters peeked inside. He could see over the shelves. The only person he saw was a man holding a towel to his head, running toward the front door.

"Hold it!" Winters shouted as the man ran out of the store and onto the sidewalk. "They just robbed me, officer. Less than two minutes ago!" the clerk yelled. "How many were there and did they go out the front or the back?" Winters probed. "There were two of them. They ran right out the front door. One had a gun, the other a knife." "Did they get into a car?" "Yeah, it was an old primer gray Chevy Impala. I didn't get the license number, but it was beat up pretty bad." "Which way did they go?" Winters asked. The clerk answered, "They went that way," pointing north. Winters made a preliminary crime broadcast, indicating the suspects were armed with a gun and a knife and that they had left the scene northbound in an older gray Chevy Impala. Communications immediately re-broadcast the information for the other units.

Winters took the clerk back inside and requested paramedics to treat the large gash he had sustained on the top of his head when he was struck by one of the suspects. Winters then did a quick cursory search of the store just to make certain there were no suspects remaining on the premises. Nolan continued to follow his every move. Next, Winters obtained a much more detailed suspect and suspect vehicle description from the clerk. He made a supplemental broadcast to go along with the preliminary information he had put on the air minutes earlier. The communications operator again repeated all of his information.

Nolan watched and listened as Winters then took the clerk through the whole robbery, one step at a time. In the midst of this exchange, paramedics arrived and treated the clerk for the gash on his head. Nolan noted that Winters displayed compassion towards the victim clerk. But, at the same time, he was firm and professional, insistent on obtaining even the smallest details pertaining to the robbery. And he did so very quickly.

Paramedics stopped the bleeding on the clerk's head and they recommended he go to the local emergency hospital for stitches. The clerk thanked the medics, however he refused to go to the hospital. At about that time, Winters acknowledged a call to their unit. Dispatch advised that one of the responding units had a vehicle stopped that matched the description of the suspect vehicle. They were less than a mile away from the store. The vehicle contained two suspects who also matched the description.

Winters told the clerk he would need him to accompany him and his partner because one of the other units may have pulled the suspects over. "Let's go see those sons of bitches!" the clerk exclaimed. "Hold on," Winters said. "I have to explain this to you. Just because we have these people stopped doesn't mean they're the right suspects. You have to look at them and tell me if it's them or not. It may not be. You have to be sure." The clerk nodded and said, "I understand, sir."

The clerk locked the store and the three walked to the police car. They drove slowly to the area where the officers had the possible suspects detained. As they drove closer, officers had the two detainees stand and face the street. "That's the car!" the clerk shouted. Winters drove closer and again reminded the clerk to look carefully and be sure. "That's them—see? The little one had the knife. Look at the tall one, officer.

He's the one that pistol-whipped me. I'm gonna go beat that son of a bitch," the clerk said as he frantically grabbed at the door handle, trying to get out of the car. He failed to realize that police cars have the back door handles rigged so as to prevent the doors from being opened from inside the vehicle.

"Winters turned to the clerk and said, "I want you to settle down, right now." The clerk took a deep breath and said, "Okay, okay, I'm sorry. I just wanted to get a little payback." "Sorry man, it doesn't work that way," Winters said. The identification positive, the officers who made the stop, formally arrested the two suspects and searched the vehicle. They recovered a handgun, a knife and the stolen money. Winters and Nolan transported the victim back to the store. This had turned out to be a great caper.

"Let's head back to the station. We've got a lot of writing to do," Winters said to his trainee. "I'm ready to write," Nolan replied. "Did you understand everything that happened?" Winters asked. "Yes I did. Everything seemed almost 'textbook.' The way you got the preliminary suspect info and put it on the air. Even the field identification admonition you gave the clerk before he identified the suspects. That was great."

"Okay, I'm glad you're enjoying yourself," Winters smiled. "You did fine. I know you were nervous. I expect that—it's your first night. But, were you scared?" Nolan paused for a moment before responding. "Well, yeah, I guess I was. I could almost feel my heart pounding. But, it was great! We still did what we had to do. Were you scared, sir?" Nolan asked his teacher. "Let me put it to you this way. If the day ever comes when you're not a little scared rolling on one of these types of hot calls, it's time to find another line of work. As long as the fear doesn't overcome you, it's a healthy thing. Keeps you on your toes," Winters replied. The officers arrived at the station. The next ninety minutes would be spent writing reports generated by the robbery.

When they were back out on the street, Winters asked Nolan, "Are you hungry?" He replied, "I sure am." "See if we're clear for code seven." Winters instructed. Nolan removed the mike from its holder, raised it to his mouth and said, "302, are we clear for code seven?" "Negative 302, handle a 415 family, 2137 Fountain Avenue." Nolan looked over at Winters as he acknowledged receipt of the call. "That's the way it goes. We'll get something later," Winters said.

When they arrived at the location, the officers made their approach to the residence. Again, Nolan studied every move his training officer made. The officers could hear a woman shouting as they moved up the walkway to the small house. "Why don't you get a damn job? All you do is sit home every day and watch TV while I work." Winters knocked on the door. A disheveled man in his forties answered the door. He had a beer in his hand. He wasn't intoxicated, but his speech was slightly slurred. "Hi officers, come in. My wife is pissed off at me again."

The officers entered the modest home and began speaking to the husband. The wife came around the corner and in a very loud voice exclaimed, "I'm Mrs. Farmer. I'm the one who called. Put him in jail. He has no job. He sits home all day drinking and watching TV. I can't take it anymore, he..." Winters interrupted the female, "Partner, why don't you talk to Mr. Farmer over here while I talk to the Mrs. over there." Nolan nodded, remembering from his academy training that the first thing you do with any combatants, verbal or physical, is separate them immediately.

Winters positioned the irate, screaming female out of the line of sight of her husband. She continued to complain to Winters about how her unemployed husband watched TV all day, and so forth. Winters got her calmed down, and during his conversation with her, he realized she was very religious and she attended church regularly. Winters suggested counseling through the couple's church. He told her that most churches or religious groups have some sort of counseling services available to them. Mrs. Farmer seemed to embrace that idea.

Winters then changed places with Nolan and laid it down to Mr. Farmer. "Look," he said. "Your wife wants you to go to counseling with her. Why don't you do that?" The man said, "If that'll get her off my ass, I'll do it! I'm in between jobs right now. I'm looking, I just haven't found another one yet. We've been together for twenty years. I've never been out of work more than a month. This time, she's really on my case. We haven't even had sex for over a month!"

Winters motioned for Mr. Farmer to stop talking. He asked Mrs. Farmer to come into the room and sit next to her husband. He told them they'd been together for twenty years and it was obvious they really cared for each other. He said they didn't need the police to referee their differences. The family counseling service would help them through this rough period. Then, *he* briefly counseled both of them, built up their hopes, and by the time he and Nolan left, the couple was holding hands, smiling and thanking the officers.

As they got back into the car, Winters said, "I'm hungry—see if we're clear for seven, now." Nolan smiled, got on the air and received clearance for code seven. Winters stopped at a quaint Mexican restaurant. "I don't usually ask rookies where they want to eat. Hope you like Mexican." "Absolutely, sir. I love Mexican food." As they walked into the restaurant, Winters told Nolan he wanted to discuss the last call with him.

Over their meals, the officers talked about the last call they had handled. Winters said, "The first thing you need to remember is the potential for danger on these disturbance calls. They are the most frequent calls for service, and you never know what you're walking into. Officers are often attacked and sometimes killed on calls similar to the 415 family we just handled. Because we have to deal with these types of calls day in and day out, it's easy to become complacent in the way we handle them."

"Also, on these 415 calls, you almost always come across people whose emotions are running high. When people are upset or on the edge, they may choose to do something they wouldn't ordinarily do—such as attack a police officer. My long-winded point; Never, never become complacent on any call, especially 415 calls." Nolan listened carefully and absorbed every word his training officer said.

By the time the officers finished their meals and got back on the street it was close to 10:00 p.m. Winters informed his trainee that by comparison to a weekend evening, this had been a relatively slow night. Winters took advantage of that to work with his new partner. He quizzed Nolan on his knowledge of penal codes, vehicle codes and department policy. Nolan had done very well in the academy, and he planned to continue to push himself and to study during any free time.

Though Winters was pleased with Nolan's "book" knowledge, he advised his young trainee, "The streets can't be learned in a book. No matter how well you did in the academy, no matter how well you think you know the laws, until you have actual street experience, you don't understand how to apply that knowledge properly. Your book knowledge is very good. I want you to keep studying. I'll give you homework and guide your studies. Then, with every shift you work, the experience portion of your education will grow and ultimately, it will begin to mesh with the book knowledge you've learned. That's what training is all about."

"I'm looking forward to all of it," Nolan said. "I'll work as hard as I can to be the best police officer I can be." The officers drove in silence for a few minutes. There was very little chatter from the radio. Nolan momentarily drifted off into thought. "I have only known this guy for a few hours, yet I want to be as good a cop as he is. He's knowledgeable, confident and has excellent command presence. He sure seems to have it all together and..."

"Oh, just great," Winters said in a loud, obviously frustrated voice that momentarily startled Nolan. "It's starting to rain and I spent two hours washing and waxing my car this morning." Winters turned the windshield wipers on and off quickly so the wipers made only one pass to remove the droplets from the windshield. "It hasn't rained for a while," Nolan said.

"Yeah, that means stand by for the traffic accidents," came Winters reply. "Unfortunately, these people just can't drive when the streets are wet. It never ceases to amaze me. During our first few rain periods every year, it's like bumper cars out here. People just don't realize that when it hasn't rained for a while, the water mixes with the oil, rubber and other pollutants on the surface of the street. That makes for a real slippery ride."

Winters turned in the direction of the police station. "Let's go to the station, make a head call, and grab our rain gear. Tell dispatch we'll be out to the station." Nolan nodded and followed his T.O.'s order. Dispatch cleared them to the station and advised them to contact the watch commander upon arrival. "What's that about?" Nolan asked. "I'm not sure, but more than likely, it'll have something to do with the robbery from earlier."

When they arrived at the station their first stop was the watch commander's office. Nolan had not met the lieutenant yet, so Winters introduced him. The lieutenant was cordial. He smiled at Nolan and welcomed him. "You couldn't have asked for a better training officer," he said. "Yes sir," Nolan replied. "I've already learned quite a bit from him and it's only my first night on the street." The lieutenant smiled and then turned to Winters. "Those two guys you and unit 306 picked up in the liquor store caper are good for at least two more robberies out of the valley. The gun came back stolen. Taken in a burglary last month. Thought you'd want to know." "Thanks Lieutenant, I appreciate you letting us know right away," Winters said.

Winters and Nolan left the watch commander's office, and they each got their rain gear out of their lockers. Back out on the street, it was raining steadily and they hadn't driven three blocks when they saw a very nice looking older VW bug slide right though a stop sign, with the driver obviously mashing the brake pedal to the floor. "Let's talk to this guy," Winters said as he turned the black and white after the VW and activated the overhead red lights. "Run the plate." "Okay," Nolan said. Nolan couldn't help but notice the fading bumper sticker on the bumper next to the license plate. It was one of his favorites. It said, "If you don't like the police, next time you need help, call a hippie." Though it was the early 1970's, "hippies" and "flower children" were still around in significant numbers.

The plate came back clean. The driver of the VW pulled over immediately. Winters got out of the police car and walked up to the driver. Nolan made his approach from the passenger side. Nolan was unable to hear all of the conversation from his position, but after a few moments, he heard Winters tell the driver, "Just slow down and take it easy. It's very slippery." With that, Winters walked back to the unit and the VW pulled away from the curb.

"What happened, sir?" Nolan inquired. "Well, it was a college student—squared- away, polite, knew he screwed up. I gave him a warning." "Oh, okay," Nolan replied. "You don't always have to write a ticket. In this case, the properly licensed violator knew he had made a mistake, honestly felt bad about it, and appeared to be genuine. By counseling him briefly and giving him a warning, it has the same or better effect than if we had written him a ticket. That's my opinion. Besides, I limited the amount of time I got wet!"

"Others would argue I should have cited him. That's what is so great about this job. You have discretion. Never abuse it and always use it wisely." "Yes sir." "Are you starting with the 'yes sir' stuff again?" Winters asked with a grin on his face. Nolan felt himself blushing, and he was glad it was dark so his T.O. couldn't see. "No," he replied. "It's just habit."

The officers handled two more simple report calls and a little less than thirty minutes prior to their "EOW" (end of watch), Winters told Nolan, "Today was been a good day for you. Continue to study the penal and vehicle code sections I gave you. Tomorrow, I'll start working you hard. I'm gonna head in to the station now. I'll show you how we secure our gear, sign out and all that stuff." "Okay," was the eager reply.

Seconds later, another call. "Unit 302, handle an injury accident involving a possible drunk driver at the intersection of Main and Stuart. One of the vehicles is reportedly on fire. Fire Department has been dispatched. 302, handle Code Three." "I knew it," Winters said. "Acknowledge the call, and give her an E.T.A. of one minute." Nolan did as instructed. "Your first code three run is going to be a short one. We're almost there."

Just before they arrived at the scene, Winters instructed Nolan to attempt to locate the other parties involved in the crash while he went to the burning vehicle. Because they were so close, Winters knew they'd beat the fire department to the scene. As they arrived, Winters unlocked the trunk using the interior switch. He exited the unit, grabbed the small fire extinguisher out of the trunk, and ran towards the burning vehicle.

Even though it was raining, people had already gathered and were milling about. "Hurry, there's people in here!" a man shouted as Winters approached the almost fully engulfed vehicle. Winters yelled for onlookers to get away from the vehicle as he ran up to it. Winters feared it could explode at any moment. He yelled for Nolan.

Nolan had seen what was happening and by the time Winters called for him, he was already running to his assistance. Meanwhile, through the flames, Winters could see two small children within the rear portion of the vehicle, an older station wagon. Neither child was moving. He also saw an adult female slumped over in the driver's seat.

Winters began working frantically to rescue the kids. Flames leaped several feet from the vehicle, but Winters hung in there with the small extinguisher, trying to get to the kids. He managed to extinguish enough of an area where he could get close enough to smash the right rear window of the wagon and get the door partially open. He felt tremendous heat and smoke exit the window as it broke. He couldn't open the door all the way because it had sustained too much damage in the accident.

As Nolan ran up, Winters was pulling the first child out of the vehicle. The child's body was limp and lifeless. Nolan shouted, "I'll get the other one." Winters nodded and then ran a safe distance from the burning vehicle, positioning the child in his arms for CPR as he ran. As soon as he stopped and placed the child on the ground, he started CPR. Seconds later, Nolan retrieved the second child. He too, ran from the still burning vehicle, carrying the motionless body of the second small child in his arms. He started CPR on the child as soon as he was a safe distance from the vehicle.

By that time the fire department and additional police units had begun arriving. Two officers and a fireman were able to get the semi-conscious female driver out of the vehicle, and other firemen immediately tended to the fire. At about the same time, two paramedics arrived and took over CPR on each of the children from Winters and Nolan. There was no time to wait for an ambulance. Winters had one of the assisting police officers seat both paramedics in the back seat of his black and white. The officer then transported the paramedics to the hospital code three while they administered non-stop CPR to each of the children.

With the utmost in speed and precision, firefighters were able to extinguish the blazing vehicle and prevent an explosion. Simultaneously, another paramedic was tending to the driver, most likely the mother of the two kids extracted from the vehicle. An ambulance arrived to transport her to the hospital. Amazingly, less than five minutes had transpired from the time Winters and Nolan arrived on the scene, to the time the ambulance arrived to transport the driver of the burned car. Initially, and in all the chaos, Winters did not have the opportunity to direct anyone to contact the other driver.

Winters and Nolan approached the striking vehicle, an older pick up truck with heavy front-end damage. Two men were holding an older man by the arms. One of the men said, "Here's the driver that hit those poor people. He was trying to leave." "Thank you, sir," Winters said humbly.

Winters took charge of the man and immediately smelled the moderate odor of an alcoholic beverage on and about the man's breath and person. The man, later identified as Robert Stevens, displayed all of the classic objective symptoms that would lead a police officer to believe he'd been driving while under the influence of an alcoholic beverage.

Winters had Nolan get the names and witness accounts of the two men who held on to the driver that had caused the horrible accident. Meanwhile, he conducted a field sobriety test on Stevens and confirmed his opinion that Stevens was "deuce." (A California law enforcement term for a D.U.I. driver. Can be used as a verb or a noun). Steven's truck had been badly damaged, and he hadn't been wearing a seat belt, however, because he was under the influence, he was "too drunk" to get hurt. Winters took him into custody for felony drunk driving.

During that time, Nolan was able to find another two witnesses to the accident. All witness accounts were essentially the same. The pickup, driven by Stevens, ran the red light and struck the station wagon broadside at forty plus miles per hour. The station wagon spun around from the impact, and one witness told Nolan she actually saw what appeared to be a spray or mist of some liquid, probably gas, cover the station wagon after it was struck. Evidently, upon impact, the truck ruptured the station wagon's gas tank. Shortly thereafter, it burst into flames and was almost immediately enveloped by the flames.

Winters was anxious to get to the hospital to see if the two children had made it. He also wanted to check on the driver of the station wagon to see how she was doing. Winters figured that in all probability, she was the mother of the two kids. He was hoping to get a statement from her regarding the accident. He asked one of the other assisting police officers to transport Stevens and see to his blood alcohol test. Then, Winters instructed Nolan as he and Nolan conducted the balance of their traffic accident investigation. After photos and measurements were taken, the vehicles were towed away and the intersection was reopened.

Nolan remembered there was little or no talking between him and Winters during the short drive from the scene of the accident to the hospital. Both veteran police officer and rookie alike were obviously shaken by the tragic scene involving the two small, seemingly lifeless bodies. Many thoughts raced through Nolan's mind. The children weren't burned, so perhaps the inhalation of all that hot smoke rendered them unconscious, maybe the CPR helped, maybe the doctors could save them, maybe...

"Let's get in there and find out what's going on," Winters said. Nolan was so lost in thought, he didn't even realize Winters had pulled into the hospital parking lot and parked. The officers entered the emergency area with hopes held high. Winters knew his way around the hospital and he was acquainted with some of the staff. The officers walked directly to the nurse's station where Winters spotted a familiar, gray haired nurse.

"Hi Betty," he said. The nurse looked up at him with a sad look on her face. She asked, "Dennis, are you here about the three traffic accident victims that came in just a little while ago?" Winters nodded his head. Betty looked at both Winters and Nolan as she told the officers what they did not want to hear. "The doctors were unable to revive either of the children. They were both D.O.A." (dead on arrival). "Shit!" Winters exclaimed as he pounded his fist down on the counter. Betty continued, "Their bodies will be turned over to the coroner's office for autopsy. But I *can* tell you it appeared the smaller one had a broken neck. Nothing you could have done. Her little neck must have snapped from the impact. The other one had severe head trauma. Neither one had a chance. I just wish they would have been in child seats."

Both officers were deeply saddened by what they had just heard. "What about the driver?" Winters asked. Betty said that the driver was, in fact, the mother of the two dead little girls, and that she was in surgery with internal injuries. Her condition was listed as critical. Hospital staff had found a phone number in her purse. They successfully notified her husband of the accident, and advised him that he needed to respond to the hospital right away. They didn't tell him his two daughters were dead and his wife was in critical condition. He was only told there had been a serious accident and that he needed to get to the hospital as soon as possible. He was on his way, and his world was about to change. A priest and a social worker would be there to intercept him.

Nolan recalled feeling almost stunned, as if he'd been hit in the head with a two by four. Winters had that same look on his face. They thanked Betty and said goodnight. They were just about to leave the nurse's station when Nolan caught a glimpse of a young, dark-haired nurse dressed in surgery scrubs walking up to the nurse's station. Her surgical mask was pulled down to her chin and she was holding a clipboard. Even though she was dressed in scrubs, it was obvious she was a stunning

Hispanic beauty. Their eyes met for a brief moment and Nolan nodded in her direction, as if to say hello. She reciprocated by smiling ever so slightly. She knew what the officers had just been told by Nurse Betty.

Winters and Nolan walked in silence to their unit. They drove slowly, almost methodically, to the station. It was well after midnight, their EOW time, however, they had several reports to write before they could call it a night. They also needed to amend the booking charges on Stevens to include two counts of vehicular manslaughter in addition to felony drunk driving.

When they arrived at the station, Winters took care of the booking charges and found out that Stevens had registered a .19% blood alcohol on the breathalyzer test. Almost twice the legal limit. (In 1970's California, the legal limit was .10%) Winters handled some of the paperwork and coached Nolan through the rest. At one point during report writing, Winters lifted his pencil from the paper and seemed to stare off into space for several minutes, motionless. "You okay, sir?" Nolan inquired. Winters shook it off and said, "Yeah, I'm okay. Thanks man." Winters then continued, "It makes no difference how many years you do this job. When you see a child hurt, or worse yet, dead, it really hurts." "Yes sir, I'm very saddened by what happened tonight."

Almost two hours had passed since Winters and Nolan started writing the reports related to the accident. When they had finally finished, Winters told Nolan, "Forget what I told you earlier this evening. Don't study tonight or tomorrow. We had a rough day. Go home. Get some rest and we'll pick it up again tomorrow." "Yes sir. Goodnight." Nolan answered. As Nolan turned to head to the locker room, Winters said, "Hey." Nolan turned to look at him. "You did great today. You should feel proud. We did the best we could." "Thank you sir, but I don't feel very proud right now." Nolan said sadly, as he turned and walked away.

As soon as Nolan arrived at home, he took a shower and then sat in front of the television. He was kind of glad he lived alone in his nice little apartment. At that moment, he wanted to be alone. Tired as he was, he knew that if he went to bed right away, he would have a tough time falling asleep. He had way too much on his mind. He found an old western movie on television, and just sat there in the dark, the only bit of flickering light emanating from the changing scenes on the television. The flickering light seemed to have a calming effect on him.

Yet his mind was running 100 mph. He started thinking about the children. He could see their innocent little faces, their lifeless bodies. He wondered if he would see this type of thing regularly. He wondered how the veteran policemen dealt with this. He heard Nurse Betty telling him and Winters the children were "pronounced dead on arrival." He wished there had been something else he could have done. He thought about the mother, in critical condition. He thought about the husband and father, whose life, by now, had been devastated. He kept seeing the kids' little faces. He was very weary. He began to weep.

A couple of hours later, he woke up, still on his couch. The television station he had been watching was now off the air and all he saw was "snow" on the screen, accompanied by the familiar hissing sound. He looked at the clock and saw that it was 5:45 AM. He got up, poured himself a glass of water, and turned off the TV. Then, he went to bed, and as he lay there trying to go back to sleep, he found himself thinking about his first day in patrol again.

He re-played the entire day in his mind, except for the accident. And with the exception of the accident, Nolan recalled feeling pleased about the way the day had gone. Suddenly, his mind focused on the beautiful nurse he saw at the hospital. Seeing her had been overshadowed by the tragic news about the children and he had forgotten about her. But he certainly remembered her now. I wonder if she's single, he thought. She sure is a classic beauty. With my luck she's happily married. She was his last thought before he fell asleep.

Chapter Four

The Break-in Period Continues

The following day, Nolan went to work early. He wanted to hit the gym in the basement of the station and get in a workout prior to his shift. Working out and staying in shape had become a way of life for him. He learned the value of a sound mind in a sound body from his parents. That concept had been reinforced by his high school football coach and then, of course, by the training at the police academy. Furthermore, training his body also helped him clear his mind of the daily stresses of life. When he had personal issues to resolve, a hard workout always seemed to get him over the hump.

Nolan pushed himself and had an extra hard workout. It helped him deal with the needless deaths of the two children the night before. He enjoyed a long, hot shower and took his time as he dressed in uniform. When he was done, he picked up his bag and walked to the briefing room. Once again, he was quite early and had the room to himself. He took a seat toward the back of the room and was looking over some of his study material when Winters walked in. He was still in civies. He inquired, "So, how ya doin' today?" Nolan knew what he meant and replied, "I'm okay. I'm dealing with it." "Good," Winters replied. "Good." Winters left to go change into uniform.

Several minutes later, Nolan once again heard the sound of approaching laughter and loud voices. The rest of the P.M. shift arrived for briefing. When Winters entered, he sat in the front portion of the room with the rest of the crew. He turned to Nolan and said, "Come on over here." Nolan complied, leaving the back of the room for apparent temporary acceptance in the front of the room. He sat next to his training officer.

Sergeant Carter entered the room and conducted briefing. When he finished, he talked about the accident the night before. "I don't know if all of you have heard yet, the two kids were DOA—the mother in critical condition. The individual responsible for all this has had three prior deuce arrests. He's never done any jail time. Maybe this time they'll lock his ass up for a while." Then, Sgt. Carter got a very solemn look on his face. He said, "I've got three kids at home and I can tell you, I hugged them all just a little tighter today. On a brighter note, I was very pleased with the way everyone handled themselves at the scene. You guys had it together, doing it right. I'm particularly pleased with Winters and his trainee. Outstanding job, fellas. I'm just sorry it didn't work out better."

A short time after Winters and Nolan left the station and were on patrol, Winters turned to Nolan and said, "What the sarge said in roll call is very true. I've got two youngsters of my own, and I live for my family. After I woke up today, I also spent extra time with the kids. More time than I normally would. That seemed to help me deal with it. Now, what about you? Are you okay with it?" Nolan thought for a moment, then said, "Well, I did have some trouble with it last night. I fell asleep on the couch. I kept seeing their little faces. Drove me nuts for a while. I'm

44

okay now though. I came in early, hit the weights for a long time, then took a long, hot shower. That's what takes the edge off for me."

They drove in silence for a few moments, when Nolan confessed, "I can't imagine ever getting used to seeing a child in distress or worse yet, dead. I've heard this job can make you hard, but I just can't see ever getting used to that." Winters replied, "Listen, I've been around for several years, and lots of guys that have been on twenty years or more will tell you the same thing. You never get used to seeing dead or injured children. No one should ever get used to that." "Thank you, sir," replied Nolan. "I guess I just needed to hear you say that again."

"Okay, enough said about that. Today's a new day. We're going to focus on traffic stops and other traffic issues today. I want you to spot violations and alert me to them." "Alright sir." In between calls for service, Winters spent several hours instructing Nolan on everything from A-Z on traffic stops. From officer safety issues, to addressing the motorist after the stop, to citation preparation, Nolan got lots of practice. Although he had learned a great deal from his training officer and they had handled many calls, his second night in the street seemed to pass almost uneventfully.

During the course of the following evening, Winters and Nolan were assigned a follow-up call to the hospital. En route to their call, Nolan felt prompted to ask, "Do you remember the other night at the nurse's station when we were talking to your nurse friend Betty?" "Yeah, I remember." Nolan continued, "Well sir, I was wondering if you happened to notice the real pretty nurse that came walking up right as we were leaving."

"She was a Hispanic girl with dark hair in a ponytail, dressed in surgery scrubs. She was absolutely gorgeous, and I was curious as to whether or not you know who she is. Even though she was in hospital scrubs, she was stunning. She's probably one of the most beautiful women I've ever seen in my life."

Winters burst into laughter, which momentarily puzzled and confused Nolan. "Sorry for laughing at you man, but that's the most you've spoken at one time since I met you. It figures it would be about a woman and not your job!" Before Nolan could react to his training officer's statement, Winters added, "Yes, I noticed her. Everyone notices her. That's Marie, Marie Martinez. She's a surgical nurse. Just about every guy in the station has tried to get a date with her. As far as I know, no one's ever gotten to first base with her. Word is, she doesn't date cops. Smart girl. She's really very nice and easy to talk to. She actually likes cops. Her sister and brother are both deputy sheriffs." "I thought you initially said she didn't like cops," Nolan said. "No, I said she doesn't *date* cops." "Oh, well, hope I get to see her again anyway," a determined Nolan responded.

When Winters and Nolan arrived at the hospital to handle their report, they simultaneously spotted Marie at the nurse's station. Nolan turned and looked at Winters, but he didn't speak. Winters looked back at him, smiled and said, "Okay hotshot. I'll get the information for the report while you strike out... I mean talk to Marie. Go ahead." "Thank you, sir."

Nolan casually approached the counter at the nurse's station. Marie saw him coming. "Hi," Nolan said with the best "Mr. Charlie Charming" smile he could muster. "Hi," Marie said, as she politely returned a smile. "Are you new? I hadn't seen you before the other night." "Yes, I just got out of the academy. This is my first week on the street. In fact, the other night, when those two little girls died... well, that was my first night on the street," he explained.

"That was terrible. I see a lot of different things here in the hospital, some good, some pretty horrible, but when it's bad and it involves kids, it hurts even more," Marie said. Nolan nodded in acknowledgment. For a few moments there was an uneasy pause in the dialogue. Marie broke the ice. "So, what's your name, Officer?" "My name is John Nolan. What's your name?" "I'm Marie Martinez." "I'm very pleased to meet you, Marie Martinez," Nolan said. "I'm pleased to meet you too, John." Nolan was starting to feel a little awkward, since they were both working and both in their respective uniforms. Though no one was within direct earshot, there were quite a few people around. Nolan sensed Marie felt a little awkward as well. "You look pretty busy and I'd better catch up to my training officer. Maybe we can talk again soon," Nolan said, hoping that Marie would respond in a positive way. "I'd like that, John." "Great. Well then, bye for now Marie." "Bye John."

Nolan was all smiles when he caught up to his T.O. "Well, what happened?" Winters inquired, as if talking to a child. "You were right, sir. She's very nice. We introduced ourselves and talked for a few minutes. I really do like her," John said excitedly. "Calm down, control your hormones. We've got lots of work to do. You keep your head on straight and think about your job," Winters warned his young trainee. "Yes sir, no problem," Nolan replied.

Less than five minutes after clearing the hospital, Winters and Nolan monitored a hot shot. "Beep, beep, beep." "Any unit in the vicinity, 459's there now, 8732 Sycamore Street. R/P (reporting party) advises two 18-20 year old male Hispanics entered the residence via a side window. Units responding, identify." Nolan reached for the mike while simultaneously looking at Winters for approval. "Go ahead. We're not that far. Give her a two-minute ETA. See who else is responding so we can coordinate with them."

Nolan followed instructions and then switched off of the main channel and onto a specified tactical channel to talk to the other responding unit— Officers Gonzales and Meyers. Since Winters and Nolan were closest and would arrive first, they would come in black (no lights, quiet approach) and cover the rear. Gonzales and Meyers would take the front while other units continued to respond as well. No one would approach the residence until the location was properly covered.

Winters and Nolan quietly rolled up to the appropriate address on the first street south of the location. This would give them the opportunity to cover the rear of the victim location without the likelihood of the suspects even realizing they were there. They waited to hear the other units announce their arrival in the front. Once the other units had arrived, officers started towards the residence. Suddenly, without any warning, the rear door of the house flew open and one of the suspects exited into the backyard area. From there, the suspect starting jumping fences as he attempted escape. Approaching from the rear, Winters and Nolan saw the suspect fleeing.

Instinctively, and with no hesitation, Nolan took off after him. Nolan was a fast runner and fences hardly slowed him down. Within the distance of a few houses, he caught up to the suspect and tackled him. A moment prior to running after his trainee, Winters saw Meyers and Gonzales grab the second suspect as he tried to exit the rear of the house to follow his buddy's escape route. Less than a minute later, Winters reached Nolan just as he was handcuffing the suspect. "Good job, partner. Congratulations on arresting your first burglar." Winters said proudly. "The second suspect is in custody too."

As Nolan got up off the ground after handcuffing the burglary suspect, he realized his arm was bleeding. Then he remembered going over a chain link fence and cutting his arm during the short chase. Winters looked at his arm and said, "That's a nasty gash. We'd better get that looked at." While escorting the prisoner back to their unit, the officers noticed that Sergeant Carter was parked behind them, apparently waiting for them. As they approached, he exited his vehicle to greet them. "Once again, nice job fellas." Winters smiled in response and said, "Hey Sarge, my trainee runs like a gazelle. Ran this guy down quick." Sergeant Carter smiled and quipped, "That's cause he's young. He's supposed to be fast."

Nolan seated his prisoner in the back seat of the black and white while Sergeant Carter talked to Winters. "Dennis, the main reason I came by was to tell you your vacation request for next month has been approved. I felt bad because you've already asked me about it several times and I kept forgetting to respond back to you." Carter pointed to Nolan and added, "We'll put Junior here with somebody else while you're gone." "Thanks Sarge. My wife will be happy. She's made all kinds of plans. We're going up north to see her folks." "Okay, good... Listen, I'm going back to the station. Give me your prisoner and I'll transport him for you. Take the kid to the hospital. Have one of the docs patch him up," the sarge said.

Once again that evening, Winters and Nolan were en route to the hospital. Winters teased his trainee. "You'd do anything to get back to that hospital to see her, wouldn't you?" Nolan grinned and said, "Come on now sir, you know I didn't plan this, but I do hope I get to see her again tonight." The officers arrived at the hospital and as they were nearing the nurse's station, Nolan saw Marie walking away with a purse in her hand. He called to her and she turned. She saw him holding his arm and walked briskly back towards him.

"What happened to you?" she asked. Before he could answer, Winters responded, "He just ran down a burglar and cut himself going over a chain-link fence." "I was just leaving to go on my break. Let me put my purse away. I'll be right with you," Marie said. "No, that's okay. Go ahead and take your break, Marie. I don't want you to go to any trouble," Nolan said. "It's no trouble John. Just give me a moment to let the doctor know what I'm doing," she said. Winters just looked at Nolan and smiled. He didn't say a word.

Marie returned after a few minutes and called Nolan into an exam room. Winters said, "I'm gonna get a cup of coffee. I'm sure you'll be code four. I'll be back." Marie cleaned Nolan's wound. He couldn't help but stare at her. She was so beautiful. He tried not to make it obvious. "This is a nasty cut, but it doesn't really need suturing. I'm going to put a couple of steri-strips on it. It'll be fine," she said. Nolan replied, "Thanks Marie. I feel bad about this. You were supposed to be on your break." Marie didn't respond. She finished cleaning the wound and dressed it. Then she asked, "John, when's the last time you had a tetanus shot?" Nolan laughed and said, "I don't have any idea." "Typical," she snapped. I'll be back to give you a shot."

Moments later, Marie returned with a syringe in her hand. "Let's do this on your non-gun hand. It'll probably be sore for a couple of days. Roll up your sleeve." "Yes, Ma'am," a cooperative Nolan said. He realized he was staring at her again. He also realized that this time, she saw him staring. "I'm sorry Marie. I didn't mean to stare at you. It's just that you're so nice and so pretty." She smiled, "That's okay John. I'm not complaining," she replied, as she administered the injection. "Do you have time for a cup of coffee?" she asked. "Well yeah, I guess so. My partner went to get a cup," Nolan said. "Maybe we'll see him in the cafeteria. Let's go," Marie said.

As they walked into the cafeteria, Nolan saw Winters talking to one of the emergency room doctors as they both sipped coffee at a small table. Nolan looked over at Winters, who returned the look and nodded. Nolan understood that as permission. He and Marie then got a cup of coffee and sat at a nearby table. Nolan said, "Marie, I heard you have a brother and sister in law enforcement." "Yes," she replied. "They're with the

Sheriff's Department. I tried to get on myself but I was told I'm too short. I'm only 5'3". Didn't meet the height requirement. So, I settled for the medical field."

"I'm sorry," Nolan remarked. "It bothered me for a while, but I'm over it now. No regrets," she said. "I decided to become a policeman when I was in high school. Boy, that seems so long ago now," Nolan sighed. Marie said, "I know what you mean. I remember I couldn't wait until I turned sixteen so I could drive. Then I couldn't wait to turn twenty-one to be legal." Nolan nodded in agreement as they both chuckled. He looked over and saw his partner getting ready to stand up. He knew it was time to go.

"Marie, I know this is kind of forward of me, but would you like to go to out for coffee, or maybe even dinner some time?" he asked. Marie's facial expression never changed. She hesitated for a long moment, as if in deep thought. Nolan's heart started sinking. Then, she looked him directly in the eyes, smiled and said, "Yes, I think I'd like that." She wrote her phone number down on a napkin and discreetly passed it to him. He immediately pocketed it without looking at it. Then he said, "Thanks Marie," and stood up, preparing to leave. Marie remained seated at the table. She smiled and said, "Hey, don't get hurt anymore." Nolan smiled at her and walked away. He was so happy, he could hardly contain himself.

Back in the black and white, Winters asked Nolan how it went with Marie. "She's so nice. I just feel comfortable around her, even though I just met her and I don't really know her yet." "Well, don't get your hopes up. She's beautiful and nice and all that, but like I told you, she doesn't date cops," Winters warned. "Well sir, I asked her out and she said yes!" Nolan said excitedly. "Wow, that's great!" Winters said. "Good for you. She really is a fine young woman." "Now, let's get back to work. The arm okay?" "Yes, it's fine. Are we going back to the station to do our paperwork?" Nolan asked. "That's affirmative, lover boy," Winters joked.

At the station, in order to expedite their paperwork, Winters assisted Nolan by booking in and recording evidence recovered from the earlier burglary. Nolan was left to write the actual crime and arrest report portion of the incident. When Winters was done with the evidence, he checked on his trainee who had not progressed very far in his report. "Look John, I know you're happy about going out with Marie, but you need to stay focused on your work. You're obviously thinking about her and not your report. I'll be back in twenty minutes. I expect you to be done with all your paper," Winters admonished his trainee. "Sorry sir, and you're right, I have been daydreaming. It won't happen again." "Okay."

Nolan completed his paperwork on time. Winters proofread the report and told Nolan it was fine. Back out in the field, Winters advised Nolan, "I'll be going on vacation in less than two weeks. I'll be gone for ten days. Sarge said he'd put you with somebody good while I'm gone. I'll load you up with homework before I go." "Yes sir," Nolan said, saddened he would be without the teacher he admired for almost two weeks. The rest of their shift was slow, and they got off on time. As Nolan was driving home, he thought about calling Marie. She finished her shift at almost the same time he did. Why not?

Nolan got home and relaxed for a few minutes. He looked at the clock—12:45 A.M. He kept staring at the napkin with Marie's phone number on it. Finally, he picked up the phone and called. Marie answered by the second ring. "Hi...Marie?" he asked. "Yes, is this John?" she asked in return. "Yes, I'm sorry I'm calling so late but I figured you'd still be awake," he explained. Marie responded, "I just walked in a few minutes ago. I'm beat. It was a long day." "I'm sorry Marie. Maybe I should call back at a better time," he said apologetically. Marie quickly said, "No, I want to talk to you. I'll tell you what. Give me a few minutes to wash up and change, and call me back." "Great," Nolan said. I'll do the same, because I just got in too. I'll call you right back." "Okay Bye."

Nolan waited several minutes before calling back. When Marie answered, the two entered into a lengthy conversation. They talked about themselves, their families, their backgrounds, interests, etc. They laughed and enjoyed their time on the phone. They spoke as though they were old friends. Before either one of them realized it, it was after 2:00 A.M. "Wow," Nolan said. "It's two in the morning. I never knew I could talk on the phone that long." "Do you have to get up early, John?" Marie asked. "No, I'm just concerned about you, he replied. "I'm off tomorrow, I can sleep in," she chuckled.

"Good, because there's something else I wanted to tell you. Marie, I know it was very forward of me to ask you out after we'd just met. That's not like me. I'm usually quiet and reserved. It's just that I really like you, and I'm not sure how to describe it, except to say that I feel good around you. So please don't be offended by my assertiveness," he said.

Marie paused before responding. "Well, in the first place, I'm not offended. If I were, I would have let you know right away. Also, it seems pretty obvious to me you're a good guy. I usually don't date policemen, but, as you so eloquently put it, I too feel good around you." "I'm so happy to hear you say that," he exclaimed. "What time do you usually wake up?" he inquired. "Whhyyy?" she asked teasingly. "Well, I thought maybe we could go to breakfast," he hinted. "Boy, you sure don't waste any time," she laughed. "No, it isn't that. I just ..." "I'm only kidding," she interrupted. "I think that's a great idea. Do you want to meet somewhere?" she inquired. "Actually, I'm from the 'old school.' I'd rather pick you up, if that's okay." "That'll be fine." Marie gave Nolan her address and they agreed on a time. It was 2:40 a.m. when they finally said goodnight.

Nolan slept like a baby and woke up happy as a lark. He hopped in the shower and got all spruced up for his breakfast date with Marie. He picked her up right on time and the two had a very nice breakfast. They continued their conversation, laughing and enjoying each others company. They had been at the restaurant for over two hours when Nolan glanced at his watch. "Aw phooey. I've got to go to work, Marie," he said disappointingly. "I know John. Let's go." They left the restaurant and Nolan drove Marie home. When they arrived in front of her apartment building, Marie gently touched Nolan's shoulder. "Thank you for breakfast John. Call me later." "Okay, I will."

After dropping Marie, Nolan rushed off to work. When he and Winters were out in the field, Winters told him he needed to discuss his performance over the past week. "Today is our Friday, the end of your first week, so I thought I'd go ahead and clue you in. We're trying a new training program. Rather than have the trainee assigned to various training officers at certain times within the allotted training period, a few of us have been selected to keep the same trainee throughout the training period. I knew you'd be assigned to me before you even got out of the academy."

"I had the opportunity to review your entire application and background package. I spoke to your background investigator and in fact, I went to your graduation and watched your behavior and interaction with others, including your parents. I had the option, but I chose not to contact you at that time." "How come?" a somewhat bewildered Nolan asked. "Well, I didn't want to give you more to think about. Didn't want to spoil the moment," Winters explained.

"I can tell you that so far, I am pleased by your performance. I'll give you your first weekly written evaluation after we're done with this discussion. So that you know, that's the form I'm required to submit to the sergeant, after we've both signed it. John, you're doing very well. Knowing your background and having observed and worked with you for the short time we've been together, I'd have to say it appears you're a natural for this job. I've trained many others before you, and it's very obvious you are definitely a cut above."

"Now, before your head swells, I can also tell you that because you've demonstrated outstanding ability in most areas, I'm going to expect more from you than I would from the average trainee. I'm gonna load you up and work you hard." Nolan interrupted, "Sir, I am a very humble person. I'm grateful for your words, but I can assure you my head will not swell. I will do everything to the absolute best of my ability. I'm very hard on myself." "Good. And because I'm going on vacation for what is essentially two weeks, I am going to accelerate your training." Nolan smiled and said, "Bring it on, sir."

The pair resumed patrol and in so doing, they simultaneously spotted a suspicious looking character going from vehicle to vehicle in a crowded grocery store parking lot. The individual would discreetly pull on car door handles and peek into windows. "What's he doing?" Winters asked. "He's looking to steal a car or do an auto burglary." "Right, Winters nodded as he positioned the unit so as to be able to continue surveillance on the subject without being detected. After looking into a few more car windows, the man made his move. He forced his way into a newer vehicle and disappeared under the dash. "Now, we go!" Winters smiled as he quickly and quietly maneuvered the unit to within close proximity of the suspect. The officers got out on foot, quickly approached the suspect, and made their apprehension just as he had finished "hotwiring" the vehicle.

Once the suspect was in custody, Nolan located the owner of the victim vehicle shopping in the market. He obtained the victim's information for reporting purposes, and then he and Winters took the prisoner in for attempting to steal the car. En route to the station Winters inquired of his trainee, "Did you notice anything unusual about our suspect?" "Yes, he appears to be under the influence of something, but

I'm not sure what yet," Nolan explained to his teacher. "He's a hype. He's under the influence of heroin. I'll show you when we get to the station," Winters said.

By the time Winters had shown Nolan how to detect, process, interview and test a hype, it was almost 10:30 P.M. Nolan typed out the arrest report and Winters helped him with the appropriate terminology applicable to persons under the influence of heroin. When he was done, Nolan made a quick call to Marie. "Hi Marie." "Hi John." "Marie, I have to get back out on the street but I found out I'm off tomorrow," Nolan offered. "So am I." "I know. Do you want to hang out?" he asked. "Yes, when?" Marie inquired. "Can I come pick you up as soon as I wake up?" "Sure," she answered. "What are we going to do?" "I don't know, we'll figure it out. I just want to see you," he confessed. "I want to see you too," she said softly. "Great," he replied happily. "I'll call you in the morning."

"There's still some time before we EOW. Let's go get a deuce," Winters said as they drove out of the station parking lot. "Okay," Nolan agreed. Working the streets within the bowels of Los Angeles County on any given evening, it's difficult *not* to find a DUI driver. Before very long, the officers came upon a vehicle traveling about 20 mph in a 35 mph zone. The vehicle had no lights on, and it straddled the white lines dividing lanes one and two five times within a space of three blocks. "Classic indicators of a drunk driver," Winters said. "Seen enough for your report?" "Yes I have, sir. Let's go ahead and stop him before he crashes."

Winters effected a traffic stop on the vehicle. Once he and Nolan got the driver out, the man displayed objective symptoms consistent with being under the influence of an alcoholic beverage. Winters demonstrated how to properly and safely administer the field sobriety tests for his partner. Ultimately, they arrested the man for deuce. By the time they got back to the station, processed the DUI driver and wrote the reports, it was time to go home. Winters gave Nolan his homework and study assignments. "Enjoy your days off," Winters said. "You've earned them, but study hard. Are you doing anything special?" Nolan simply smiled at Winters. Winters laughed and said, "Going out with Marie, huh?" "Yes sir." "Have fun—see you in a couple of days." "Thank you, sir."

The following morning Nolan got up and wasted no time in preparing to see Marie. By 10:00 A.M. he was ringing her doorbell. She opened the door and invited him in. "Good morning, John," she said as she gave him a little peck on the cheek. "Good morning to you too, Marie. I missed talking to you and being around you," Nolan said. "Well, I must confess, I missed you too. I kept thinking about you," Marie offered. "We haven't known each other very long but, we sure seem to get along," Nolan said with a smile. "It sounds kinda mushy, but maybe we've got that 'chemistry' thing going on here," he laughed. "I think you may be right," she concurred.

"Okay, what would you like to do today?" he asked. Marie answered, "I've got a couple of errands to run...you know, cleaners, market, gas my car, that kind of boring stuff. Do you mind?" Smiling, Nolan rubbed his chin, squinted his eyes and said, "Hmm... well, I don't mind at all, as long as you let me take you to a movie and dinner when we're done." "You got a deal mister!" Marie laughed. The two set out to take care of her errands. They continued to talk and laugh and take pleasure in each other's company.

By late afternoon they headed to the movies. While watching the movie, Marie reached for Nolan's hand and held it throughout the entire show. He couldn't have been happier. As the movie ended, he gently pulled Marie's hand to his lips and kissed it. The two then looked into each other's eyes for a moment, but said nothing. They got up and walked out of the theatre, arm in arm.

At a nearby restaurant, they ate a leisurely dinner and carried on with more dialogue and laughter. Then, it was time to go. Nolan drove the pretty lady back to her apartment. She invited him in and fixed some coffee. They sat on the couch and watched television for a bit. She snuggled next to him, and he put his arm around her shoulders.

After a while, he started stroking her beautiful hair. She turned to look in his eyes. They kissed gently and briefly. "We should go slow, John. I don't want either one of us to get hurt," she said softly. "I agree, but I have never felt this way about anyone before. It just feels good to be with you," he replied. "I know Sweetie, I know," she whispered in his ear.

After they finished their coffee, John stood up to leave. It was late. Marie put her arm around his waist and walked him to the door. They embraced and kissed. "Goodnight, Marie," he said. "Thank you for a beautiful day, John," she replied. "You really are a nice guy." "Thank you." As Nolan drove home that night, his mind was racing. He didn't want to be away from her. Was this love? Could he fall in love that quickly? He hadn't lied to her. He had never felt this way before about anyone.

When Nolan arrived home he took a long, cool shower. He hadn't paid attention to his studies all day. He knew he had better play catch up otherwise, Winters would have a chunk of his backside. He spread out his material and began to review it. Staying focused was a problem. He couldn't get her off of his mind. He forced himself to study but, eventually, he fell asleep on the couch. When he awoke a few hours later, it was still dark outside. He was surprised he felt as rested as he did, for having slept only a few short hours. Nolan put on a pot of coffee and studied hard for well over an hour. Then, he went on a long run.

As he ran, he thought about several issues. First, of course, he thought about Marie. Then, he thought about his job and his studies. As he headed back home, it occurred to him, he had not called his parents in a few days. That was unlike him. By the time he shaved and showered, it was 7:30 A.M. He knew his folks would be up. His mother answered the phone and he could tell she was upset with him. "I'm sorry I haven't called. It's been very busy at work and uh...oh, never mind, Mom. I don't have an excuse. Please forgive me. How's Dad?" he said all in one breath. His mom laughed. She couldn't be mad at him for very long. "Your dad and I are fine. When are you coming over?" "Well, I'm off tonight, but..." "Good, tell me what you want for dinner," his mom insisted. "Make whatever you want mom. I'll be there by 6:00, I promise."

A few seconds after he hung up the phone, it rang. "Hello," he answered. "Hi handsome, how are you?" Marie asked. "I'm great, now that I'm talking to you," he replied. "What are you doing?" he inquired. "Well, I just called to say hi. I have to go do laundry. I'm gonna kill two birds with one stone. I'm taking my laundry to my mom's. That way, I can visit with my folks while I wash my clothes. I have to be at work at 3:00 this afternoon. What about you?" she asked.

"I got most of my study work done. I went on a long run this morning, and then I called my parents. I'm gonna go see them tonight. I was kind of hoping we could see each other before you went to work," he hinted. "Well, you told me where you live...how about if I stop by for a cup of coffee on my way to my mom's?" "Perfect. Can you come over now?" he chuckled. "I'll be there soon," she said.

When Marie arrived, John went out to greet her. She was wearing a tight pair of faded blue jeans and a tight red sweater. She had almost no make-up on and her beautiful dark hair glistened in the sun as it hung halfway down her back. "God, you're pretty," were his first words to her. "Thank you," she smiled. They walked arm in arm to his apartment. She gave herself the nickel tour of the place. "Sorry if it's messy, the cleaning lady hasn't arrived yet," he joked. "You've got a nice place here. It figures you'd have good taste. "I do have good taste," he said. "I picked you." Marie walked over to him and they embraced and kissed.

Before they could get all hot and bothered, Marie said, "Okay buddy, where's that coffee you promised me?" "John played along, "It's right here lady," he said as he walked over to the coffee pot and poured her a cup. They sat at the table and talked. After a while, Marie looked at her watch and sadly said, "I'd better go." Then, she paused for a moment, got a big smile on her face and said, "Come with me!" "To your mom's house?" he asked. "Well, I've never taken a man to my parents' house before. And, from the way we seem to be getting along, they'll probably know about you soon enough. Please say you'll go with me." "You know I can't say no to you, but shouldn't you call them first?" he suggested. "Yeah, you're probably right. It'll scare the heck out of them if I just show up with you," she smiled. She made the call.

.When they arrived at her parents' home, Marie immediately introduced John to her mom and dad. She referred to him as her friend and described how they had met. John noticed several pictures on the wall in the front room as soon as he walked in. There were three in particular that caught his eye. The first picture was of Marie in a pair of scrubs with a stethoscope draped around her neck. The second and third were pictures of her sister and brother, each in their sheriff's uniform. Nice family, John thought as Marie was chatting a mile a minute with her folks. Within a few minutes, Marie's Dad turned to John saying, "They talk too much. I get a headache." "Oh, be quiet Dad," Marie smiled at her father.

John and Marie's dad moved to the couch and settled into light conversation while Marie and her mom talked and tended to Marie's laundry. Typically, as most moms do, Marie's mother prepared some food. She served John a huge burrito with rice and beans and all the trimmings. It was probably the best burrito he had ever tasted. As he continued to speak with her father, John overheard Marie's mom quietly asking her questions in Spanish. She must think I can't hear her, he thought. Marie answered in Spanish, and John realized that was the first time he had heard her speak other than English. She has a sweet voice in any language, he thought. He was still engaged in conversation with Marie's dad when she announced it was time to go.

Marie and John loaded up her freshly laundered clothes and left her folks' house with plenty of time for her to make it back to John's apartment where she could pick up her car and head off to work. As they drove, John said, "Your parents are very nice. Made me feel right at home. They remind me so much of my parents. Just plain good people. My mom would have done exactly what yours did—fix food right away." They both laughed. "Man, that was a good burrito. She sure can cook." "Why thank you, sir. I know she'll be pleased to hear that." "Maybe soon you could meet my mom and dad. They're gonna love you." Marie pretended not to hear John's comment.

"My parents liked you, John." "What makes you say that?" he asked. "My mom told me in Spanish she knows I obviously care for you. Like I told you, I've never brought a man to their home. My mom said you are a very nice young man, and my dad wouldn't have sat and talked to you for so long if he didn't think so too." "Well, thank you, I sure appreciate that." When they arrived at Nolan's apartment, he carried her laundry to her car for her. They hugged and kissed for several minutes before Marie got in her car and rushed off to work.

Since Nolan had a couple of hours before he would leave for his parents' house, he hit the books again. He shined his gear and began to mentally prepare himself for the following day with his training officer. He went to his parents' house as promised and had a delicious dinner with them. Afterwards, they had some of Mom's pastries and talked in detail about his first week on the street. His parents echoed their feelings about him being a policeman. They were as proud as parents could possibly be about a child and yet, at the same time, that pride was constantly overshadowed by the fact that they could not stop worrying about him. Nolan understood his parents' worries, but he also reassured them that he did everything by the book, and that he was fortunate to have a superb training officer in Dennis Winters.

The discussion then turned to Marie, and Nolan told his mother and father how they had met and that they had been together as much as possible since meeting each other. Fearing he might hurt their feelings, Nolan left out the part about him having already met her folks. His parents saw the gleam in his eye and watched his facial expressions as he spoke of her. He was so excited and happy as he carried on about her.

They knew this was obviously a very special woman in their son's life. They were happy for him because they knew he had been lonely. Typical of loving and caring parents, their first question, as posed by his mom was, "So, when do we get to meet her?" Then, "Why don't you bring her to dinner?" John explained that he and Marie had difficult schedules, but he promised his parents he would arrange a meeting as soon as he could.

That evening, Marie called when she got home from work. They talked for a long time on the phone before calling it a night. The following day, Nolan went to work early, allowing himself plenty of time for a hard workout, after which he prepared for his shift. Following briefing, he and Winters readied their unit and received their first call before even driving out of the station parking lot. "302 handle, 415 females, possible prostitution activity, at the Blue Sky Motel, 3718 Garner Street. R/P is the clerk / manager." After he acknowledged the call, Nolan listened as Winters explained, "The motel we're going to is a typical flea-bag hooker motel. The girls usually have an arrangement with the manager of the place to get rooms by the hour. Generally, they pay either a discounted room rate, cut the manager in for a portion of the money received from each trick, or provide sexual favors for him and his associates. But, if the girls have a pimp, he'll usually handle the financial arrangements with the management. This particular motel is especially dirty and more often than not, the hookers have VD or some other disease or infection. They're usually hypes or "coke whores," so don't touch anyone or anything unless I tell you."

Upon arriving at the motel, the officers could hear the ruckus emanating from within as they walked towards the office. They entered and separated the parties. The "manager," was a foul-smelling, filthy looking, overweight and balding white guy. He was arguing with two hookers, one black, one white. Winters had Nolan keep the females at the far end of the relatively small lobby while he talked to the manager. Winters had talked to this creep once before, and the guy knew better than to give him a bad time. He told Winters the argument started over the two girls sharing the cost for the room. The manager wanted a fee from each girl, and they didn't want to pay it.

Nolan calmed the two girls down and told them he and his partner would take care of the problem as best they could. The girls both smiled and starting coming on to Nolan. He immediately got embarrassed, which made them laugh and call him a "rookie." Where Nolan was standing, he was able to see out onto the parking lot of the motel. He saw a sixties model Lincoln convertible with the top down pull in and park.

The Lincoln was spotless and had beautiful wheels with "gangster" whitewalls. The lone male occupant exited the vehicle and approached the motel office. He was a tall, muscular black man dressed just like a pimp. Nolan called to Winters by saying, "Partner." Winters turned to look at Nolan who gestured with his head and eyes toward the office door as the man approached. Winters looked at the man just as he opened the front door to the office.

"What's goin' on here?" the pimp demanded, as he eyeballed the motel manager, whom he obviously knew. "The ladies are upset about our room rates," replied the manager. Winters immediately told the pimp to go outside and wait. The pimp glared defiantly at Winters as if to challenge him. Seeing this, the black girl stepped toward the pimp and said, "Honey, we didn't want no trouble here. Just do what the police tell you."

As soon as she finished talking, the pimp slapped her across the face with enough force to send her reeling across the room and into a wall. She screamed and collapsed in pain. Instinctively, Nolan stepped toward the man, and before he could react, Nolan grabbed him and slammed him face down on the ground and into handcuffing position. Winters ran over and helped his partner handcuff the now quiet pimp.

The manager shouted, "Hey, he didn't have to do that!" "Shut your mouth!" Winters ordered. "Yes officer," the manager replied. Nolan left his prisoner lying on the floor while he hurried over to see how the hooker was doing. He helped her to her feet. She looked him in the eye and started crying even more. "Please let him go, Officer," she pleaded. "He'll kill me." Nolan called the white girl over and had her tend to her friend.

Nolan then offered to call for medical help, however, the girl declined, repeating her plea to Nolan for him to let her pimp go. "I'm not going to press charges," she said as she wept. Winters had just finished talking to the manager. He walked up and said, "We figured that." "Partner, why don't you take him out and put him in the unit?" Nolan nodded and complied with his partner's request.

Winters got whatever names and other identifying information he could from the two girls even though he knew that hookers rarely had any valid form of identification on their person. He also knew that when dealing with police officers, they usually give bogus information. Once again, he briefly admonished the manager, as well as the hookers, as he exited the office. The three promised to resolve their differences peacefully.

As Winters approached the unit, Nolan informed him he had already run the pimp who had several AKA's and an outstanding felony warrant for ADW (assault with a deadly weapon). "Good job, partner," Winters commented. "What's his real name?" "My name is James Dixon," the arrestee replied before Nolan could answer. Directing his remarks to Winters, Dixon said, "I ain't gonna give you no trouble. I just do what I have to do to keep my bitches in line. But your partner slammed me hard."

Nolan turned as if to respond, but Winters raised his hand to silence him. Winters then told Dixon, "My partner was nice to you. If I'd been closer, you'd be on your way to the hospital right now for what you did to that girl." "Okay man, I understand how you feel. No problem. Look man, I don't care about going to jail, but I'm worried about my car. Can you tell the manager to watch after it?" Dixon asked. "Yeah, we can do that," Winters said. "I'll go tell him," Nolan said. "Okay partner," Winters agreed. "Thank you, Officer," Dixon said.

After they had transported and booked Dixon, the officers got right back out on the street. It was a busy evening and they were needed in the field. En route to their next call, Winters asked, "That was a nice, quick take-down on that guy. Where'd you learn that? I know you didn't learn it in the academy." "My dad taught me. I just reacted. After we hooked him up, I started worrying about whether or not you'd be mad at me for being so aggressive," Nolan said with concern. "Not at all. Even though I had told you not to touch anyone unless I told you, the situation changed and required quick, decisive action."

"You took the right action. He was the aggressor—you took him down, we hooked him up and it was over. I'm not at all upset. You did exactly what you were supposed to do," Winters said. "Whew, thank you sir." Winters smiled in frustration, "Look John, I know you're having trouble getting away from the 'sir' crap, but, I'll tell you again, call me Winters or partner. In fact, now that I'm seeing that you've pretty much got your shit together, and you're squared-away, you can even call me Dennis. Just quit calling me 'sir' in every other sentence." Nolan smiled and said, "Thanks partner, I fully understand, and I'll make it a point to stop doing that." "Good."

After handling another couple of calls, the officers noticed the radio seemed to have quieted down. "Now that there's a lull in the action, lets go eat. Find out if we're clear for seven," Winters instructed Nolan. They received clearance and after being seated in the restaurant, Winters tested Nolan on some of the study homework he had been assigned. After several minutes, Winters said, "Well, I see you took your studying seriously. That's good John."

Winters changed the topic. He smiled and asked, "So, how was the date with Marie?" Before he replied, Nolan couldn't help but get a great big grin on his face. "It was perfect. She's absolutely great. I really enjoy being with her." "Does she feel that way about you?" Winters inquired. "I think so. We spent as much time together as possible. I even met her mom and dad," Nolan said proudly. "Wow! Aren't you guys going a little fast?" "Oh no," Nolan laughed. "It's nothing like that. I just accompanied her to her parents' house. She does her laundry over there on her day off while she visits." "Oh," Winters replied. Nolan added, "We do get along very well and we seem to share the same beliefs and philosophies. We talk for hours on end."

"Falling in love, huh John?" Winters asked. "It sure looks that way," Nolan confessed. "I just love being around her and I miss her terribly five minutes after I'm away from her. I even miss her after we've just talked on the phone." "Oh, you've got it bad, son," Winters joked. "I know," Nolan said. "I've never felt like this before." "Well, the best advice I could give you would be to proceed slowly. That goes for the both of you." "Thanks. Marie and I talked about that too, and we decided we'll do just that."

The officers finished their meal and headed back out on the street. Even though it was quiet on the air, the remainder of the evening seemed to pass quickly. Winters reminded his partner he would finish that week and work the following week with him, after which he would be gone on vacation for two weeks. "I haven't figured out yet who the sarge is going to put you with while I'm gone. I need to ask him, so that I can talk to whoever it is about you, before I leave."

They headed for the station when it was time to go EOW. They carried their gear downstairs and changed into their civies. "Goodnight, partner," Nolan said with a smile on his face as the two walked out of the building and headed towards their personal cars. "Yeah, goodnight partner to you too," Winters chuckled, pleased that Nolan didn't call him "sir" again.

The next few days were busy, but they passed relatively uneventfully. However, with each day, Nolan learned more and gained more valuable experience. He was like a sponge, absorbing whatever input was sent his way. Winters was an excellent training officer, and Nolan knew he was

71

fortunate to have been assigned to him. He also knew he had one more week with Winters before he would go on a two-week vacation. Nolan was anxious to learn to whom he would be assigned during Winters' absence.

Because of conflicting schedules, Marie and John did not have the opportunity to see much of each other during the rest of that week. However, they did manage to go to breakfast once in that time period. They also called one another as often as possible, talking about anything and everything. The two were rapidly becoming very close. They were very excited as the week drew to a close because they knew they would have two days off together that following week. They could hardly wait to spend some quality time together.

Chapter Five

Love Is In The Air

Nolan woke up early on his first of two days off. His first thought was of Marie and the fact she would be off with him. Though they had not made any definitive plans as to what they would do on their days off, it was understood they would spend as much time together as possible. He did not call her when he first woke up, because he knew she had worked until 2:30 A.M.

Instead of getting out of bed, he laid there thinking, reflecting on what was going on in his young life. Notwithstanding the tragedy he witnessed his first night on the street, he kept things in perspective and reaffirmed his career decision. He was an idealist, and in his eyes, being a policeman was not only an honorable profession, it was one in which he could actually help others.

His focus returned to Marie. We really haven't known each other for very long but, I can't stand being away from her, he thought. I feel a sort of emptiness when I'm not around her. When I close my eyes, I picture her face and hear her voice. Geez, am I falling in love, or what, he mused. Is this how it's supposed to feel? Suddenly, he laughed out loud as he lay there thinking how this could be a romantic story on one of the soap operas his mother loved to watch. He decided it was time to get out of bed.

Nolan readied the coffeepot and jumped in the shower. Once he was dressed, he poured himself a cup and decided it was time to call Marie. To his surprise, there was no answer. Nervous anxiety immediately kicked in and he felt his heart skip a beat. That's very unusual, he thought, and he began to worry. He hung up and dialed the number again. Still no answer. She's probably in the shower, he reasoned. I'll give her a call again in a few minutes. He finished his first cup of coffee and went to get another when the doorbell rang. "Just a minute," he shouted as he finished pouring his second cup. He walked toward his front door and asked loudly, "Who is it?" There was no response.

He opened the door anyway and there stood the woman of his dreams with a big smile on her face. "Surprise!" she said cheerfully. "Are you happy to see me?" He pulled the door open the rest of the way and embraced her. "Of course I'm happy to see you. I called you just a few minutes ago, and there was no answer. I got worried. Then I figured you were in the shower. I was just about to call you again when the doorbell rang."

They walked into his apartment, still embracing. John closed the door and turned back towards Marie. They hugged once again and kissed for a long time. "It's so good to see you," he said. "I know, I couldn't wait anymore. I jumped out of bed and got ready as fast as I could. I wanted to surprise you," she whispered. For a few moments, neither one said anything. They just stood there tightly embraced in each other's arms. Then, John started slowly stroking Marie's hair, pushing it back off her forehead. They gazed into each other's eyes. He started to smile.

"What?" she asked as she smiled back at him. "I was just thinking. The anticipation is killing me." "We've been pretty good, huh?" she asked. "Too good," he replied. They laughed.

"Okay, so what do you want to do today?" he asked as they broke their embrace. "I hadn't thought about it. I just wanted to be with you," she said. "Well, let's go do something, maybe get something to eat and then later...we'll see," he suggested. "Let's go somewhere we can walk around and talk and hold hands," she said. "I know, we can go to a museum or even to the zoo," he offered. "The zoo. Yes, the zoo! I haven't been there since I was a kid," Marie said excitedly. "So what are we waiting for? Let's go," John said as he grabbed his car keys.

They spent the next few hours at the zoo doing just what Marie had said she wanted to do. They walked around, looked at all the birds and animals, held hands and talked. They ate junk food and had an absolutely great time together. Toward the end of the afternoon, it was time to leave.

"Do you want to get something to eat?" John asked as they walked to his car. "Is that all you think about... food?" she chuckled. "Actually, no," he said as he stopped, turned Marie towards him and stared hungrily up and down her body, making exaggerated head and eye movements to be sure she saw exactly what he was doing. She grinned and said, "Okay, okay, I guess I walked right into that one." "Uh-huh," he said, as they resumed walking to the car hand in hand. "Why don't we pick up something to go, take it back to my house, eat and watch a little TV." "That sounds good, but first, stop at my house so I can pick something up," Marie said. "Okay," he replied.

Nolan parked in front of Marie's apartment building, and the pair walked up to her apartment. "What do you have to get?" he asked as they approached her door. Marie didn't answer right away. She waited until they were inside her apartment before she replied, "Well, by you suggesting we go to your house to watch TV, I was thinking we might possibly get romantic." "Well yeah, I hope so. I mean, I was looking forward to it," he stammered shyly. "Well, I need to have something to change into in the morning Sweetie," she hinted. "Oh, okay, I didn't get it," he said, as his face flushed with embarrassment.

Marie hurriedly threw a few items into an overnight bag. Back in the car, they decided to forego their planned food stop. They drove directly to John's house. On the way, John reached over and held Marie's hand. "God, I feel like I'm on my first date," she said. "Me too. I've got butterflies in my stomach," he volunteered. "We're pathetic, aren't we?" she giggled nervously. "No, we're not pathetic. It's just that we care for each other and we know it's real," he said. She didn't reply. She just squeezed his hand.

At John's apartment, Marie went to freshen up while he got a bottle of wine and a couple of glasses. By the time Marie was done, he had poured the wine, dimmed the lights and turned on the TV. "Oh my," she said in a surprised voice as she entered the room. "Thought you might like a glass of wine," he said as he handed her a glass. "I would," she replied. John got his glass and they toasted each other, "Here's to the most gorgeous woman in the world," he smiled. "And here's to my handsome blue knight," she replied. They sipped wine and sat on the couch in front of the TV.

Before very long, they had shared the entire bottle of wine and were wrapped in each other's arms watching an old World War II movie. "Do you want to go lie down?" he asked softly. "Yes," she whispered. John carefully carried Marie into the bedroom. They continued caressing one another and spent the better part of the night entwined in passionate lovemaking. Neither one had ever experienced anything so intense or so wonderfully romantic.

Very late the next morning, the two lovers awoke. They kissed and said good morning to one another. They were each happy and very relaxed. Marie stretched lazily and then jumped out of bed saying, "I'm gonna go wash up and make us some breakfast. I'm starving." "Me too! There's plenty of stuff in the fridge. I'll get the coffee going," John added. "Okay," she replied as she closed the bathroom door. By the time Marie got out of the bathroom, John had put on the coffee, poured orange juice and set the table. Marie walked into the small kitchen and hugged him, not saying a word. He responded by kissing her forehead and stroking her beautiful hair. Then it was his turn to go wash up.

John could smell the bacon and eggs as soon as he emerged from the bathroom. Marie was busy. She ordered him to sit and served them both a very nice breakfast. They ate and talked and continued to enjoy the pleasure of each other's company. "We should go see my parents," Marie said. "Okay, I'll go see yours, if you go see mine," John said teasingly. "Do you think I'm ready for that?" she asked nervously, referring to her meeting his parents. "Definitely," he replied. "You *know* I told my parents all about you. They can't wait to meet you. I'm gonna call my Mom. They wanted me to bring you to dinner, so why don't we take care of all our errands, visit your parents and then go to dinner at my parents' house?" "Okay, let's move it then. It's already noon," she said as she glanced at the clock on the wall.

They spent the next couple of hours taking care of their respective errands and chores. Once again, they stopped at Marie's apartment so she could pick up her dirty laundry to take to her mom's. When they arrived at Marie's parents' house, John was welcomed with open arms by her mom and dad. Also visiting her parents that particular day was Sylvia, Marie's sister, and John had the opportunity to meet her as well.

Marie and her sister were very close, and Marie spoke often of her. They all chatted and had a pleasant visit while Marie tended to her laundry. During the course of the visit, John and Marie gazed lovingly into each other's eyes on a number of occasions, as only lovers do. Marie's mom noticed the way the two looked at each other, and she knew they were lovers. She was happy because even though she hadn't known John very long, she sensed he was a fine young man. Not because he was a policeman, but because it was obvious he came from a good home with a good upbringing. It was time for Marie to settle down with a good man. Maybe this was him!

Sylvia, a deputy sheriff, and John, were entertaining Marie's dad as they exchanged their personal academy torture stories. The three guffawed loudly as the various stories unfolded. Seeing this as an opportunity, Marie's mom went to help her daughter fold her clothes so she could question her. "So tell me, how do you feel about John, Marie?" her mom inquired as they both folded clothes. "Well Mom, it's always been hard to hide anything from you," Marie laughed, "but, I guess you could say we're falling in love with each other." "Does he feel the way you do?" Mom asked protectively. "Yes, I truly believe he does. We just enjoy being together, and we seem to click. We've become very close friends." "Good. He seems like a fine young man." "He is Mom, he really is," Marie beamed.

As he sat and talked with Sylvia and her Dad, John looked at his watch. 5:15! He promised his mom he and Marie would be there for dinner by 6:00PM. It was about a twenty-five minute drive from Marie's folks' house to his folks' house. A few minutes later, Marie came into the room and John reminded her of the time. "I'm almost done," she smiled. "We'll leave in just a few minutes." "Okay," John returned the smile.

Sylvia said she had to get going too, and started saying good-bye to everyone. She kissed her parents good-bye, and as she was leaving, she stopped to shake John's hand. She looked him in the eye and said sternly, "It was very nice meeting you, John. Be good to my little sister." "You have my word," John replied seriously. Sylvia smiled and left. Marie's dad then turned to John and asked, "Where are you guys off to?" "We're going to go to dinner at my parents' house," John responded. "Oh, that's nice. Have they met Marie before?" "No sir, but I've told them all about her. They're very anxious to meet her," was John's answer. "You and

Marie *really* like each other, I can tell. Just don't ever hurt my little girl," he said as he smiled. "No sir. That could never happen."

It was just about 6:00 o'clock when John and Marie pulled into his parents' driveway. Marie admitted she was a little nervous. "Come on now," John coaxed. "They're gonna love you. I've already told them all about you." "Do they know I'm Hispanic?" she inquired. "Yes, they do, and it's not an issue in this house," John retorted. "Don't be mad, John. It's just that I've experienced prejudice before and it's ugly." "You don't ever need to be concerned about that with my family and if anyone else has a problem with us being together, they can see me about it," he replied.

John took Marie's hand and raised it to his lips. He kissed her hand gently, paused and said, "I'm sorry if I seemed to snap at you just then. It's just because...well...I've really fallen deeply in love with you, Baby." Marie reached for John's hand as tears began to stream down her face. "I'm in love with you too, Sweetie," she said, crying happily. John chuckled as he quietly backed his car out of his parents' driveway.

"Don't want to meet them with tears in your eyes, do you?" he joked as they drove around the block. Marie managed to compose herself quickly and wiped her face with a tissue by the time they had returned. The two then held hands and smiled at each other as they pulled back into the driveway. "Come on, ma'am," he said, "there are some really nice people who are very anxious to make your acquaintance." "I believe I'm ready, sir," she said confidently.

John rang the doorbell. His mom and dad both responded to the door expecting to see him and to meet Marie. "Come in, come in," they both said excitedly as they opened the door. John introduced Marie to his parents, and they all went inside. "We've heard so much about you, dear," John's mom said as the four sat in the living room. "And you're just as beautiful as he described you," John's dad added. Marie looked over at John and they grinned at each other. "Thank you," she said. John offered Marie something to drink, and the four had a nice chat for several minutes. Then, John's Mom said, "Let's eat," as she got up and headed towards the kitchen. "Can I help you?" Marie offered. "Sure," John's mom replied. "Thank you for asking."

"John told us you went out of your way to patch him up when he hurt himself chasing someone," his mom said. "I wanted to thank you for that," she said as she and Marie readied the dinner table. "Oh, I didn't do anything special—he's so sweet." "We worry a lot about him being a policeman." "I know," Marie said, "but he loves it so much." "You're right, my dear, he really does love it." Marie smiled and said, "He also loves to eat." "I heard that," John said, as he came strolling into the kitchen. "Speaking of which, I'm starving." "Okay, okay," his mom said laughing. "Let's sit and eat."

The four of them sat down to a delicious, full course meal. John's mom had prepared enough food to feed a small army. Marie felt very comfortable with his parents, and she realized her initial apprehension about meeting them was unwarranted. As they ate, the conversation remained light and filled with laughter. When everyone had eaten their fill, John's mom excused herself and began removing plates from the table. Once again Marie offered to help. "No, No, you sit and relax," his mom said. "I'd really prefer to help you," Marie insisted, as she stood up and gathered the remaining dirty dishes. John's mom didn't offer any further resistance. She just smiled at Marie.

Shortly after dinner, John's dad put on a pot of coffee and, within thirty minutes of them finishing their meal, John's mom summoned everyone back to the table for pastry and coffee. "I'm stuffed," Marie whispered to John. "Come on, you've got to have a coffee and a pastry. You wouldn't want to hurt my mom's feelings, would you?" John asked teasingly. Marie smiled and playfully punched his shoulder as they walked to the table.

After dessert and coffee, Mom broke out one of the picture albums. "No, Mom!" John protested. Despite his protests, Mom starting showing Marie his baby and childhood pictures. John threw his arms up in the air and walked out of the room. He and his dad left the ladies alone and watched the news on television.

When it was time to go, John's mom hugged Marie and said, "You're a very fine young lady." "Thank you ma'am," Marie answered, blushing. John's dad hugged Marie as well and told her he was happy she was able to come and meet them. In the car on the way back to John's apartment, Marie said, "Your parents are so nice." "Thanks," he replied, "and they loved you, just like I knew they would." "They made me feel so comfortable. I wasn't nervous at all."

Marie rubbed her tummy and asked, "Sweetie, can we go for a walk? I'm still so stuffed," she laughed almost painfully. "I guess I'm just not used to eating that much," she explained. "Yes ma'am, we will go for a walk," John replied.

They parked the car at John's apartment and went for a leisurely stroll, hand in hand. Once inside the apartment, Marie asked, "John, did you really mean what you said to me?" Knowing exactly what she meant, he embraced her and replied, "I meant every word. You're the woman of my dreams and I've been looking for you for a long time. I love you very much!" They kissed and held each other for a long time. Eventually, they made their way to the bedroom, where they enjoyed another wonderful night of passionate exploration and incredible lovemaking.

Chapter Six

The Replacement Training Officer

The following morning, John and Marie woke up in each other's arms. They kissed and reaffirmed their love for one another. Looking at the clock, John said, "I've gotta start getting ready for work." "Me too, Sweetie. I'll fix a quick breakfast for us then I'll get going," Marie said sadly. "Okay," John replied with a somber look on his face as they both got out of bed.

After Marie left, Nolan reviewed his study materials and shined his gear in preparation for a new week. In keeping with his routine, he left early and trained hard in the basement gym. He hit the shower, dressed and patiently awaited his training officer in the briefing room. He reflected on his days off with Marie and felt that it couldn't have gone any better than it did. I really do love her, he thought. She is the perfect woman. He had only been away from her a few hours, he couldn't wait to talk to her and see her again.

Winters arrived for work early as well. He wanted to talk to Sergeant Carter prior to the start of watch. He was concerned about who would have his trainee during his two week absence. Winters liked working with Sergeant Carter and thought he was squared away. He was fair and consistent and had a great deal of experience. Winters entered his office. "Hey Sarge, how ya doin?" "Hi Dennis, doing fine, thanks. What brings you in so early?" he inquired. "I wanted to ask you who's gonna take my trainee during my vacation." "Well, I looked at that earlier. The choices are very limited. I'm going to have to put him with Ernie Davidson." "Ernie Davidson!" Winters exclaimed in amazement.

"Come on Sarge, isn't there anyone else? I mean, I don't have anything personal against the guy, but he's not a T.O. That kid's sharp. His training is going very well. Can't you put him with anyone else? What about Gonzales?" Winters asked. "He'll be away at narco school," the sergeant patiently replied. "How about Meyers?" Winters asked. "He's going to be on stand-by for a homicide trial. The D.A. called me last week and asked that he be in court every day next week. Look Dennis, I'm not going to play twenty questions with you. I understand your concern, but Davidson is the best I can do right now."

Winters didn't reply. He just stood there for a moment. "Tell you what," Sergeant Carter said, "I'll make it a point to watch out for the kid while you're gone, okay?" he smiled at Winters. "Now get out of here while I work on some other schedule changes," the sergeant said, grinning at Winters. "Okay, thanks Sarge," Winters replied quietly as he left the office.

Winters was definitely not pleased with the fact that Nolan would be assigned to Davidson. He was one of those guys more concerned with meeting women and being "bitchin'" than caring about any trainee. Winters changed into uniform and met up with Nolan in the briefing room, but he didn't say anything about Davidson. After roll call, Winters had Nolan set up their unit. "You drive today," Winters told Nolan. "Really?" Nolan asked, grinning like a kid with a new toy. "I usually don't let new guys drive for several weeks, but since you've done very well and I'll be gone for a couple of weeks, I'm gonna have you drive me around. My treat," he smiled. "Thanks partner," Nolan said, getting comfortable in the driver's seat. Wow, this is pretty cool, he thought as he pulled the shift lever into reverse.

Before very long, Winters and Nolan got their first call of the evening. It was a 415 fight call at a local rowdy bar named "Bill's Tavern." "Great," Winters said sarcastically. "Haven't gotten called to that dump in two or three weeks. It's one of the regular places you'll get to know real well. Lots of assholes hang out in there. When we get there, stay close to me." One other unit was assigned to the call, but they had a long roll. Winters and Nolan arrived and went in. They immediately saw that one fellow was down on the floor just inside the entrance. He was apparently unconscious and he was bleeding from the head. Glass was strewn about him and it appeared that someone had done him with a beer bottle. With all the yelling and commotion going on in the darkened, smoke filled bar, it took a few moments for patrons to realize the police had arrived.

Two other guys were just about to gang up on one fellow when Winters yelled out, "Hey, knock it off. Get your hands up and walk over here." "Fuck you, pig," replied the bigger of the two aggressors. He turned his attention to Winters and started towards him. Winters drew his baton out of the ring and the big man laughed, "What are you gonna do with that, pig?" he shouted, as he continued his approach, fists clenched. When he got close enough, Winters stepped forward towards him and drove the tip of his baton into his sternum. The big man dropped like a sack of potatoes.

Seeing that, his buddy yelled and charged at Winters. Nolan stepped in front of Winters and met the fellow with a front kick to the chest. The man staggered backwards, but recovered and came again, loudly threatening to kill Nolan this time, as he charged. Nolan met him with a front kick to the abdomen this time, doubling him over. Nolan then grabbed the man and delivered two quick and powerful knee strikes to the abdomen and the chest. He collapsed on the floor, writhing in pain. Nolan readied himself for two more coming towards him as Winters shouted, "Heads up, partner."

Back up Officers Gonzales and Meyers had arrived at the entrance of the bar in time to hear the second attacker shouting threats to Winters and Nolan. They hustled over toward where Winters and Nolan were standing. These were both big, burly officers. When the two men who were in the process of charging Winters and Nolan saw them approaching, they stopped dead in their tracks. Gonzales and Meyers were more than happy to deal with those two, while Winters and Nolan handcuffed the two men who had actually attacked them.

Immediately thereafter, they checked on the man down. Nolan said, "I'll get the medics rolling." "Okay," Winters acknowledged. Meanwhile, Gonzales and Meyers arrested the two subjects who had started to attack Winters and Nolan. "Thanks, guys," Winters said to Gonzales and Meyers. "Our pleasure, sir," Gonzales laughed. All four suspects were transported to the station for booking.

Paramedics arrived and rendered aid to the victim of the bottle attack. He regained consciousness, however, he was too intoxicated to remember what had happened to him. An ambulance responded and transported him to the hospital. During the course of their investigation, Winters and Nolan determined that it had been their first attacker, the big man, who had in fact, broken a beer bottle over the victim's head. Several witness statements supported that determination. Therefore, in addition to assault on a police officer, he would be charged with ADW (assault with a deadly weapon).

Prior to leaving the bar, Winters turned his attention to the bartender and co-owner of the bar. Winters had dealt with him numerous times in the past. This guy hated the police and permitted his establishment to be a hangout for dope fiends, dirtbags and other assorted ne'er-do-wells. Winters had noticed at least two "A.B.C." licensing (Alcoholic Beverage Control) violations in the bar, and he issued a citation to the bartender for those violations. Simultaneously, he had Nolan run him for warrants, and he was pleased to learn the bartender had an outstanding battery warrant. Winters couldn't help but smile as he told him he was under arrest and hooked him up.

Winters and Nolan headed in to the station to book the bartender and handle the arrest reports and all of the accompanying paperwork related to the bar incident. After they finished and went back out in the field, Winters quizzed Nolan. "John, tell me why you stepped in front of me to take out the second attacker." "Well, I'd been standing just off your left side because there were two guys yelling at you from that side, and I wanted to be in position to protect you in the event they decided to attack while you were engaged with the big guy."

"But then, after you laid the big guy out and his buddy started towards you, I focused on him. I could see you in my peripheral vision, but I wasn't sure you had recovered from the first attacker, and I just didn't know if you were ready to deal with another one. I didn't want to take the chance on him getting to you. Sorry partner," Nolan said. Winters shook his head, "No, no, don't be sorry. I appreciate what you did. I just wanted to understand your reasoning behind it. Again, your evaluation of the situation and your response were right on. Good job, man." "Thanks partner."

"Why don't you see if we're clear for seven. I've got some other things to talk to you about," Winters advised Nolan with a serious tone in his voice. Nolan thought, "Oh shit, what did I do wrong?" as he requested clearance for them to go eat. They received their clearance, and Winters selected his favorite Mexican "hole in the wall" restaurant. "I'm starving. Think I'll have one of their gigantic burritos," he laughed. Nolan didn't respond. As they were exiting their unit, they received a radio call to phone the station. "I'll call from inside," Winters said.

The hostess seated Nolan while Winters asked permission to use the phone. It was Sergeant Carter who had made the request for him to call. "Dennis, I've looked at the schedule," Carter said. "The easiest way for me to transition Nolan into Davidson's schedule is for Nolan to work one more day with you and then take the next day off. The following day he'll start with Davidson on the mid-watch." "Alright Sarge, I'll let him know," Winters said, "If that's the case, since I won't be with my trainee anyway, can I take the balance of this week off and extend my vacation? I've got plenty of time on the books." "Yeah sure, that'll work. I'll amend the paperwork," Sergeant Carter replied. "Alright Sarge."

Winters returned to the table and sat down. He had a sad look on his face. "What's wrong," Nolan asked of his training officer. "That was the sarge," Winters said. "He's changing your schedule so you can fall into your interim T.O.'s schedule. His name is Ernie Davidson, and he works the mid-watch. I don't think you've met him. You'll work with me tomorrow and take the following day off. The day after that you'll report to Davidson on the mid-watch. You'll be with him until I get back," Winters explained. "Okay partner, whatever you say," Nolan replied with a forced smile on his face. "Look John," Winters added, "Davidson wouldn't have been my first choice as your interim training officer, but it's only for a couple of weeks. You'll be fine," he reasoned. "Is that what you were going to talk to me about?" Nolan asked. "Yes."

The officers ate their meal, cleared, and promptly received two report calls. They handled a traffic accident and a 415 family before their shift came to an end. The following day, Winters and Nolan were noticeably quieter than usual. Though they had not been partners very long and Nolan was a trainee, they seemed to work well together. Both men knew it would be their last shift together for more than two weeks. It was a busy evening and they seemed to go from call to call. By 8:00 p.m. they had amassed quite a bit of paperwork and Nolan asked Winters if they could head in to the station so he could take care of it.

"Sure, advise communications we'll be out to the station." They picked up some food on the way in, and Nolan took care of all the paperwork they had. Then, he called Marie at the hospital. "Hey lady, my schedule changed. I'm off tomorrow. Since you're working nights again this week, how about if I pick you up for breakfast?" Nolan asked. "Sure Sweetie, I'll be ready by 10:00...I gotta go, we're real busy, there's a full moon." "Okay, bye," Nolan said. "Bye."

By the time they got back out in the field, Winters and Nolan only had a couple of hours left on their shift. Nolan had read somewhere that a full moon usually meant an increased level of activity for police, fire and hospital personnel. He thought it was a myth. He inquired of his partner, "I know this is going to sound like a stupid question, but is it normally busier during a full moon?" "Well, that's really not a stupid question," Winters chuckled. "The fact is, it's almost always busier when there is a full moon. There is no scientific data that I know of. I only know that in emergency service circles, it's common knowledge that a full moon goes hand in hand with increased levels of activity. Just that simple."

Winters paused and then inquired, "What made you ask that?" "After I finished all of our paper, I made a quick call to Marie. She told me they'd been very busy and nonchalantly mentioned it was because there's a full moon," Nolan explained. "Well, see, there you have it." Winters nodded. "By the way, how's it going with you two?" he asked. "We've really hit it off. We spend as much time together as possible and...well, she's simply the greatest," Nolan smiled. "We're very comfortable with each other." "I'm happy for you man," Winters said sincerely. "Thanks."

The officers made a couple of traffic stops, wrote a citation and handled two more 415 calls prior to their shift coming to an end. On the way in to the station at EOW, Winters reminded Nolan about working with Davidson, "Just do what you've been doing. Do it right, do it by the book, and do it on time. You'll be fine and I'll see you in two weeks. Oh yeah, keep up on your studies and if I get back early, I may give you a call." "I sure appreciate you watching out for me, partner," Nolan said in response. Winters smiled and said, "You're an excellent trainee. You've got a good attitude and you're proving yourself to be a worthy partner." "Thanks Dennis. Enjoy your vacation."

As he did almost every night since they met, Nolan called his dream girl when he got home. "Hi Baby, when did you get home?" he asked. "I got in about forty-five minutes ago," she responded wearily. "You sound tired, Marie." "I am. It stayed busy all night. I took a shower, and I'm already in bed. But I knew you'd call, so I waited up." "Okay then, get some sleep and I'll be there at 10:00 o'clock to pick you up. I love you," John said. "I love you too, Sweetie," Marie purred. "Goodnight."

At 9:50 A.M. John was knocking on Marie's door. She answered the door with a big smile on her face. She was still in her robe, "You're early, I'm still putting on my make-up," she chuckled. "I keep telling you, you don't need any make-up. You're too damn pretty for make-up," John said as he embraced her. They had not seen each other for a few days and they began hungrily kissing each other. Though they had intended on going out to breakfast, they didn't make it. Instead, they got caught up in the heat of passion, as lovers often do. By the time they finished making love, it was too late to go out to breakfast because Marie had to ready herself for work.

John lazily got out of bed. "Since it's too late for us to go to breakfast, I'll make it for you. Got anything in the fridge?" he asked, joking sarcastically. "Of course I do," Marie said, as she threw a pillow at his head. "My fridge is stocked as well as yours." She also got out of bed, and the two laughed and embraced once again. "I sure love you," she purred in his ear. "And I adore you," he replied softly. John managed to put something resembling breakfast together and served Marie when she finished dressing. They ate hurriedly, and then Marie had to leave. John left Marie's house and then visited his parents. He stayed at their house most of the day.

As instructed, Nolan went to work on the mid-watch the following day. Getting dressed in the locker room, he was approached by an officer he had not seen before. "You're Nolan, right?" "Yes, that's right." "I'm Davidson. You're working with me for two or three weeks. Get all your shit and meet me in the parking lot," he snarled. "I'll be right there," Nolan replied. "You address me as sir, or Officer Davidson. Is that clear?" "Very clear, sir," Nolan replied. Davidson turned and left. Nolan finished changing and responded to the parking lot as Davidson had ordered. This is gonna be loads of fun, he thought, as he approached Davidson's unit. Nolan put his bag in the trunk and seated himself on the passenger side just as Davidson started the car.

Davidson did not say a word to Nolan for several minutes. Nolan felt uneasy. He knew this guy didn't want him in his car. They were assigned a 459 report. Nolan reached for the mike to answer. Davidson smacked his hand and angrily said, "In my car, you don't touch anything unless I tell you to." Nolan did not respond.

When they arrived at the residence, the female victim met the officers. A very beautiful black lady in her mid-thirties, she led them into the house, and the officers immediately noticed it had been ransacked. Taken was jewelry and money from a jewelry box she had on the dresser in the bedroom. Nolan started asking the victim questions for the report, however, he was interrupted in the middle of a sentence by Davidson, who growled, "Go check the point of entry." Nolan excused himself and walked outside. What an asshole, Nolan thought. Just so he could act like a big shot in front of this attractive woman, he makes a monkey out of me.

Within a couple of minutes, Davidson joined Nolan outside at the point of entry, the bathroom window. Davidson grumbled, "Go ahead and get the information from her. I changed my mind. I'll check for prints (latent fingerprints) here." Nolan went back inside to re-contact the victim and to obtain information for the report. She seemed more upset than when he had spoken to her just minutes earlier. She said, "My husband is due back tonight. He was away on business. I'll sleep much better tonight, knowing he's home. Silly, but somehow, I feel violated." "Ma'am, a burglary is, in fact, a violation. It's an intrusion into your private domain. Your reaction is perfectly normal."

She smiled and said, "Thank you, officer, you're much nicer than your jackass partner." "Ma'am?" a surprised Nolan replied. "Less than a minute after you went outside he asked me if he could come over when he got off work. I told him he'd have to check with my husband who is 6'5" and weighs 245 pounds with not an ounce of fat. I don't think that was what your partner wanted to hear." "I'm truly sorry ma'am. I'll take it up with him," Nolan said, as he tried to appease the woman. "Look, it's obvious you're new. I saw the way he treated you, and I heard him talk to you in that condescending tone. Don't say anything to him. It's okay," she said, almost protectively.

Nolan completed his investigation and recorded all of the information he needed for the report. He told the lady that if she discovered any other items missing, she should call and request that a supplemental property report be filed. Then, as he was leaving, he urged the woman to have the shrubs trimmed and cut back away from the windows in the back of the house as they provided perfect concealment to a burglar trying to gain entry. He also suggested lighting for the rear yard and at least two locks for each window and door in the house. He thanked the lady and bid her farewell. Davidson was waiting in the unit.

Nolan got back in the unit and Davidson drove off in a hurry. "She was a bitch," he said. "She was pretty nice to me, sir," Nolan replied. "You being a smart ass?" "Not at all, sir. I just said she was nice to me, that's all," Nolan said. Man, this guy is a loser, Nolan thought to himself. How did he ever become a policeman? "Look Nolan," Davidson said moments later, "I don't like being strapped with a trainee. I like working a one man car. I didn't ask for you, don't want you and I resent you, or any other trainee, being in my car." "I understand, sir. I felt that from the moment I got in your car," Nolan replied. "Good, then just sit there and keep quiet. Maybe this two weeks will pass quickly." "Yes, sir."

Their next activity was a call to assist parole agents searching for a "parolee at large." Officers responded to the meet location, a corner mom-and-pop grocery store parking lot, where they made contact with Steve Delgadillo, the parole agent in charge on this outing, and his crew of three additional agents. They had their briefing and passed around a photo of Pedro Gonzalez, who had originally been incarcerated for armed robbery and assault. He had served three years of a seven-year sentence and had been on parole only two months. He had not reported to his parole agent, as required, and he also failed to show up for a mandatory urinalysis to determine if he had been using drugs. His last known address was an apartment within a large complex about a block away.

After a plan had been formulated and agreed to by Davidson and Delgadillo, the group converged on the parolee's residence. When all possible escape routes were covered, two agents and Davidson knocked on the front door. A female eventually answered and claimed that her boyfriend, Gonzalez, was not at home. The agent explained that under the law, agents had the right to conduct a warrantless search of the premises for the parolee. She pulled the door open and stepped aside. Delgadillo and another agent, along with Davidson and Nolan entered the apartment.

Nolan followed Davidson who quickly scanned the small apartment for the parolee with negative results. He was satisfied the woman had told the truth and was ready to leave. Although the parole agents seemed a bit more thorough, they too completed their search very quickly. When

Nolan exited the bedroom of the small one bedroom apartment, he looked directly at the girlfriend, watching her body language. She was obviously preoccupied and didn't notice Nolan watching her. She had her arms folded as she nervously smoked a cigarette. When she took a puff of the cigarette, she inhaled deeply and then raised her head so that when she exhaled the smoke, it would be directed towards the ceiling. Nolan watched her do this twice and each time, as she finished exhaling, but with her head still looking up, her eyes moved quickly to one side. She was glancing at the attic access panel in the hallway!

Nolan quietly advised Delgadillo of his observations. Delgadillo summoned two of his agents and positioned a chair to access the attic. As the agent lifted the ceiling panel, Delgadillo announced, "Gonzalez, if you're up there, come out now. If we have to come up after you, there will be a permanent mark on your prison record. You'll never be eligible for parole again." There was a pause and then, "Okay, I'm coming down." With that, Gonzalez crawled down and was taken into custody. A quick records check of the girlfriend revealed she had an outstanding shoplifting warrant and she, too, would spend time at the gray bar hotel.

Delgadillo expressed his thanks to Davidson and Nolan. He told Davidson, "You've got a sharp young partner there." "Thanks," Davidson replied. As Davidson and Nolan were driving away, Davidson noticed a vehicle ahead of them with a taillight out. At the next red signal, he pulled up next to the vehicle so as to be able to look inside. The vehicle contained two nice looking women. Davidson effected a traffic stop on the vehicle. "Stay in the car," he told Nolan, as he got out to contact the driver. A few moments later, Nolan saw Davidson laughing and carrying on as he stood at the driver's door, obviously trying to pick up on the females.

Okay, I get it. This asshole uses his badge to exploit every opportunity to meet women. It's like he's on a mission, the sick son of a bitch, Nolan thought. Then he saw Davidson writing something in his notebook. The vehicle started, and the two women drove away. Smiling, Davidson got back in the unit and announced, "Alright, gonna get laid tonight." Nolan didn't bother to respond because he was too disgusted. So much for me thinking all policemen live to a high standard with impeccable morals, he thought, as Davidson asked clearance for code seven.

Davidson stopped at a burger place. "Get your food to go," he said. Nolan didn't respond and waited until Davidson had ordered before approaching the counter. He noticed that Davidson had ordered two burgers, two fries and two cokes. He wondered what that was all about. Driving out of the burger restaurant parking lot after picking up their food, Davidson said, "I'm gonna go eat with my girl. You stay in the car and eat."

Davidson drove for a few minutes before stopping in front of an old dilapidated house on the edge of the district. A young white woman exited the house and met Davidson. They hugged as they walked back towards her house. She was dressed like a floozy, and Nolan thought she might have been a hooker. Nolan ate his food in the unit and felt disgust and contempt for his partner.

About thirty minutes later. Davidson came walking out of the house. He got into the car and drove off without saying a word. Nolan noticed he had the faint odor of cheap perfume about him. A few minutes later. Davidson exclaimed, "Shit! I forgot my wallet and my notebook!" What is this fool talking about, Nolan thought. Davidson hurriedly drove back to his "girlfriend's" house. He ran in, but returned a few minutes later, smiling and holding the two items for which he had returned. "Must have fallen out of my pants," he chuckled as he drove off once again. Just great, Nolan thought. I sit in the car while this asshole goes and gets laid by his floozy girlfriend.

"Don't you have some reports to write?" Davidson asked. "Yes sir," Nolan replied. "Okay, I'm going to drop you off at the station. Have them call me in when you're done, got it?" "I got it," Nolan answered. Davidson dropped Nolan off at the rear of the station and drove off. Nolan wrote his reports, however, he was in no particular hurry to go back out in the field with Davidson. He telephoned Marie and they talked for several minutes. He expressed his unhappiness with his temporary training officer. Marie sensed his frustration and felt bad for him. She and John had become very close and, in fact, in addition to being lovers, they had quickly become each other's best friends. Marie gave him an old-fashioned pep talk, advising him to take it a day at a time and that before he realized it, Winters would be back.

Marie's words of encouragement seemed to refresh Nolan's attitude, although his opinion of Davidson did not change. After he hung up with Marie, he submitted his paperwork and asked that Davidson be called in to pick him up. He waited and waited. By the time Davidson finally got back to the station, it was time to go EOW. "Did you turn in all our shit?" Davidson demanded as they cleared out the unit. "Yes, I did, sir." "You know, you're not so bad, kid. You did pretty good today," Davidson commented. "Thank you, sir," Nolan replied. Nolan wanted to speak to this excuse for a policeman as little as possible.

It was almost 4:00 a.m. when Nolan got home. The 7:00 p.m. to 3:00 a.m. mid-watch would definitely take some getting used to. It was too late to call Marie, and he couldn't sleep, so he went on a long run. When he got back, he took a shower and had something to eat. He finally went to bed at 7:00 a.m. and slept until it was time for him to get ready for work. Nolan's next shift with Davidson was relatively uneventful, although Davidson continued to treat him as though he was his personal servant. Nolan's resentment for Davidson grew.

Their third day together proved to be a busy one. Their first call was a 415 family in which the husband had struck his wife. The R/P (reporting party) was a neighbor, concerned about the screaming and crying she had heard. When the officers arrived at the victim's residence, they knocked and she responded to the door. They immediately saw that she had a bloody lip, a swollen cheek, and she was crying almost uncontrollably. They went inside and found that the husband had been drinking heavily. He displayed a belligerent attitude towards the officers.

(It is important to note here that there were no "domestic violence" laws which, in effect, empowered police to arrest a spouse or domestic partner for any sign of physical trauma for at least another decade in the state of California. In the 1970's, the incident described above would have been deemed a "415 family dispute" with a misdemeanor battery. Under current California law, with few exceptions, police officers can only arrest for a misdemeanor committed in their presence. Using this case as an example then, the officers would have needed a signed "citizen's arrest" complaint form, signed by the victim wife, before they could have taken the husband into custody for battery. In contrast, by today's standard, officers would have arrived, seen the trauma suffered by the victim and, once it was determined that the husband inflicted the trauma, he would have been immediately arrested and booked for a *felony*. The victim/wife would have no say in the matter, nor would she be required to sign a complaint).

While Nolan interviewed the (suspect) husband, Davidson explained to the woman she could leave or she could sign a complaint, allowing officers to arrest her husband for hitting her. The woman refused to sign a complaint against her husband, stating that the last time he hit her, *she* had been the one that called police.

During that prior incident, she signed the complaint form and the police arrested him. Released within two days, he returned and promptly beat her more severely than he did during the incident for which he had originally been arrested. She said because of that, she would never again summon police to help her when her husband beats her. She also indicated she would not leave her home and, further, she declined medical treatment.

Davidson had Nolan stay with the woman while he took the husband into the bedroom and closed the door. Nolan heard a faint grunt followed by a thud. A few moments later, the bedroom door opened. Suspect and officer emerged. The husband was rubbing his stomach, but he displayed a much nicer disposition. Gone was his belligerent, challenging attitude. Davidson knew he could not force him to leave, however, as he and Nolan were leaving, Davidson pointed to him and said, "Remember what I told you."

The man looked at Davidson, but he did not respond. Davidson then turned to the woman and said loudly, making sure the husband could hear, "I know it wasn't you that called and I understand what you told us, but you don't have to keep taking beatings. If he hits you again, please... call us back here." He turned, stared down the husband, and left the residence, followed by Nolan.

As they drove away from the location, Davidson explained the term "battered wife syndrome" to Nolan. "All it means," he said, "is that for one or more of many possible reasons, the woman doesn't leave or take any affirmative action to remove herself (and children when applicable) from that situation. She stays with her husband, trying to convince herself he won't ever beat her again. She tries to rationalize and find the good in her husband. But deep down, she knows another beating or some other form of abuse will come again, all too soon. Usually, her self-esteem is all but gone. Do you understand?" Nolan answered in the affirmative and Davidson continued, "The common denominator with all these women is that they *fear*. They fear that if they leave, the husband will find them and beat them. They fear he'll track them and hurt the kids or hurt his in-laws. They fear they won't be able to make it financially. The bottom line is they fear the piece of crap that's hurting them, so they stay on. They rationalize that it'll be okay." "I understand," Nolan said.

Nolan asked, "Sir, what happened in the bedroom?" "As cops, we get very frustrated with these situations. We know the wife-beater needs to go to jail, but if the victim/wife doesn't sign a complaint, there's not much we can do. So, on rare occasions, we violate the rules a little on behalf of the woman, especially if we keep returning to the same location, week after week."

"Like what I did back there. I made it appear to the guy that I took his wife-beating personal. I took him into the bedroom and advised him I wasn't going to tolerate him pounding on his old lady. I punched him in the gut and slammed him into the wall. He got scared. I told him that every time he abuses his wife, she gets even more scared than he just did. I asked him if it made him feel manly when he beat his wife, trying to get a remorseful response from him."

"Then I warned him, if I had to come back, he would require booking in the hospital jail ward. Hopefully, that might buy the woman a few days of peace without being beaten. Maybe, just maybe, she'll make a decision to leave. That's all we can hope for. Oh, and fortunately, this time, no kids were involved. When children are involved the situation is even worse. But Nolan, don't ever do what I did. The fact of the matter is, what I did by smacking the guy was wrong. Even though my intentions were good and I was trying to find a way to help the lady, I could get into a lot of trouble because I laid my hands on him."

Nolan was surprised Davidson actually took the time to explain something to him. Maybe the guy has a heart after all, Nolan thought. Their next call was a 415 business dispute at a shoe store in a strip mall. When they arrived, they found an irate woman trying to get a cash refund on a pair of shoes. The store manager had refused, stating that the store policy was "no cash refunds." He even pointed to a sign, conspicuously posted on the cash register for all customers to see, that clearly read, "NO CASH REFUNDS" in large capital letters. Davidson instructed Nolan to talk to the manager to see how far he might be willing to go to resolve this situation and satisfy the customer while he spoke separately to the female.

Within a few minutes, Nolan convinced the manager to bend as far as he could to resolve the situation. The manager agreed to give the female "store credit," but he would not refund the money since she had already worn the shoes. Meanwhile, Davidson calmed the angry woman down. She explained that she had purchased many pairs of shoes from that particular store in the past with no problems. This time, just a couple of days after purchasing her new shoes, she wore them for the first time and after a few minutes, they hurt her feet.

She said she explained that to the manager, but he didn't seem to care. That really made her mad. Also, she was under the impression the police could force the store manager to return her money. Davidson explained that this was a civil matter, and that all the police could do was try to help the parties find a viable solution to the situation. The police had no power to force the store manager to refund her money. Davidson began to advise her regarding civil administrative remedies, however, when Nolan came over and said the manager would be willing to give her store credit towards another pair of shoes, she was satisfied with that, and went about looking for another pair. Problem solved.

Upon clearing their call, Davidson and Nolan were assigned a vandalism report at a bridal shop, a business specializing in wedding dresses and other formal wear. Thereafter, they made a couple of traffic stops and arrested one of the drivers for several thousand dollars worth of outstanding misdemeanor warrants. When they cleared, they got something to eat and before very long, the shift was over.

At EOW the next day, Nolan realized he had made it through the first week with Davidson. One more week with him, Nolan thought as he drove home. He was off for the next two days, but Marie was off only one day with him. They spent as much time together as they could, and essentially took turns staying at each other's apartments on their days off. John and Marie both realized their friendship and romantic relationship had blossomed very quickly. They were strongly committed to each other and they each knew this was the real thing. Not only did they trust each other, they constantly reaffirmed their love for one another. They were very happy together.

Nolan kept thinking about working with Winters again as he drove in to work for the start of his second week with Davidson. Davidson started the week off by getting Nolan loaded up with reports and miscellaneous paperwork. Then, he returned Nolan to the station so that he could file his paperwork. Meanwhile, Davidson spent several hours in the field by himself. Sergeant Carter caught wind of this because he saw Nolan in the station for several hours. He approached Nolan and asked, "How come you're still in the station?" "I'm just writing my reports and doing what I'm told, Sarge." "Where's Davidson?" "I think he's out in the field," Nolan replied. Hearing that, the sergeant turned and walked away. He checked on Davidson's status and quickly figured out that he had loaded up the kid with reports so he could dump him off and be alone.

Sergeant Carter was upset. He called Davidson in, and when he arrived, he took him into the office and closed he door. "Look Davidson, I know you didn't want a partner. But, I told you I didn't have anyone else to put the kid with. I know what you're doing to limit the amount of time you have with him. Here's my warning. I gave you an assignment to work with this kid for two lousy weeks. If I catch you trying to find a way to weasel out of it again, I'll write your ass up and go formal with a complaint. Do I make myself real clear?" Davidson hung his head and replied, "Yeah, Sarge." "Further, you will treat this trainee and anyone else I may assign to you properly, or you'll again be dealing with me. Take him out in the field, now!"

Davidson found Nolan writing in the report room. "Let's go," Davidson said. "Five more minutes and I'll have the last report done, sir," Nolan said. "Let's go, now," Davidson insisted. Once they were out on the street, Davidson asked Nolan if he had approached the sergeant to beef him. "No sir, not at all. I don't operate like that. The sarge saw me in the station for a long time, and he came and asked me where you were. I told him I thought you were out in the field. Then he walked away, but he seemed pretty upset."

The next couple of days passed without incident, but on the third day, midway through their shift, they were patrolling in a residential neighborhood when Davidson blacked out and pulled the unit into a long narrow driveway behind a small house. "What are we doing, sir?" Nolan asked. "Sit tight for just a minute," Davidson said, as he shined his spotlight through one of the windows, brightly illuminating the interior of the residence. A few seconds later, a very voluptuous blond woman emerged, smiling as she approached the unit. "Hi Ernie," she cooed. "Hi Diane," Davidson replied. "I see you brought a friend. Bring him and come on in. My sister is here too."

"Let's go," Davidson said excitedly. It was not difficult to figure out what was going on, but Nolan asked anyway. "Sir, what is this?" "Sarge said I have to have you with me all the time. I'm gonna get laid. There's a broad here for you too. Now let's go," Davidson snarled. Nolan got angry. "I'm not interested!" "Fine, suit yourself. I'll be back."

Davidson got out of the unit and disappeared into the house. Minutes later, an equally voluptuous brunette exit the residence. She looked a little younger than the first woman, probably about twenty-three or twenty-four years old. She approached the unit on the passenger side where Nolan was seated.

"Hi," she said as she casually leaned inside the open window. "My name is Carol, what's your name, handsome?" "I'm John. John Nolan." "John, why don't you want to come inside?" "Uh, I'd rather just stay out here. Thanks anyway." Carol leaned a bit further into the unit, causing Nolan to have to lean away to avoid physical contact with her. Seeing that, she pulled her top up, fully exposing her magnificent bare breasts in an attempt to entice Nolan and lure him into the house. "Come in, John— you won't be sorry," she cooed. Nolan became annoyed. "Look Carol, you're obviously a very beautiful woman. It's not personal, but I just don't want to come in…okay?" Carol didn't utter another word. She quickly pulled her top down and angrily stormed back into the house, slamming the door behind her.

About fifteen minutes later, Davidson emerged. He got back in the unit, backed out of the driveway, and out onto the street. He drove for several minutes without saying a word. Nolan remembered the tension in that police car was so thick, it was almost unbearable. Finally, Davidson sneered, "So what's your fucking problem, don't you like girls?" That was it for Nolan. He was really pissed off then. "Yeah, I like girls alright. I'm also very picky about when, where and most of all, with whom I sleep. Is that okay with you?" he shouted angrily. "Hey rookie, don't get shitty with me. I'll kick your ass," Davidson bellowed. Nolan snapped back, "If you try, you'll be very sorry. Listen, why don't you take me back to the station? I want to talk to the sarge—this is all bullshit."

Davidson thought about the consequences of Nolan's demand for a moment. He took a long, deep breath and said, "Look Nolan, let me try to bring this back down a notch. I don't need any more hassles with the sarge. I'm already riding another beef and I just don't need any more shit right now. I'll back off and leave you alone. You have my word.

Besides, I think we've only got a couple more days together. How about it?" Nolan thought for a moment and then replied, "Okay."

Nolan stuck it out with Davidson and happily, the end of that week came quickly. Winters had returned from his vacation early, and he called Sergeant Carter to cancel the extra time off he initially requested. Sergeant Carter was a good man, and he let Nolan know that when he came back from his days off, he would be with Winters once again on the P.M. shift. Nolan was grateful to the sarge and went on his days off, a happy man.

As with the previous week, Marie had only one day off with John, and it was her turn to spend the night at his place. He hadn't told her about what happened with Carol, and that whole situation with Davidson having sex on duty, and exploiting his badge. John saw no need to upset her. And, as it had been since they first met, they had fun together, doing anything and everything. They were becoming more and more dependent on each other, and their love was growing deeper and stronger with every passing day.

Chapter Seven

The Conclusion of Training

Nolan was happy as he drove to work. He knew he'd once again be working with a very professional police officer—his training officer, Dennis Winters. He went in early, had a great workout, and awaited his partner's arrival. Winters arrived and he seemed genuinely pleased to see his trainee. They shook hands and exchanged pleasantries.

"Ready to go to work?" Winters asked as they loaded their unit for the shift. "Yes, I am," Nolan grinned. "How was it with Davidson?" "Dennis, if it's okay with you, can we talk about that later? I'd rather just get out there with you and do some police work for a while." "No problem, we'll get to it soon enough. Toss me the keys, I'm driving," Winters exclaimed with a big smile. "Here you go, partner," Nolan said as he tossed him the keys.

After they had been out in the field for a while, Winters started telling Nolan about his vacation. "We went up north to visit Jenny's parents. They live in Oregon. They're really nice folks. It was a great visit, and the kids had a nice time with their grandparents. Jenny waited till we were there to tell me she's pregnant again," he beamed. "I'm so happy. My daughter Linda is three, my son Jason is two and I can hardly wait for this next one," he said excitedly.

"Wow, that's fantastic news, Dennis. I'm very happy for both of you," Nolan said as he shared in his partner's enthusiasm. "Do you guys want a boy or a girl?" "You know, we really don't care. At first, I thought Jennifer might be hoping for another little girl. But when we talked about it, she said she has absolutely no preference, as long as he or she is healthy. And that's exactly how I feel," Winters said philosophically. "That's beautiful," Nolan said. Then, momentarily, Nolan thought about how he would feel if he and Marie were married and she announced she was pregnant. As strange as it seemed at the moment, Nolan was certain that if Marie told him she was pregnant, he'd be elated.

As the sun was about to settle into the western horizon, Winters and Nolan received a call to handle a burglary report in a residential district close to a large municipal park. Unfortunately, it seems many perverts, weirdos and drug dealers like to hang out in parks. Because of that fact, Winters had already taught Nolan to patrol the parks whenever possible and check on the kids. As the officers were driving by the park en route to their call, they automatically scanned the area looking for suspicious activity. Each of the officers noticed a suspicious looking character peaking out from behind the men's restroom. He was a male white in his thirties, clean shaven with collar length hair. He was wearing a short sleeved red shirt.

Nolan began to tell Winters about the fellow, but Winters cut him short, "I saw him too John. If I slam on the brakes now he'll spook and have time to make his escape before we can get turned around. I'm watching him in my mirror. He doesn't realize we saw him. Don't turn around yet because he's looking right at us." Seconds later, when the man had apparently ducked back inside of the restroom, Winters said, "Okay

John, now turn around and watch for him. I didn't see him walk away from the bathroom. He probably went back in. He thinks we just kept going. I'm gonna flip a "U" and come back around. I'll park close, but we'll make our approach on foot." "I'm ready to go," Nolan said eagerly.

As they approached the restroom area on foot, they heard the muffled, painful screams of a child. Both officers immediately knew what they had heard, and they sprinted the remaining few yards to the bathroom area. Upon charging into the restroom, the officers saw the suspicious man they had seen moments earlier. He was holding a young boy against the wall with his body weight, effectively pinning him there. The boy's pants were pulled down below his knees and while he held one hand over the child's mouth, the molester was holding his erect penis in his other hand, trying to force it into the petrified and struggling child's anus. There were blood smears on the child's buttocks and blood on the head of the molester's penis.

Before the molester could react, Winters stepped into him and delivered a forceful punch to his temple. He instantly let go of the child and dropped to the floor of the bathroom. Nolan grabbed the child and carried him out of the bathroom. Winters momentarily "lost it" and repeatedly punched the molester, who cried for mercy. Only a few feet from the restroom, but completely out of view, Nolan put the boy down. He quickly pulled the boy's pants up and assured him he'd be okay. The boy hugged Nolan tightly and wouldn't let go. Nolan heard the molester crying for mercy. Nolan yelled into the restroom, "Partner, code four?"

It took a second for a response, but finally, an out of breath Winters yelled back, "Yeah, it's okay partner." Nolan then heard the distinctive ratcheting sound of handcuffs being applied. Winters emerged from the restroom holding the handcuffed and crying molester by the arm. As soon as he came into view, the child got startled. "Easy," Nolan reassured him. "He won't hurt you again. I promise." Winters motioned for Nolan to come over. "Partner, please…take this piece of shit away from me. I'll stay with the boy. Take this asshole and go get the unit. Request paramedics for the child and another unit for transportation." "You got it, partner," Nolan said as he nodded in acknowledgement.

(In the early 1970's, police officers did not yet normally carry portable radios, and obviously, they had no cellular telephones. Communication was either via the two-way radio in the police car, or by "landline" telephone).

Nolan walked the molester back towards the unit. No words were spoken as they walked. However, as Nolan opened the rear door of the unit and told him to be seated, the molester, having apparently regained his composure, smiled and turned towards Nolan. As he was positioning his body to sit in the back seat, the molester defiantly said, "The boy liked me. I will be seeing him again." Without thinking, Nolan instantly grabbed the molester by the throat with one hand in a "C" clamp. As he squeezed tightly, Nolan advised the molester, "Listen, you filthy piece of shit, keep your mouth shut or you'll wind up in a body cast." Nolan purposely held a tight grip on the molester's throat until just before he was ready to pass out. Then, he let go. As the molester recovered, he wisely chose not to speak anymore.

In the few moments it took for Nolan to drive the unit from where they had left it, to Winter's location, he had requested the paramedics, requested another unit for transportation and advised communications of what he and his partner had. He also requested that their original call of a burglary report be reassigned. Meanwhile, Winters had talked to the boy and found out his name was Kevin. Kevin was ten years old and when Winters asked him what had happened, he said that after school, he rode his bicycle to the ball diamond to play baseball with some of his friends, as he did two or three times per week. He knew he had to get home before dark, but he needed to use the restroom.

After leaving his friends, he rode his bicycle over to the restroom and went inside. He said he wouldn't have stopped there if he'd seen the man hanging around, but he didn't see him until he went inside. He got scared and turned to run out, but it was too late. The molester grabbed him and began his attack. Kevin cried as he recounted the moments leading up to the attack and the attack itself. Winters hugged him and consoled him. He asked Kevin if his parents were home, and the boy replied his mom would be there.

Paramedics arrived and looked after the boy. Another unit responded and transported the molester to the station for Winters and Nolan. After the medics were done treating Kevin, Winters and Nolan loaded his bicycle into the trunk of their unit and transported him to his nearby home. There, Winters made contact with his mom and advised her of the situation. He and Nolan then transported the boy and his mom to the hospital for a medical evaluation.

This served two purposes. First and foremost, the victim needed to be treated for his injuries. Second, in order to present a complete case for prosecution, the detective and district attorney would require an immediate and appropriately documented medical examination of the victim as well as the proper securing and safeguarding of any items of evidentiary value, including any bodily fluids.

At the hospital, Nolan looked for Marie, and when he found her, he explained the situation to her. Marie took charge of the youngster and got him in to see the doctor as soon as she could. Shortly thereafter, Kevin's dad arrived at the hospital, and as most fathers would, he expressed the desire to have five minutes alone with the molester. Winters tried to appease the distraught man by telling him, "I understand what you're saying, sir, and if it were up to me, you'd get your wish. The fact is, we have to allow the system to do its work. We have an excellent case against him, and he's going to go prison for a while."

Marie brought Kevin out after just a few minutes. Kevin stayed with his mother while the attending physician, Doctor Silverman, spoke to the officers and Kevin's father. The doctor advised them that there had been some tearing of tissue when the molester tried to force his penis into the child's anus, however, the damage was not severe and physically, the boy would recover quickly. Dr. Silverman also said there was no evidence of ejaculate, which was consistent with the account given by the police officers, as they interrupted the attack on the boy. The doctor strongly suggested counseling for Kevin and emphasized that even though physically he would recover quickly, he was more concerned with Kevin's mental well-being. Kevin's dad promised the doctor he would definitely follow up on his advice and take him to counseling.

As the doctor excused himself and walked away, Kevin's dad said, "I'm really sorry I didn't thank you guys first, for what you did. I was so angry, all I could think about was the fact that I want to kill the son of a bitch that hurt my son. I can only imagine what would have happened to him if you guys hadn't been there. How could I ever thank you or repay you?" "You just did," Winters smiled. Kevin's dad gratefully looked each officer in the eye as he shook their hands and then embraced them. While he was shaking Winters' hand, Winters said, "I know this will be hard, but try to let your anger go. Otherwise, it'll drive you nuts. Kevin will sense your anger, and he'll begin to feel that *he* did something wrong."

Kevin's dad didn't respond verbally to his advice, however, judging from his body language, Winters knew the message had hit home. Kevin's mother came over and embraced each officer as well. She started crying, and Kevin went up to her and said, "It's okay mom, I'll be okay." The officers then took turns saying good-bye to Kevin. Even though he was only ten years old, he fully understood what had happened and without being prompted to do so by his parents, he thanked each of the officers for helping him. Then, just before Kevin and his parents left the hospital, Marie came over with a lollipop and a large bag of M&M's.

Kevin's eyes lit up as he took the candy, and he thanked and hugged Marie as well.

After the family left, Winters turned to Nolan and said, "I think we deserve a cup of coffee." Nolan smiled and said, "I agree." Nolan turned to Marie and asked if she could join them. Marie said, "I'd love to. I'll take my break now." The three went to the cafeteria for coffee, and they couldn't help but engage in conversation about what had happened to Kevin. Nolan explained how his T.O. had taught him to check the parks whenever possible. Marie said, "You guys are great. No telling what else would have happened to that little guy if you hadn't come along." Winters responded, "We were just doing our jobs. We just happened to be in the right place at the right time."

Marie looked at Winters and asked, "What's going to happen to the piece of crap that did this?" "Well, I haven't seen his rap sheet yet, but more than likely, this isn't the first time he's been caught for some type of sex crime against a child. Unfortunately, our prison system here in California is such that even if he is sentenced to several years, he'll probably only end up doing half or less than half of his original sentence," Winters explained. "Then what?" Marie inquired further. "Parole. He'll get out of prison and be placed on parole. As a condition of parole, he'll have to register as a sex offender. It's all a bunch of baloney because everyone, from the D.A. to the defense attorney to the judge and to his fellow inmates, everyone knows there is no rehabilitation for a pedophile. Psychiatrists have studied and analyzed them for years. Even the most liberal psychiatrists will admit that pedophiles cannot be cured."

As he looked at Marie, Nolan interjected, "You know how I value human life and I try to see the good in people, but I have to tell you, I wanted to kill that guy for what he did to that little boy." Before Marie could reply Winters added, "And that's precisely why they have to keep child molesters out of the "general population" in prison. Even hardened criminals like murderers and robbers have absolutely no tolerance for child molesters. If given the opportunity, they'll kill them."

"So then in your opinion, what should do we do with child molesters?" Marie asked. Winters replied, "Well, since we know a molester cannot be rehabilitated, we also know that simply means when the molester gets released from prison, he'll find another victim, or two or three, or more, until he's caught again. He can't help himself. He is driven and he must continue to molest. Essentially, what we as a society are doing, when we release a child molester from prison, is insuring the fact that at least one more child will be victimized, traumatized, and damaged for life."

"Although the recidivism rate for ex-cons in general is high in this state, for child molesters it is incredibly high, which simply supports the fact that the molester *will* molest again. So, my long-winded answer to your question is this; In my humble opinion, convicted child molesters should be executed. That is the only way to insure they don't ruin any more children's lives. I think that when one of these molesters is found guilty, a review panel consisting of at least two judges and one high-ranking member of the D.A.'s office should review the finding of the court to eliminate any possibility he might have been wrongly convicted. Once that's done, the molester should be put to death, quickly."

Marie looked over at Nolan, took a sip of her coffee and asked, "Do you agree, John?" "Marie, it doesn't matter whether you call them pedophiles or child molesters, the bottom line is they are monsters, predators whose prey is innocent children. You should have seen some of the cases they showed us in the academy. It was unbelievable and it turned my stomach. All I can tell you is these monsters will stop at nothing to achieve their mission. I have to reiterate... I do have a healthy respect for life, and I believe in our society, but I also believe we have a duty to protect our society. In my opinion, execution of these monsters is the only way to protect our society's children."

Marie absorbed what she had just heard, however, she made no comment. She excused herself from the table and returned with the coffeepot. After refilling all of their cups, she smiled and declared, "Okay fellas, as we drink this cup, let's discuss something not quite so deep." Winters and Nolan each chuckled and agreed with the lady. Nolan did not quite remember how the conversation evolved, or what the catalyst was, but Marie and Winters ended up laughing and joking about his beat-up old sedan. He remembered telling them, "Hey, my old jalopy gets me anywhere I need to go." He also remembered confessing that he could hardly wait to save enough money for a down payment on a new car. The three of them especially enjoyed that second cup of coffee before going on with the rest of their workdays.

It was late in the shift before Winters and Nolan had finished their paperwork regarding the child molestation. Winters was right again. The molester did have a lengthy rap sheet. Winters used the rap sheet as a tool to instruct his young partner. "Look at his first offense. It's for loitering around a school, and for indecent exposure. Next, he graduated to lewd and lascivious activity. Following that, another indecent exposure and then, his first actual molestation. Now, imagine all the other crimes he attempted, or actually committed, without being apprehended. Or how about the crimes he perpetrated that no one reported?" Nolan listened carefully as his teacher continued, "Unfortunately, the rap sheet only shows the crimes for which he's been arrested. But in general terms, you can usually see a pattern of behavior as these creeps graduate into actual molestation or other sex crimes. Also, in order to surround themselves in a target-rich environment, many molesters will seek any type of employment that will expose them to children, lots of children."

Nolan absorbed every word his partner taught him. Nolan asked, "Dennis, what about rapists?" Winters replied, "Frequently, a rapist's rap sheet will reveal a similar pattern in his evolution as well. He may start with indecent exposure, prowling, "peeping tom" activity, sexual battery, and so on. If you look carefully, you can usually see a pattern. Keep in mind that especially with the rapist, his rap sheet will probably not reveal anywhere near the true number of crimes he's committed. The reason is that many women are too embarrassed or ashamed to come forward and report the crimes. Also, in far too many cases, rapists are known to their victims, and in this country, our courts permit character assassination of victims of sex crimes. And, as is the case with child molesters, our system does little, if anything, to prevent any of these creeps from moving up into full-blown rapists."

Back out in the field, Winters told Nolan to refresh himself on his book knowledge of court procedures. He laughed and warned, "Study hard—there will be a test tomorrow." Nolan returned the smile and said, "I'll be ready. Is this because we got our subpoenas for that burglar we caught?" "Yes and no," Winters replied. "I always cover court proceedings, court demeanor and testimony with new guys. In this case, since we've already been subpoenaed on a preliminary hearing, I'm going to ask the handling deputy district attorney to remove me as a potential witness and keep me as the investigating officer, or I.O."

That way, when the defense attorney makes a motion to exclude all the witnesses in the case, and they almost always do, I won't have to leave the courtroom. Besides, you actually participated more in this case than I did, and I didn't see anything that you didn't see. So, eliminating me as a witness shouldn't be a problem in this case. I need to watch you testify." Nolan rubbed his hands together, smiled and reported, "I'm a little nervous about testifying, but I'm ready." "We'll talk more about it tomorrow, but of course, the main thing to remember is, always tell the truth." "That's never been a problem for me," Nolan said. "I know that," Winters answered.

"What I want to talk about right now is your time with Davidson," Winters said, with a serious tone in his voice. "I let you avoid the question earlier, but I want an answer now." Nolan paused, took a deep breath and said, "Well Dennis, in my opinion, he shouldn't have anything to do with the training of new police officers. In fact, I don't think he has the right morals for this job. I mean, he knows his stuff, it's just that he uses this job as a tool to find women." "Easy now, you're making some pretty strong statements for a new guy. Tell me what happened."

Nolan went on to explain about Davidson's skirt chasing and on duty sexual escapades. He talked about the pretty burglary victim and how Davidson came on to her. He described the scene at Diane's house and explained how he felt when her sister bared her breasts as she leaned into the window of the unit. Nolan cited some of the other incidents and told Winters it made him have second thoughts about being a police officer because he had always naively believed all police officers were beyond reproach, that they did things right and clean all the time.

He also briefed Winters about how Davidson would dump him off at the station and disappear for hours and that Sergeant Carter had chewed Davidson's butt for that. Nolan concluded by saying, "Look Dennis, I feel bad enough about this as it is. I'm not a snitch, and I wouldn't have said anything about it, but since you asked me, I wasn't going to lie to you. I don't lie. I dreaded the time I was with him, and I couldn't wait for you to get back. Can we just let it go now?"

Winters was very angry. Not at Nolan, but at Davidson. He had respectfully voiced his opinion to Sergeant Carter that Davidson was not a good choice as a temporary training officer. Davidson's fellow officers all knew he was a little different. Winters thought for a moment and then announced, "I'm gonna take it up with Davidson as soon as I can." "Please Dennis, I don't want any problems and I don't want..." "Drop it, John. I said I was going to take it up with him. What he did was pure bullshit, and I won't stand for it," he said in a loud voice.

The officers were both upset, and they drove in silence until came upon a DUI driver. They made a traffic stop and arrested him. By the time they finished processing the deuce and all of the required paperwork, it was time to go EOW. Nolan drove home that night with a heavy heart and called his best friend—Marie. They talked for almost an hour. Marie helped John put things in proper perspective and expressed her love and support for him.

The following day, Nolan arrived for work, only to find Winters already there. They talked briefly in the locker room as they prepared to go to work. "I'm kind of glad Davidson wasn't working yesterday. I was really pissed and if I would have found him, I may have done something I would have regretted later... like punch his lights out. I came in to talk to the sarge about the whole mess. Not to beef Davidson, just to talk to the sarge about the way he treated you. I wanted to make sure he wouldn't get the opportunity to screw with any more trainees. Anyway, Carter cut me short. He told me not to worry about it for right now. I guess Davidson is riding a pretty heavy beef from something that happened prior to you working with him," Winters said. "Yeah, Davidson did mention something about riding a beef right now," Nolan confirmed.

"Well anyway, in addition to the rest of his problems, I guess the husband of the burglary victim you talked about came in and beefed Davidson for trying to pick up on his wife. So stand by. Internal Affairs may eventually want to talk to you about this." "Shit!" Nolan exclaimed. "I don't need this, Dennis. I just want to get on with my training."

"Well, don't sweat it. You didn't do anything wrong. Besides, why worry about something over which you have no control. I.A. will either talk to you, or they won't. No big deal." "Yeah, but I'm still a probationary officer," Nolan said. "I've heard some major horror stories about what happens to probationary officers who get involved in internal affairs investigations." "Doesn't matter what you heard," Winters said. "I'm telling you straight; if you didn't do anything wrong, you'll be fine." "You know I didn't do anything wrong, don't you?" Nolan asked. "Of course I know that," Winters replied.

Once they were out in the field, Winters asked, "Now, are you ready to talk about our court system?" "I am," Nolan replied with a big grin. Winters asked Nolan a series of questions concerning court proceedings, the answers to which he learned in the academy. Then Winters asked, "You're subpoenaed to court next week for a preliminary hearing, right?" "Yes, it's next Wednesday morning," Nolan said. Winters continued, "What exactly is the purpose of the preliminary hearing and where does it take place?" Nolan cleared his throat and offered his reply; "The preliminary hearing takes place in municipal court. The purpose of the hearing is to present the case in shortened, or somewhat abbreviated form so as to give the court (the judge) the opportunity to hear the evidence against a defendant who has been arrested and charged with a *felony* crime."

"If, after hearing the testimony and other evidence, the judge rules that there is sufficient evidence to go to trial, the judge will declare that the defendant is, 'Held to Answer.' The case is then sent out for trial to the

Superior Court handling that particular jurisdiction." "What happens to the defendant?" Winters queried his student. "The defendant is either remanded to the custody of the Sheriff (county jail), or released on bail." "Very good, partner," Winters smiled. "Okay, you passed the test. Now, let's go find some bad guys."

Winters and Nolan finished out a very busy week, making several felony and misdemeanor arrests for an assortment of crimes ranging from theft, to possession of heroin for sale. Nolan continued to be a sponge, absorbing everything his veteran partner taught him. Because he believed Nolan was capable, Winters continued to push him harder than he had ever pushed a trainee before. He was very pleased with Nolan's progress.

In fact, at the end of that week, when he prepared Nolan's weekly evaluation, Winters noted that Nolan's people skills were excellent and that he was long on common sense. In addition, he rated Nolan's judgement as outstanding and gave him an overall rating of "outstanding." The following week, Winters would begin to allow Nolan to drive every day and handle most every situation. He would simply act in the role of back up officer and occasional advisor.

John spent as much of his weekend with Marie as he could. She had only one day off with him that week, but as usual, they made the most of it. They were very much in love, and their commitment to each other was rock solid. Jokingly, John asked Marie to be his girlfriend. Her response was, "I already am your girlfriend, silly!" The two laughed and kissed.

Then, John surprised her with a beautiful gold bracelet. He enjoyed seeing the look on her face as she opened the box, exposing the bracelet.

Momentarily speechless, she hurriedly put the bracelet on her wrist. After it was securely fastened, she held her hand up and admired it from every possible angle. John was pleased with her response. He loved buying things for her. He felt total happiness whenever he was around her.

The following week, Winters watched Nolan testify for the first time. Winters was seated at the attorney's table just to the right of the deputy district attorney. He was functioning in the role of investigating officer, simultaneously watching his partner. Nolan followed all of his teacher's advice and did an excellent job on the stand. After he was excused, Nolan left the witness stand and walked past the table where his partner was seated next to the prosecutor. "Good job, John," Winters whispered to Nolan as he walked by. "Thanks," Nolan whispered back. A few minutes later, the burglar was held to answer and he was remanded to the custody of the Sheriff.

On patrol that night, Winters and Nolan monitored a communications broadcast advising of a homicide that had taken place earlier in the evening in the Sheriff's Firestone area. The suspect vehicle was described as a 1968 to 1970 Dodge Charger, green in color, with a partial license plate number of 492. There were two suspects. One was described as a male Hispanic in his twenties; the other a male black or dark skinned Hispanic, also in his twenties.

The homicide was the result of a market robbery gone bad. Apparently, during the course of the robbery, one of the store clerks tried to disarm one of the robbers. As the store employee struggled with the one robber, the other robber came up from behind and shot him point blank in the head, killing him instantly. The robbers made good their escape in the described vehicle.

A little more than two hours later, Winters and Nolan had just cleared a call in the business district when Nolan spotted a 1968 or 1969 green Dodge Charger up ahead. Winters was riding shotgun that night, and he was recording their last call disposition in their log, when Nolan alerted him to the fact that they were coming up on a green Charger. As they approached, Winters said, "Come on baby, be the right car." Sure enough, as soon as they were able to read the plate, they saw the numbers 492. "Yes!" Winters shouted. The vehicle was occupied by two males, both seated in front. When the driver saw the police unit in his mirror, he must have alerted his passenger, because he turned almost all the way around in his seat to look at the officers.

Winters advised communications they were following a possible 187 P.C. (homicide) suspect vehicle and requested at least one additional unit. No sooner had he done that, then the driver of the suspect vehicle slammed on the brakes and quickly slowed from about 35 mph to about 15 mph. He evidently wanted to see if the police unit would go by, or stay back. Obviously, if the unit stayed back, the suspects would know the cops were on to them. Nolan slowed down and stayed behind the Charger, keeping a safe distance from it. "Come on buddy, what are you gonna do?" Nolan said out loud as he shadowed the vehicle.

Suddenly, the driver of the Charger floored it, causing the vehicle to accelerate very rapidly. Nolan punched it, activated the units' emergency lights and siren, and the chase was on. Winters began broadcasting the pursuit, giving expert and precise position reports. Initially, the pursuit stayed on surface streets, however, after about five minutes into the pursuit, the suspects made their way to the Harbor Freeway and got on going northbound with Winters and Nolan right behind them.

The pursuit continued only briefly on the freeway. The suspects exited in the downtown area, after which the vehicle began executing all kinds of turns, never going more than one or two blocks before making either another right or left turn. The driver was very erratic. He drove the wrong way down one-way streets and even drove onto the sidewalk a couple of times.

Fortunately, it was late at night and there was very little traffic to contend with in the downtown area. The suspects stayed in the area, continuing their frequent turns for several more minutes. By this time, four additional units had joined in the pursuit. Then, while the driver of the Charger was in the middle of executing a right turn, the passenger suspect leaned out of his window, pointed a sawed off shotgun at the pursuing police unit, and fired.

Winters and Nolan heard some of the pellets hit their unit. "That asshole just shot at us!" Winters exclaimed angrily. As Winters was voicing his reaction to the suspects shooting at them, Nolan's simultaneous reaction was to slow the unit, thereby increasing the distance between his unit and the suspect vehicle. Winters, doing an excellent job of broadcasting the pursuit, advised they were taking fire from the vehicle, and that their unit had been struck. He also unlocked the shotgun, removed it from the rack, and kept it between his legs for quick access.

After his accomplice fired his shotgun at the pursuing police officers, the driver of the suspect vehicle drove even more erratically. He increased his speed, made more exaggerated turning movements, and ultimately, lost control of the vehicle while making a left turn. The Charger went careening up over a curb and crashed into a building. It took Nolan only a split second to react. He brought his unit to a stop in the best tactical position the situation would allow.

But before the suspect vehicle had even come to rest, the passenger pushed his door open and jumped out, shotgun in hand. He immediately turned towards the police unit and began raising the weapon into firing position as he stared directly at Winters. However, Winters was too fast for him because he had already popped his door open and held it open with his right leg as Nolan brought the unit to an abrupt stop. Winters jumped out of the unit while pumping a round into the chamber of his shotgun. Just as the suspect was pulling his weapon up to his shoulder and into firing position, Winters fired one round striking the suspect, who went down immediately.

After the suspect vehicle crashed, the entire shooting incident involving the passenger suspect and Officer Winters played out in only a few seconds. By the time he saw his buddy going down after being shot by Winters, the driver suspect had opened his door and had exited the vehicle. Nolan jumped out of the unit, weapon in hand. He pointed his weapon at the suspect and ordered him to stop. He could see the suspect's hands, but he did not see a weapon at that time.

The suspect failed to heed Nolan's warning to get down on the ground and instead, fled on foot. He was a fast runner. As Nolan took off after him, he called out to Winters, and shouted he was going after his suspect. Nolan never took an eye off of his fleeing suspect. He had seen the passenger suspect go down after Winters fired, and he knew Winters would be okay. In addition, units were pulling up and several officers were arriving on the scene.

Nolan sprinted after the suspect. He remembered thinking how dark it was, and how, even though he was within a few hundred feet of his fellow officers, he suddenly felt very alone. Nolan had seen his quarry duck down a small, dark alley. Prior to entering the alleyway, Nolan stopped, peeked around the corner, saw nothing and advanced. Winters had taught Nolan about the advantages of being silent, using a flashlight only as needed, and never making any unnecessary noises like jingling keys or walking or running with "heavy" footsteps.

The alleyway was lined on both sides with overflowing, smelly trash cans. Nolan knew his suspect could not have gotten very far ahead of him. He kept advancing in a crouched position, carefully, slowly, and very quietly. He listened to every sound and made a conscious effort to control his rapid breathing and slow his heartbeat.

Nolan recalled that there was absolutely no lighting in the alleyway, nor was there much in the way of moonlight that night. Nevertheless, he did not use his flashlight, relying instead on what little ambient light there was. Suddenly, less than twenty feet ahead of him, Nolan's eyes caught the movement of a man's silhouette. It was the suspect, and he had jumped up from his hiding place in between two trash cans. Nolan instinctively crouched lower to the ground just as the suspect fired at him. Nolan heard the round hit the wall close to him and immediately thereafter, he heard the sound of footsteps running away from him.

Nolan stood, holstered his weapon and started running as well. He was angry, and he wanted that suspect. He could barely see the suspect up ahead of him, however, he was determined to catch him. He ran like the wind and closed the gap quickly. He got close enough to clearly see his prey slow down and look back over his shoulder. Though he continued running, Nolan could see by the way the suspect carried his body, he was tiring very quickly. Nolan knew he would be stopping soon.

Nolan continued running after the suspect and pulled his weapon from its holster. Moments later, the suspect stopped and without delay, he sought a position against the wall of the alleyway, turning to face his pursuer, gun in hand. Nolan immediately stopped as well and dove to the ground on his belly. The suspect fired at Nolan again. Nolan quickly aimed at his target and returned fire. He fired all six from his revolver and quickly reloaded. He paused for a moment. There was no sound coming from where he knew the suspect was. In the distance, he could hear sirens. They're looking for me, he thought as he lay there momentarily, trying to look and listen for any evidence that the suspect was still a threat.

After a few seconds had passed, and with his gun still aimed at the now motionless suspect, Nolan stood up and inched forward toward him. The suspect was in a slumped over, semi-seated position against the wall. His head was resting awkwardly on his shoulder. His right hand still held his weapon, but his hand was down by his leg, and the barrel of his weapon was actually touching the ground. Nolan was completely focused on the suspect as he slowly moved forward.

Suddenly, Nolan was momentarily startled by the noise of a low flying helicopter. They found me, he thought, as he reached the still motionless suspect, now brightly lit by the helicopter's powerful beam. He stepped on the suspect's gun so as to hold it down in the event the suspect was feigning injury and was waiting to ambush him. Nolan reached down and checked for a pulse but could not find one. That was when he saw a bullet hole in the suspect's head.

Winters came running up, gun in hand. "You okay, John?" he asked as he surveyed the situation and re-holstered his weapon. "Yeah, I'm fine. He's dead, partner, I had to shoot him," Nolan replied calmly. "You did a great job pal, just great." "Is the other guy dead too?" Nolan asked. "Yeah, he's dead," Winters replied.

Within moments, Sergeant Carter and several additional officers were on the scene. Sergeant Carter had already called out an officer involved shooting (O.I.S.) team for Winters' shooting. As he had done at the first shooting scene next to the suspect vehicle, the sergeant secured the area to preserve it for the shooting team.

Although it was close to their EOW time, Nolan and Winters would spend the next several hours going over every minute detail of their individual shootings with investigators from the O.I.S. team. Winters called home to let his wife know he had been involved in a shooting and that he was okay. Nolan made a call to Marie to let her know what was going on. They had an agreement that no matter what happened, Nolan would call her as soon as he could.

"Hi Marie," John said calmly. Marie knew her man and knew by his voice something was up. "What's wrong, John?" she asked anxiously. "I just shot a homicide suspect. He's dead." "Are you okay?" she asked, trying to project an air of calm. "Yes, I'm okay, but I'll be out here with the O.I.S. team for several hours. They said it'll probably be dawn, maybe later, before we get everything done out here."

Marie asked, "John, is there anything you want me to do?" "No, I just needed to hear your voice," he replied. Those words started her crying and she repeated, "Are you sure you're okay? What about Winters? Where is he?" "He shot the other guy. They're both dead. We're both fine. I'd better get going now. Please don't worry, everything is fine. I'll call you as soon as I get home tomorrow morning." "Okay John, I love you." "I love you too, Baby."

Winters and Nolan knew their shootings were righteous. However, it wasn't until several days later that they got the official word. The shootings they were involved in were determined to be justifiable and within department policy. The district attorney's office rendered a similar decision, calling the shootings justifiable homicide.

That same day, Winters and Nolan also received word that Nolan would not be called upon by internal affairs investigators with respect to Officer Davidson. It seemed yet another woman had come forward to complain about him. Riding three beefs, one of which was very serious, Davidson decided to resign, in lieu of possible termination.

The next several months passed quickly. Nolan completed his training and passed his probationary period. He was now a bonafide, "regular" police officer. He and Winters remained partners and that made both of them happy. They obviously worked exceptionally well together, they trusted one another and they became very close friends. In fact, Winter's wife, Jenny, and the love of Nolan's life, Marie, had become very close as well. The couples got together regularly for dinners, movies, barbecues and the Winters' children's birthday parties.

John and Marie continued their love affair with tremendous intensity. It was obvious to both of them they would be together for the rest of their lives. John asked Marie to marry him and, of course, she accepted. They were so happy together. Both sets of parents gave their unequivocal blessings to John and Marie. Then, the four parents became actively involved in helping the couple plan their wedding. And, coming as no surprise to anyone, John asked his partner to be his best man. Marie also asked Jenny to be her maid of honor. It would be a beautiful wedding.

Chapter Eight

A Brother Passes

Nearly two and a half years had passed since John and Marie got married. She was eight months pregnant with their first child, and they could hardly await the baby's arrival. The two of them had worked hard and had saved enough for a down payment on a nice starter home in a modest area of the San Fernando Valley. They particularly liked the street on which their house was located because it was quiet, had lots of trees and everyone in the neighborhood seemed to take very good care of their property.

By the time escrow closed and they finally got to move in, John and Marie realized they only had a month or so to get everything ready in the baby's room. John and Marie's dads, along with Dennis and John, were able to effect minor repairs, and get all of the house painting done, while the moms, Marie's sister, and Jenny focused on the actual decoration of the baby's room. Through the team effort, they completed everything on time. Marie gave birth to a beautiful baby girl whom they named Samantha.

Nolan could not have been happier. He was married to a beautiful, caring woman and he was a new father. He had a great job, and he was fortunate enough to have a partner whom he regarded not only as a friend, but also as the brother he never had. Winters and Nolan were as close as friends and partners could be. About a year earlier, in order to continue working with his best friend. Winters had passed on an opportunity to be assigned to detectives. Nolan remembered having mixed emotions about Winter's decision.

Of course, he wanted nothing more than to continue working with Winters, but on the other hand, it was time for Winters to move on. After all, he had already been a policeman for ten years and spent all of that time in a radio car.

Winters and Nolan had exemplary records on the police department. The quantity and quality of their work was frequently praised, not only by their supervisors, but by their peers as well. One Friday afternoon, as they sat in roll call preparing for their shift, the sergeant read a notice inviting qualified personnel to apply for detectives. Nolan looked over at his partner and jokingly punched him in the shoulder. "That's for you, Dennis," he whispered. "Don't you pass on it this time around." "Quiet, knucklehead," was Winter's response. "I'll make my own decision." The two chuckled quietly as the sergeant continued briefing.

Out in the field that evening, the topic of discussion was Winter's decision. Would he apply and leave his partner? "Dennis, in all seriousness, you've got to apply for that position. You know you'll make an excellent investigator. With your experience and people skills, you'll shine just like you do in patrol. Besides, think of your family. You'll have better hours, and more often than not, you'll be home on the weekends," Nolan rationalized with a sense of urgency. "You know, I think I'd really like to give it a shot this time. The only thing is, that obviously means we don't work together anymore," Winters said.

"Look man, we're still best of friends. That won't ever change and we both know that. This is your time, pal. Don't pass on it this time. Talk to Jenny. We both know she'll agree," Nolan said confidently.

Their conversation was interrupted by a hotshot: "Beep, beep, beep." "Any unit in the vicinity, back-up unit 308 with approximately twenty 415 subjects at the Pacific Roller Skating Rink." "Let's roll on that partner," Winters said as Nolan simultaneously floored it and activated the unit's rear-facing amber lights. Nolan always made it a point to remember to activate the amber when he intended to "hot-foot it" to a call. It served two functions: First, amber, or yellow, is the universal sign for caution. Second, it functioned as a courtesy, notifying the motoring public the unit was being driven a little more aggressively to get to a hot call.

Arriving at the scene quickly, the officers saw that Gonzales and Meyers were trying to control more like thirty teenagers. Additional units arrived to assist as well and, within a few minutes, the officers had everyone under control and order was restored. After interviewing several of the detainees, officers determined that the fight initially started with two guys fighting over a girl, and it blossomed rapidly from there.

Fortunately, no one had been hurt. The teens were strongly admonished regarding self-control, respect and consideration. Then, the majority of them were sent on their way. However, officers continued to detain four of the males. These teens exhibited some bizarre behavior. They appeared to be intoxicated, yet there was no smell of any alcoholic beverage on their breath or person. Instead, officers smelled a strong odor of a chemical substance consistent with the odor of ether.

As they examined the most noticeably impaired teen, officers saw that his eyes moved about rapidly, bouncing from side to side, up and down and in a circular motion. He walked with a sort of stiffened gait and seemed impervious to his surroundings. Officers tried to speak to him but it seemed as though could not understand what they were saying. The chemical smell was much stronger on this particular young man than on the others, and his strange symptoms and movements were much more profound.

Although it was a relatively cold evening, the teen was clad only in his pants. Prior to the arrival of the police officers, he had removed his shirt, his T-shirt, and his socks and shoes. It was plainly obvious to them he was under the influence of some type of chemical substance. They just didn't know what that substance was.

When officers tried to handcuff him, he resisted. He wasn't a very big boy, and he could not have weighed more than one hundred and twenty-five pounds, soaking wet. And yet, it took the very husky and powerful Gonzales, his partner Meyers, and another officer to bend his arms and hold on to him long enough for yet a forth officer to handcuff him. This little guy had put up quite a struggle. Officers were astounded by his exhibition of near superhuman strength. After he was handcuffed, the teenager made the strangest, guttural noises any of the officers had ever heard. He didn't sound human. He sounded more like some kind of animal.

Police officers were receiving a firsthand education about a relatively new drug making its debut in the neighborhoods of Southern California.

Prior to its introduction on the streets, this very potent drug had been used for years by veterinarians as an animal anesthetic. *Phencyclidine* was its formal name. However, on the street, it was known by several different names, and it could be acquired in different forms.

P.C.P. and Angel Dust, were but two of the common street names. When handled by mid-level street dealers, the drug normally came in liquid form. It was amber in color and called, "juice" on the street. In fact, during its heyday in the 1970's and early 1980's, police officers came across PCP in this form quite often. Dealers usually kept the liquid in small vials. However, they would keep the majority of their stash elsewhere, in baby bottles, refrigerators, or anywhere they thought they could secret the substance from police in the event they were discovered, and a search warrant was executed at their residence or "place of business."

But for the majority of actual users, P.C.P. was acquired in cigarette form. Dealers would take a package of "Kool" brand menthol cigarettes and dip individual cigarettes in the liquid P.C.P. The cigarette would then be allowed to air dry, after which it was commonly wrapped in aluminum foil. Hence the name, "supercool." To get high, the user would simply smoke the cigarette, ingesting the drug by means of inhalation. The same concept applied to the "sherm." This was a brown wrapped "Sherman" brand cigarette prepared in the same manner as the Kool cigarette.

Although available in other forms, these were the most popular. Users liked P.C.P. because it was a relatively cheap high. Dealers liked it, of course, because they made lots of money. Manufacturers or "cookers" liked it because they could "cook it up" from readily available chemicals and then sell it to the dealers, making a small fortune in the process. Their P.C.P. labs were very dangerous because of the volatility of the chemicals they used to produce the final product.

In its final liquid form, the drug was dangerous as well because it could be absorbed into the body through contact with the skin. Unfortunately, several officers learned this the hard way and actually got high as the direct result of skin contact with the liquid as they handled it during arrests and through the booking of the substance into evidence. Phencyclidine is a hallucinogenic, therefore, once the initial high was over, a user, or unfortunate police officer, could experience "flashbacks" at any time.

Police in the Southern California area had a name for people under the influence of P.C.P. Aptly named for the drug itself, users were called "dusters." P.C.P. was a major law enforcement nightmare. People under the influence of this drug usually had little or no reaction to pain, and more often than not, they exhibited superhuman strength.

Officers witnessed previously unheard of feats, such as a handcuffed "duster" ripping his handcuffs apart. Of course, he broke his own bones and badly lacerated his hands, but he felt no pain while he was under the influence. One duster literally peeled a welded metal bunk from its attachment to a wall in a jail cell. Another duster was apprehended ripping young trees right out of the ground, roots and all. As police became more and more familiar with the effects of this drug, no account of user activity, no matter how bizarre, seemed unusual.

The police never knew when a duster was going to "go off." A duster could be docile and relaxed one moment. and in the blink of an eye, turn into a raving and extremely violent madman. Sometimes they would just snap, while other times a loud noise or bright lights might set them off. When a duster did go off, it was difficult for the police because during that time period they had very little in the way of non-lethal type weapons. That meant brute force and sheer body weight were normally the methods used to subdue and effect arrests on dusters who were aggressive or combative.

After assisting Gonzales and Meyers, Winters and Nolan cleared and took up where they had left off in their conversation about Winters testing for the detective position. "I've already discussed applying for detectives at length with Jenny. She's all for it. She was for it last time too," Winters announced. "Good, then you'll apply?" Nolan pressured. "You know, you're rapidly becoming a pushy son of a bitch," Winters chuckled. "Yes, I will apply." "Alright!" Nolan exclaimed. "Now that that's settled, let's grab something to eat. I'm hungry." "My treat today," Winters declared. "Bullshit, you paid last time," Nolan argued. The partners laughed and bickered back and forth over whose turn it was to pay for dinner.

The following day Winters submitted his application for detectives, and he was almost immediately selected. Within two weeks of submitting his paperwork. Winters was shopping for suits and ties to wear on his "new" job. Nolan, Gonzales and Meyers planned a sort of congratulatory, and going-away party at a local restaurant, and all of those who attended had a great time. For laughs, Nolan presented Winters with a Sherlock Holmes detective kit, which included the signature hat, pipe, magnifying glass and lookalike coat. Gonzales and Meyers had a "Junior Detective" certificate made and framed. It looked very official. They also "issued" Winters a Junior Detective badge, complete with leatherette holder. Between all of the storytelling, the jokes, and the gifts he received, Winters laughed so much his face muscles hurt.

Then it was time to get serious. Sergeant Carter stood and called the group to order. He praised Winters for his professionalism and for his abilities as a police officer. He told him he was a good man who would be sorely missed. Carter congratulated him and wished him well. Several others stood and congratulated Winters as well.

Gonzales and Meyers, of course, wished him the best of luck, and thanked him for being a real friend. Anthony Clark, one of the black officers on the PM shift, got up and thanked Winters for always being there, in support of him. Clark briefly reminisced about his days as a rookie, when Winters took him under his wing, and taught him the ins and outs of the job. Jin Park, the only Korean officer on the PM crew was next. He stood and addressed the group. "Okay, I see how this minority stuff works. First the Mexican officer talks, then the Black officer talks and last, but not least, it's the Oriental's turn." Everyone laughed. "How come we're always last?" Park laughed.

Park was one of those funny, jovial guys who made everyone laugh. Nolan and the others often told Park he'd missed his calling. He should have been a stand-up comedian. And then, Park got serious, and he very graciously, and very eloquently, paid tribute to his friend Dennis. But he couldn't stay serious for very long. As his parting comment, he chuckled and said, "Dennis, I also want to thank you for being the only guy on our watch who never made a comment about me driving DWO, or driving while oriental. The rest of these bums always tease me." Everyone laughed and applauded Park who promptly bowed in response and took his seat.

Finally, it was Nolan's turn to speak. Initially, he had planned a somewhat longwinded narration of his feelings for his partner. Instead, he decided to keep it short, primarily because he didn't want to become too emotional in front of his buddies. Looking directly at Winters, Nolan said, "You are the best partner a cop could ask for. You are the epitome of professionalism. You're an honest, good man and you're the best friend any man could ever want." Then, he raised his glass high in the air and proposed a toast. "To my brother Dennis, here's to you. May you find happiness and success wherever you go." They all raised their glasses and drank.

Finally, Winters stood up and addressed the group with a few short, but emotionally charged words. He closed by offering his heartfelt thanks to all for their support and encouragement. He assured his friends he would visit with them often.

Sergeant Carter was in dire need of another training officer on his watch, and he knew Nolan could capably fill that position. He also believed Nolan would make an excellent teacher, mentor and role model for young police officers. Nolan had an exemplary record, and he was known for making quality arrests. He was respected for his honesty, his professionalism and his self-imposed high standards.

Carter had no trouble obtaining the lieutenant's endorsement for training officer certification school for Nolan. Within a few of weeks of losing his partner to the Detective Bureau, Nolan found himself in Field Training Officer (FTO) school. Upon completion of the two-week certification class held at the academy, Nolan returned to his crew. The very next week, a brand new trainee by the name of Steven Villanueva was assigned to him.

Meanwhile, Winters was well into his second month as a detective, and coming as no surprise to anyone, he was doing quite well. He had assimilated into the world of investigations, and he was already proving himself very adept at his job. However, he missed his ex-partner and best friend. The two spoke frequently on the telephone, as did their wives.

Winters sometimes spoke of returning to patrol division, and resuming his role of radio car partner to his pal Nolan. But, whenever he spoke of returning, Nolan would become furious with him. "You worked a radio car for more than ten years. You were the best. It's time for you to be an investigator. You like it, don't you?" a frustrated Nolan would ask. "Yes, I like it very much. I enjoy putting cases together—kinda like a puzzle. Review the evidence, conduct the interviews, make all the pieces fit, and then present the case for filing with the D.A.'s office. I do enjoy it. But, I also miss my pal. I miss rolling on calls with you, bullshitting with you, drinking coffee with you, and all of that," Winters explained.

"Dennis, you know I miss you too. You're the brother I never had. But this is good for you and the family. You're home with Jenny and the kids at night, you're doing investigations, and you even admit you like it.....just stay with it. Listen, why don't we have a barbecue at my house this weekend? I've got lots of time on the books. I'll take Saturday off and my trainee can ride with someone else for the night. What do you say?" Nolan asked.

"Actually, that sounds great John," Winters replied. "Done deal. I'll see you guys in a couple of days." "Wait, what do you want us to bring?" Winters asked. "Hey Sherlock, you're a detective. Haven't you figured it out yet? You ask the same thing every time. I give you the same answer every time. Bring yourself and your family. That's it," Nolan said with authority. "Aw, the hell with you. I'll have Jenny call Marie. She's much more sensible than you are. I still can't figure out what a beautiful woman like her ever saw in a homely geek like you!" Winters teased.

In spite of missing his partner terribly, Nolan did enjoy his new role as a training officer. It was an opportunity for him to teach, and to share his knowledge and experience. He welcomed the responsibility, and never lost sight of the fact that only a few years earlier, he was in his trainee's shoes. Now *he* was the teacher. Nolan was pleased with Villanueva. He was eager to learn, intelligent, street-smart, and he had a great attitude. He was also fluent in Spanish. That helped a great deal as the demographics of the district they were working were quickly becoming primarily Hispanic. Though Nolan understood quite a bit, his ability to properly express himself in the language was limited.

In California, having the ability to speak Spanish is a great advantage. He and Marie had decided early on that their children would be fluent in Spanish. Of course, it would have to be Marie's job to teach them.

While he trained Villanueva, Nolan often spoke fondly of his own training officer. In the couple of weeks they had been together, Nolan had begun to assess the young officer's ability to deal with stressful situations. Nolan liked what he saw, and though he was brand new, the young man interacted well with people and displayed a strong command presence. He was humble and respectful, yet, at the same time, he was also very confident. Nolan had already formed the opinion that, barring any unforeseen developments, this young man would eventually make a fine police officer.

"Steve, I'm going to take this Saturday off. The sarge will put you with someone else for the night. He might even have you work the desk. But tomorrow, I want you to meet me at the range at 10:00 o'clock. We're going to do some shooting and get our qualification out of the way," Nolan advised his trainee. "Yes sir," Villanueva replied. "By the way, did you study the penal code sections I assigned you?" "Yes I did, sir," Villanueva responded quickly. "I'm ready for you to test me." "Well, in that case, I'll assign you more reading for tonight, and I'll test you on both assignments tomorrow," Nolan snickered. "I'll be ready," Villanueva said, smiling confidently.

That Saturday afternoon, the Winters arrived at the Nolan home right on time. Armed with a cake and a couple of pies for dessert, Dennis made his way to the kitchen followed by Nolan. "I thought I told you not to bring anything," Nolan said. "Since when did I care about what you told me?" Dennis retorted. The two men laughed and jokingly insulted one another as they arranged the cake and pies in the refrigerator.

John and Marie hugged and kissed the three Winters children and Jenny. Jenny was in a hurry to see the baby. "Marie, I want you to take it easy today. Linda is almost five years old. She'll help me watch over Samantha. You need to have a good time and relax." "You guys are so sweet," Marie said. "But I'm fine. I love being a mother. I don't feel stressed or overworked at all."

Marie and Jenny settled in and began chatting while the children played. The women had grown very close over the past couple of years, and they thought of each other more as sisters than friends. John and Dennis tended to the barbecuing duties out in the back yard. "I'm glad we got the families together today," Winters said. "Me too, it's been too long," Nolan answered. "Hey, how's your trainee doing?" Winters asked. "He's a good kid. Doing great. He has all the tools, and it's obvious he comes from a good home. His value system, morals and judgement are right on. He'll make a good, solid cop." "Glad to hear it. He's lucky to have you as his training officer," Winters said. "Thanks Dennis," Nolan replied humbly.

"What about you, man? How's your case load?" Nolan inquired. "Well, I've been working closely with the dope guys, even though theoretically, I'm assigned to the burglary crew, with Dave Kawolsky as my partner. You remember him don't you?" "Yeah, he's a good guy," Nolan said. "Yeah, he really is," Winters confirmed. "Anyway, I've got a snitch giving me information on these two brothers who sell P.C.P. whenever they can. When they don't have any P.C.P. to sell, they do burgs. Right now they're in burglary mode. The snitch said they had a falling out with their fence, and for the time being, they're storing everything they steal at their pad.

Next week, Kawolsky and I are going to surveil them to see if the snitch's information is accurate. We'll see how it goes. We'll either have another one of our teams help us or we may just have the dope guys help us follow them around for a while to see if they score more juice and start selling again. That way, when we write the search warrant, we can get them for the dope and the burglary/receiving stolen property capers."

"They're supposed to be real bad asses. Hopefully, we can put them and their supplier away for a while." Winters explained. "Well, you watch your ass out there, Dennis. Remember, you don't have me to protect you anymore," Nolan smiled.

Marie and Jenny went out to the back yard to check on the progress of the chicken and burgers. Jenny was proudly holding little Samantha. "You boys cooking or talking shop?" Marie asked while grinning. "A little bit of both, Baby," John confessed. "Sweetie, we've got some hungry kids here. Can we expedite the process, please?" she pleaded. "You got it lady. Coming up right away." Nolan complied with his wife's request and finished the cooking without further delay.

Then, they all sat and enjoyed a very fine barbecued meal with all the trimmings. When they finished, the adults pitched in to get the cleanup done. The older kids were served cake and ice cream for dessert, after which they played quietly in the front room. The younger ones went down for their naps, and the adults took advantage of that time to sit at the table, drink coffee, and talk about everything. Everything, but police work. The four of them talked for a long time, and by the time the Winters left that night, the adults had polished off two pies and three pots of coffee. All of them were stuffed, but as always, they had a great time together.

Back at work in his role as training officer, Nolan and his trainee received their first call of the evening right out of briefing. It was a call of a suicide victim inside of a residence. Further information on the call was that the wife of the victim had come home and discovered her husband's body in the garage. En route to the call, Nolan commented to his partner, "Suicide is bad enough in and of itself, but when a family member discovers the body, the ensuing grief, devastation and feelings of guilt can be even worse."

"Our primary role here, of course, is to preliminarily determine whether or not there was any foul play. More often than not, a suicide is just that - a suicide. However, as you may know, in order to hide his crime, a murderer might attempt to make his crime of homicide, appear as a suicide. I say that to emphasize the importance of the preliminary examination of the scene and the body."

"Also of extreme importance, is the fact that as police officers, we must be compassionate and considerate of the family, in their time of grief." "I understand sir, and I have a lot of questions about suicide in general. They talked about it in the academy, but I was left with many unanswered questions." Villanueva replied. "Good. Remember them, and we'll discuss them after we handle this call." "Yes, sir."

Upon arriving at the meticulously maintained residence, the officers made contact with the reporting party, Mrs. Abernathy, wife of the victim. She was a well-groomed lady in her sixties. Her eyes were red, watery and swollen, and it was obvious she had been crying. Fighting back more tears, Mrs. Abernathy pointed the officers to the door leading to the garage. "Robert is in there," she said as she began to weep. She was holding several tissues in one hand and a folded piece of paper in the other. Before entering the garage, Nolan gently touched Mrs. Abernathy's shoulder and asked softly, "Ma'am, is there a family member or a friend or neighbor I could call for you?" "No thank you, dear, my daughter is on her way over from work. She should be here any minute." "Yes Ma'am. Uh, that paper you're holding, is it..." "Robert left me a letter explaining why he did this. I've read it over and over, and I still don't understand. We loved each other so much." "Yes, Ma'am." "But he's been very ill lately. He's got a lot of medical problems. Here, you read this," Mrs. Abernathy said as she handed Nolan the suicide note.

Just then Nolan heard a car race into the driveway followed by a car door slamming and a woman's running footsteps. He motioned Mrs. Abernathy towards the front door. "It's my daughter Julie," she said as she wept even harder. Julie entered the house and immediately embraced and comforted her mother. She looked directly into Nolan's eyes. "Can I see my father?" she asked. Before Nolan could respond, her mother loudly said, "No Julie, I don't want you to see your father like that because every time you think of him, you'll remember that horrible sight!" "Your mother is right, Julie," Nolan said. "It would be best if you stayed out here with your mom. Let us take care of this." Julie hung her head and said, "Okay officer."

Nolan and Villanueva entered the garage from the narrow doorway off of the laundry room. There were no cars in the garage, and it was maintained as meticulously as the house. There were some tools hanging on wall-mounted pegboard, but other than that, the garage appeared empty and clean. "Don't touch anything yet. Just look carefully. Take in the entire scene and then focus in on details," Nolan instructed. The sun had not set yet and there were several windows in the garage, allowing lots of light to enter. In spite of that, the officers used their flashlights to enhance their ability to see detail.

Nolan saw that Mr. Abernathy was hanging from a relatively thin utility type rope that he had fashioned into a sort of hangman's noose. His body was swinging slightly and there was a small amount of blood trickling down the right side of his face from a small wound near his right temple. He had strung the rope around the tops of the wooden roof supports, or rafters, that met and crossed right in the middle of the garage. In order to accomplish his task, Abernathy had apparently used a small stepladder. He would have had to stand on the very top step in order to secure the rope around the rafters and his neck. The ladder was lying on its side as if it had been tipped over. On the floor, a couple of feet to the right of the hanging body, was a small caliber automatic handgun with the hammer back in the cocked position. A single expended shell casing was lying a few feet in front of the body, near the large (drive-in) garage door.

"Tell me what happened here, Steve," Nolan asked of his young partner. "Well sir, it looks like the victim secured the rope around the rafters and his neck by standing on the ladder. Then, he shot himself in the temple. When he did that, the shock caused him to lose his balance. I guess that's when he moved off of the ladder and tipped it over. My guess is that the rope then hung him and finished the job. It looks like he really wanted to make sure he died." "Good job, Steve. That's pretty much exactly how this played out," Nolan commented.

"A couple of things though: First of all, do you see the black marking around the wound in his temple?" "Yes, I see it." "That's called tattooing. It happens when a weapon is fired within very close proximity to the victim, or actually touching the victim. Essentially, it's a gunpowder burn. Next, the wound is on the right side of his head. The weapon is located on the floor to the right of the body and, on this particular brand of .25 caliber automatic, the expended shell casing is ejected to the right. That's why we found the shell casing near the large door. When he fired, the casing was ejected to the right, or in front of the body. All of which supports your theory of how this happened."

"Remember that seventy percent of the population is right-handed, so more than likely, he was right-handed, and actually did do this to himself. But one of the questions you'll need to ask of Mrs. Abernathy is—was he right-handed. You called it on the ladder. I believe that's precisely what happened and how it came to be lying on its side like that."

"Next item: we'll need to do a gunshot residue test (GSR) on the victim's right hand. That way we'll know for certain whether or not he actually fired the weapon. After I finish talking to you, we'll call the Coroner's office and get an ETA. If they have an extended ETA, we'll do the GSR ourselves. If they don't quote a delay, we'll have the deputy coroner do the test. The reason? The more time that passes, the less reliable the GSR test becomes. The chemicals dissipate from the skin within hours. From the looks of him, he hasn't been here that long."

"Another question for the Mrs.—When did she leave, when did she return and discover the body? Is this stuff making sense to you?" Nolan asked. "Absolutely sir. It all makes sense," the young officer replied. "Good. You need to also remember that if we even suspected foul play, we would immediately seal this as a crime scene and request detectives," Nolan continued. "Yes, I understand," Villanueva answered.

"When you talk to Mrs. Abernathy get the name of the treating doctor and when he saw him last. We'll need a list of all his prescription medications and their dosages. We've already read the suicide note explaining briefly that he killed himself because of his pain and suffering, however, we'll examine the note again to make certain we didn't miss anything," Nolan said.

"Do we cut him down?" Villanueva asked. "Normally, we don't cut them down. That works well in the movies. But the coroner needs to do that, because if we cut him down, that will change the settling of bodily fluids, the temperature of his body, and potentially destroy evidence. The deputy coroner will appreciate us leaving him hanging intact. However, if we were in an open area, if there was no way to shield children from seeing this, or if there were other reasonably mitigating circumstances, you could cut him down. But, stand by for a beef from the coroner's office if you do."

"One last thing," Nolan continued instructing his partner, "He hung himself with his back towards the interior of the house. That is, he's facing the drive-in garage door. Quite possibly, he made a definitive psychological decision to do that. You see, he had obviously already made the decision to kill himself in his own home, but it would appear that possibly, he wanted to be as far removed as possible. He wanted to somehow limit the shock value of his wife's discovery of his body."

"In his mind, by hanging himself in the garage, facing the street, he was carrying out his task in a less offensive manner than if he had simply blown his brains out in their bed." "I see what you mean," Villanueva said. "I guess he loved her and, in his own way, he wanted to shield her from as much pain as possible," Villanueva added. "Exactly, but again, that's just theory and conjecture at this point," Nolan reiterated. "We'll probably never know that part of it for sure."

"Okay, I'm going to call the coroner's office," Nolan said as he looked up the number in his field officer's notebook, an item he always kept in his back pocket. A few minutes later, he returned and informed Villanueva, "The coroner's office quoted no delay, only driving time from their office. We'll let them do the GSR test, Steve," Nolan said. "Okay sir, I'm going to go ahead and talk to Mrs. Abernathy. Do you want to monitor my conversation with her?" he asked of his training officer.

"Since this is your first suicide, I'll stand by while you talk to her, but I'm sure you'll do just fine," Nolan assured his trainee. "Wait just a couple of minutes until I shoot some pictures of the scene," Nolan said as he prepared the camera he had retrieved from the trunk of the unit.

As Villanueva was completing his conversation with Mrs. Abernathy, the deputy coroner arrived. Nolan instructed the young officer to watch carefully as the coroner conducted his "field" investigation. Villanueva assisted the deputy coroner in cutting the body down and placing it in a body bag. The deputy gave Villanueva a coroner's case number, and also explained the ultimate disposition of her husband's remains to Mrs. Abernathy.

After they had cleared, Villanueva asked, "Are suicides always coroner's cases?" "Yes they are. Suicides and homicides are always considered coroner's cases." "Have you handled many suicides, sir?" "Sadly, yes I have. And unfortunately, for too many people, they see suicide as the only way out when they're overwhelmed and they've given up trying to find their way," Nolan reflected in a somber tone. Villanueva continued to pick his training officer's brain, "Is there any specific age group or occupation in which people are more prone to commit suicide?" "Yes, although there are no absolutes."

"For example, the number of teen suicides in this country each year is very shocking. Worse yet, the numbers have risen dramatically every year while the actual ages of the victims has fallen as well. That trend has been continuing for several years now. It's bad enough when a sixteen or seventeen year old kills him or herself. But when a twelve or thirteen year old kills him or herself you find yourself wondering, what in the world is going on here?"

"Also, certain professions seem to have a dramatic impact on the suicide rate. The first one that comes to mind is police officers. As a profession or group, we commit suicide at a far higher rate than most other professions. The numbers are staggering. Perhaps, it's the constant exposure to the miseries of humanity that drive some of our brothers and sisters to the brink. Perhaps, it's the repeated disappointment in the legal system. And consider this; police work is very hard on marriage and family. Certainly, dissolution of family is also a major contributing factor to the high suicide rate in our profession."

"You know, Steve, there are dozens of books written on this subject. If you're still interested, you ought to check out your local library," Nolan advised his partner. "I'm fascinated, and saddened by the subject at the same time," Villanueva said with a puzzled look on his face. "Then maybe you should do some follow-up reading," Nolan said. "It'll clear some things up and give you a better understanding." "Sir, one last question then I'll get off it, if that's okay?" Villanueva asked. Nolan smiled, pleased with his partner's enthusiasm and desire to learn. "Go ahead, Steve." "Other than the obvious, such as depression, withdrawal, loss of a loved one, and so on, are there common, tell-tale signs that would indicate a person might be contemplating suicide?"

"Well again, there are few completely fixed patterns or absolutes. Suicide can be spontaneous or it can be planned out over a long period of time. But, there are some common denominators. Experts say teenagers are generally harder to read, but in addition to the ones you've already mentioned, there are some indicators that should raise immediate concern. Some of those are: a new or different set of friends, slipping of grades, change in study habits, attitude, a decline in grooming habits, and frequent mood swings."

"Something else that seems fairly common amongst suicide victims of *all* ages is the suicide note. Victims feel compelled to explain to their loved ones why they must take the action they are about to take. For the victims, I guess it brings about a sort of closure. That's why, when I saw that folded piece of paper in Mrs. Abernathy's hand, I was almost certain it was a suicide note. Also, many suicide victims feel it necessary to give away their personal belongings in the days and hours prior to their self-destruction. Now Steve, you need to keep in mind, my responses to your questions have been very generalized. I still recommend you go to the library and learn more about this, if you're so inclined."

A couple of days later, Nolan was at home having a leisurely breakfast with the two women in his life, Marie and baby Samantha. Thanks to the shift rotation, it was his first of three days off in a row. It was a bright, sunny summer morning, and as they ate, John and Marie discussed what the three of them would do that day. They were finalizing their plans when the phone rang. "Hello," Nolan answered. "John?" a man's deep voice on the other end of the line asked. "Yes," Nolan replied. "John, this is Dave Kawolsky, Dennis Winters' partner," the voice on the other end said sadly. Nolan's heart instantly skipped a beat and his mind began racing. In a split second, Nolan determined there could be only one reason Kawolsky would call him.

"John, Dennis and I were serving a search warrant in Sylmar this morning and as we made our entry..." "What is it Kawolsky, what's happened?" Nolan interrupted, raising his voice. Marie stopped what she was doing and stared at her husband. "John, I'm so sorry to have to tell you this. Dennis was shot as we made our entry. He's dead John. I'm sorry." "No! No way man...it can't be, not Dennis." Nolan started crying. Marie immediately broke out in tears as well.

"John, listen to me, please!" Kawolsky pleaded. "This just happened a little while ago. We're here at Valley Medical Center. The paramedics worked him up and transported him over here, but he was DOA." John wept quietly as he listened carefully while Kawolsky spoke. "Everyone knows how close you guys were..." "What about the asshole that shot him?" Nolan interrupted. "He's dead. Him and his brother. They're both dead."

"Listen John, we haven't called Jenny yet. All of us, including the lieutenant, thought it might be best if you notified her and brought her down here. The lieutenant said it's your choice, John. If you're not up to it, it's not a problem. He'll notify Jenny and send a black and white to pick her up. "No, no. I'll call her right away. She's gonna need us by her side. I'll bring her down there right away," John said as he tried to compose himself. "We'll be here waiting," Kawolsky said.

John hung up the phone and just stood there in silence for a moment. Marie stared at him. "Marie, Dennis is dead! He was shot and killed a little while ago. I can't believe it! I just can't believe he's gone. Get the baby ready. We have to get Jenny. Hurry, Marie," John said almost frantically. Marie was openly weeping as she lifted Samantha from her high chair and rushed off to the bedroom to get her ready to go. John followed and said, "I don't want to call Jenny until we're ready to leave. I'll take you over there so you can watch the kids."

"Will you call my mom and see if she can watch all of the kids?" If she can, take them all over there and then you can meet us at the hospital. Jenny is gonna need you, Marie." "You know I'll be there for her," Marie said, as she tried to control her crying. "Call her now and see if she's home. She likes to get her shopping done in the mornings. I'm just going to wrap Samantha in a blanket." "Okay, I'll go call her right now," John said as he walked back toward to the kitchen.

In order to regain his composure before making the call, Nolan took a couple of deep breaths prior to dialing. "Hello," said the female voice at the other end of the line. "Hi Jenny, this is John." "Hi John," Jenny said warmly. "What are you guys doing?" she inquired. "Jenny, I have to talk to you," John said sadly. From the tone of John's voice and the few words he spoke, Jenny instantly knew that something was terribly wrong. "What's wrong, John, what is it?" Jenny asked with a trembling voice.

"Jenny, it's Dennis," John replied very solemnly. Jenny starting crying, "Tell me John, please." "Jenny, Dennis and his partner were serving a search warrant this morning. There was a shooting... Dennis...Dennis is gone. I'm so sorry." Jenny was crying hysterically. "No John, he's not dead. How could this happen? Where is he? I have to see him," she blurted out, crying uncontrollably. "Jenny, they have him at a hospital close to where the shooting took place. Marie and I will be there in ten minutes to get you. I'll take you to him right away." Jenny was crying hysterically and did not respond. She simply hung up the phone.

Fortunately, the drive to the Winter's home that morning took less than ten minutes. John took care of getting the baby out of the car while Marie ran to the front door. Jenny opened it right away and the two women embraced each other and wept. Marie gently stroked the side of Jenny's face and said, "I'll watch the children. You go with John. I'll try to get John's mom to watch the kids. She's here in the Valley. If that doesn't work, I'll call my mom, but I'll be there as soon as I get the kids settled."

Jenny didn't respond verbally. She just looked Marie directly in the eyes and squeezed her hand. Tears continued to roll down her face from her red, puffy eyes. John handed Samantha over to Marie and embraced Jenny. No words were spoken at that moment. None were necessary. But after a few seconds, John took Jenny's arm. "We need to go now," he said softly as he started walking her to the car. Jenny took a few steps, paused and turned back toward Marie. "I didn't tell the children anything yet. I couldn't," Jenny said quietly. "I won't say anything, Jenny. You'll tell them when you're ready," Marie said as she stood in the doorway holding Samantha. She watched as John and Jenny drove off.

It didn't take very long for John to get Jenny to the hospital. When they arrived, they were met by a priest, a hospital social worker and the hospital administrator. Captain Whitmore and Lieutenant Singer had just arrived from the police department as well. They were standing with Kawolsky. Captain Whitmore approached Jenny. "Mrs. Winters, I'm very sorry for your loss. Dennis was an excellent policeman, and we're all devastated by his death." Jenny touched his shoulder and thanked him. "Captain, I'm grateful to you and everyone here. But, I'd much rather just be alone with my husband. Can you please arrange that?" Jenny pleaded. "Yes, yes I can arrange that, Mrs. Winters."

Jenny turned to John. "I want to see him now, John," she whispered. "Okay Jenny," John replied. John looked over at Kawolsky and when their eyes met he said quietly, "I need to talk to you." "I know," Kawolsky replied. "I'll be right here when you're ready." Then, John turned towards the administrator and motioned inquisitively with his hands, while silently mouthing the words, "Where is he?" The administrator responded immediately. "Follow me, I'll take you to him." John held Jenny's arm as they walked.

When they reached the room, John stopped, released his grip on Jenny's arm and pushed the door open for her. "Come in with me," she said as tears started rolling down her face once again. "He loved you like a brother." John nodded. They entered the room and saw that a sheet had been pulled up over Dennis' head as he lay on the gurney. Jenny looked at John, and he immediately understood. He slowly pulled the sheet back, uncovering Dennis' face and upper body. There were several thick layers of blood soaked gauze bandages around the upper portion of his head starting just above the ears.

Jenny lost it and started screaming and crying hysterically. John began sobbing as well. He ran around the gurney to where Jenny was standing, but before he could embrace and support her, she bent over and cupped her husband's now cold, clammy face and head with her hands and began kissing his cheeks. John didn't interfere. He knew that Jenny was doing what she needed to do. He went back around to the other side of the gurney and placed his hand on Dennis' shoulder. He stared at his brother's face and wept quietly.

At some point during the time that John and Jenny were in the room saying farewell to Dennis, Marie arrived at the hospital and was directed to their location. John exited the room first, leaving Jenny alone to have some last moments with her deceased husband. "Hi Sweetie," Marie said compassionately, seeing the anguished look on her husband's face. She hugged John as hard as she could and held on to him. "Your mom is watching all the kids. How's Jenny doing?" Once again, John took a moment to compose himself. "Under the circumstances, I guess she's doing as well as can be expected. But, she's gonna need you as soon as she walks out that door." "I'm here for her. I'll take good care of her," Marie said with a determined tone in her voice.

"I have to find out exactly what happened out there. Since you're here now, I'm going to find Kawolsky," John said firmly. "Okay Sweetie. Listen, there's a room just the other side of the nurse's station. It's used for situations like this. I'll take Jenny over there. Meet us there when you're done," Marie said. "Okay, I'll see you in a bit."

Nolan found Kawolsky right where he said he'd be. "What happened out there, Dave?" "We were working these two brothers. They were burglars, but they also sold dope whenever they could get it. Anyway, Dennis and I worked up the case and wrote a search warrant for their pad. We knew they had a reputation for being bad asses. They're both ex-cons, each with a lengthy history of physical violence. They liked fighting and beating people. Because of that, we took of couple of gorillas with us, and we thought we had taken all of the appropriate precautions."

"When we hit the door, it didn't open right away. Turns out it was a heavy-duty metal reinforced door, painted out to look like a standard wooden door. There was no way of knowing that. It looked just like a regular door. It took a while to get through it. We lost our element of surprise, and gave them plenty of time to make a decision. When we finally got the door open, Dennis was the first one through. He didn't take more than a couple of steps before shots rang out. He fired before he went down, and he hit the first one. When the second suspect saw that his brother was down, he charged at the rest of us, screaming and firing his handgun. That was it for him."

Nolan didn't respond immediately. Instead, he just stood there for a brief moment, digesting everything Kawolsky had just said. He was just about to speak when Kawolsky said angrily, "It's my fault. I was the senior detective. Dennis is gone because of me, damn it!" Nolan shook his head, "No, it's not your fault. You guys were doing your job. Blaming yourself is not going to bring Dennis back to us. Don't do it." The men hugged each other and Kawolsky started crying.

"I need to talk to his wife, but I've gotta get back out there. I was just notified that Homicide and the OIS team (officer involved shooting) are at the scene." "I'll let Jenny know. There will be plenty of time for you to talk to her. I'm sure she'll have questions for you too. Maybe its better this way," Nolan reasoned. "Here, take this bag," Kawolsky said as he offered a large plastic bag to Nolan. "It's everything Dennis had with him except for his weapon." "I'll see that it gets to Jenny."

Not unlike a brother and sister, John and Marie stood by and supported Jenny. In the hours that followed her husband's death, Jenny decided it was time to let the children know their father was gone. At her request, Marie and John were present in the room when she informed them of his death. Nolan recalled it was a gut-wrenching experience to see the painful expressions on their little faces as they listened to what their mother said. He would never forget their agonizing cries of horror and disbelief. The Nolans helped Jenny comfort, hug and reassure the children, although it didn't seem to reduce or stop the flow of tears.

Immediate attention had to be given to making family notifications and funeral arrangements. The department would handle most everything with respect to the funeral, but Jenny had to make choices as to the church, burial location, and so forth. In adherence to department policy for an officer killed in the line of duty, the funeral would be military style, with full honors.

A few days after his untimely death, Detective Dennis Winters was laid to rest. In keeping with the police department's policy and in following the strictest military protocol, the funeral was an example of the manner in which our police and military pay tribute to a fallen hero in this country. It was a precision event, carried out with honor and attention to detail on a warm and sunny Southern California morning. In addition to family, friends and other civilians, hundreds of uniformed police officers from all over California and the rest of this country were in attendance. Each officer wore a black band spanning the width of his or her badge in recognition of a fallen brother.

At the appropriate time in the services, Nolan was called upon to eulogize his best friend. Nolan gave a moving and emotional speech in which he praised Dennis as a man, as a friend, as a police officer, and a fallen hero. He was able to keep his composure during his oration, however, at the gravesite later in the services, Nolan felt a lump in his throat and fought back the tears when the Police Chief presented Jenny with the precisely folded flag of our nation. He continued fighting back the tears as several police helicopters, flying overhead, executed the "missing man" formation. Then, toward the end of the ceremony, when the bagpiper played the traditional "Amazing Grace," Nolan lost it and tears flowed freely down his face. He was not alone.

Nolan had difficulty handling his best friend's death. After all, Dennis was the brother he never had. They were as close as friends could ever be and when Dennis died, a part of him died too. In the weeks and months following that tragic event, Nolan admittedly lost the edge. His normally strong, positive attitude was shaken. He just wasn't the same happy guy. In order to get back on track he would have to do some deep soul-searching. His faith in God was undaunted and strong as ever.

Nevertheless, he couldn't have done it alone. Fortunately for John, Marie was there for him, as always. She helped him through his time of grief and depression with patience and perseverance. Because of her support, he was ultimately able to put things back into perspective and get on with life. John felt lucky and very proud to have had a friend and a brother like Dennis Winters. He would always cherish Dennis' memory. As for Marie, the woman of his dreams, John felt it was a blessing to be married to her. In his mind, she was the epitome of womanhood.

Chapter Nine

The Angel of Death Returns

Several years had passed since the death of Dennis Winters. Jenny and the kids had long since moved to Oregon to live near her parents. Jenny thought it would be best if the kids were close to their grandparents. Besides, after her husband's death, there was no reason to stay in the area. The only thing she missed about California was her close relationship with the Nolans. She was eternally grateful to them, not only for their loyal friendship, but also for their help and support after Dennis' death. She missed them terribly, but she made it a point to stay in close touch with them. Jenny and Marie wrote to each other as often as they could, and via telephone, they spoke on average once every couple of months.

The Nolans were very proud of Jenny. She was a remarkable woman and a wonderful mother. She had shown great courage and strength in the way she dealt with her husband's death. Jenny would never let the children forget their father. She had family pictures that included Dennis in several areas of the house, and she made it a point to talk about him frequently with the children. She would not allow his memory to die. When her husband was alive, her goal in life was to be the best wife and mother she could possibly be. Now that he was gone, her mission to be the best mother she could be was even more intense. Indeed, the Winters children were very fortunate to have Jenny as their mother.

167

John and Marie had another baby girl whom they named Kimberly. Samantha, their older daughter, was a very beautiful child. But Kimberly had bright blue eyes, the same color as her grandfather's and, coupled with her mother's olive skin and dark hair, she was an absolutely gorgeous little girl. On numerous occasions John told Marie he would have trouble when the girls became teenagers. "By the time a boy reaches his middle teens, he's not thinking about toys anymore. He's thinking girls, girls, girls and sports, but mostly...girls!"

"Oh relax, John, you're such a worrier," Marie would tell him. "The girls will be smart. We'll see to that. Besides, my sister and I did just fine. What you should be worried about is your sanity. You're going to be surrounded by three women in the same house!" "That's okay, Baby," John would smile. "The next one is going to be a boy. That'll help even up the score."

Nolan was working day watch and was still assigned as a training officer. An officer whom he had trained years earlier, Steve Villanueva, was also assigned as a training officer on the same shift. Nolan was especially proud of Villanueva. He turned out just as predicted. He was a very sharp and squared-away police officer. The team of Gonzales and Meyers, with whom Nolan had worked on the P.M. watch for years, ultimately ended with Gonzales' transfer to the detective bureau. Meyers remained on the P.M. shift, preferring to work a "one-man" car, rather than break in a new partner. He just wasn't ready for that yet.

In the 1980's, there was a significant increase in the number of female police officers being hired. Steve Villanueva had just been assigned his first female trainee. She was a strikingly beautiful woman named Alicia Mendoza. Nolan didn't have a trainee at the time, and he watched as Villanueva began training this new officer. Almost immediately, Nolan noticed that Villanueva treated her differently than any of his previous trainees. His voice was softer and less demanding. He didn't insist upon nearly as much discipline and conformity as he had from previous male trainees. Nolan was worried that perhaps Villanueva was infatuated with this woman.

After watching more interaction between Villanueva and Mendoza, Nolan became convinced his young friend was enamored with his new trainee. Though Villanueva was single and unattached, Nolan worried that his attraction to this female might be detrimental to both their careers. Nolan didn't relish the idea of sticking his nose in someone else's business, however, he decided the issue was important enough, and he knew he had better talk to Steve. One morning after roll call, Nolan told Villanueva he wanted to talk to him alone. Villanueva gave Mendoza an assignment to keep her busy, while he and Nolan went to a nearby restaurant to talk.

Over a cup of coffee, Nolan said, "Steve, I've known you for several years now, and you know I think you're an excellent policeman, as well as my good friend." "Oh-oh, this doesn't sound good. What's this about, John?" Steve asked with noticeable concern in his voice. "Well, I've been watching the way you and Mendoza interact. You're not treating her like you've treated your male trainees. And, by your body language and the tone in your voice when you address her, it's not hard to see you like her." "Jeez, John, is it that obvious?" "Yes, yes it is, Steve, and I'm worried about you," Nolan said. "Well, I can't help myself. She's drop-dead gorgeous, she's a sweetheart, she's single and she's shown interest in me. I know I have a potential conflict here, but I think I can work through it."

"Well Steve, a couple of things immediately come to mind. First of all, if you can't treat her the same way you've treated other trainees, there is a conflict. Second, how well do you know this girl? I mean, is it possible that she's acting as though she's interested in you to help facilitate her training and make it easier on herself?" John asked. "Man, you go straight for the jugular, don't you?" Steve said, smiling weakly. "It isn't that, Steve. I just don't want to see your feelings, or your career get hurt. I feel the same for Mendoza. She's a trainee, and I'd like to see her get the best training possible."

"Right now, you ain't thinking training. You're thinking..." "I know what you're gonna say, and you're absolutely right, John. You know, with the exception of my dad, I have more respect for you than for any other man on this planet." "Thanks, Steve," John said humbly. "You've been my training officer, my friend, my mentor and my advisor. What do you suggest?" Steve asked.

"She's only been with you for a couple of weeks, right?" John asked. "Yes, that's right." You said she's interested in you. Does that mean you guys have already gone out with each other?" he inquired further. "No, but we have talked about it a couple of times. I really think she likes me, and I don't think it's an act." "But the conflict already exists, Steve.

Don't you see? Suppose you are able to deal with this and you go about your role as a training officer properly. What if she doesn't cut it? What if she can't make the training program? Will you judge her fairly, or will you let her slide?"

"If you don't let her slide and hold her to the same standard as everyone else you've trained, you'd have to fail her, right? At that point she could just go to your superiors and say that she might have made it except that you were more interested in getting in her pants than in training her. Then guess who the bad guy is pal? On the other hand, if she can't cut it, but you *do* let her slide because you're romantically involved with her, you're compromising your standards, the standards of the department and, last but not least, you're violating a trust. The trust that was given you when you became a training officer."

"Man, I never looked at it that way," Villanueva admitted. "Look Steve, I'm not trying to hurt your feelings, or insinuate anything bad about Mendoza. I'm just trying to point out a conflict and the possible consequences of that conflict. You asked for my advice. Well, my best advice is for you to go to the sarge and discreetly let him know you don't think you should train her because of this situation. More than likely, he'll reassign her to another T.O."

"Either way," Nolan continued, "be aware that since she is a beautiful woman, you might as well expect the guys to be sniffing around her, trying to get some action. Especially the younger ones. They're all horn-dogs, just like you," Nolan said smiling. "Steve, I just don't want to see my friend get into any kind of a bad situation..." Nolan told his friend with obvious concern. Villanueva thanked his mentor for his advice and his concern. "I'm not sure what I'll do yet," he admitted. "Take a day or two to think about it. I know you'll do the right thing," Nolan said.

A few hours later, Nolan was in the field and he monitored a hot shot. "Beep, beep, beep." "Any clear unit... Report of two suspicious subjects inside the savings and loan at 7314 Oceana Boulevard. The reporting party is the assistant manager. Units responding identify." Nolan advised he would respond as did Villanueva and Detective Gonzales. Once she had at least three units responding, the communications operator continued, "Units responding, suspects are described as two male Hispanics in their twenties, one wearing blue jeans and a plaid shirt, the other wearing black pants and a light weight jacket. We still have the assistant manager on the line. The suspects have split up. One is standing and writing at the customer table at the east end of the bank. The other is doing the same thing at the west end."

Nolan asked the communications operator to have the responding units come up on a tactical channel. Nolan called to Gonzales, "I'm about thirty seconds away," he advised. Gonzales replied, I'm less than a minute too." "I'll make my entry from the east." That works for me. I'll come in from the west," Gonzales said. Villanueva advised he was still three (minutes) away. As Nolan arrived he asked the communications operator if they still had the assistant manager on the line. "Affirmative, and there is no change." Nolan and Gonzales then entered the bank from opposite ends.

Nolan walked up silently behind his suspect, and as he approached, he saw what the suspect was writing. "This is a Robery. Gimme the money." Nolan quickly and forcefully shoved the barrel of his weapon into the suspect's ribs. He advised him he was under arrest. The suspect complied and was arrested without incident. Nolan took the suspect's note as evidence, but he made it a point to tell the suspect he had spelled robbery wrong. The suspect did not find the policeman's comments very amusing.

Meanwhile, Gonzales had already engaged his suspect, and he was in the process of arresting him. Villanueva and his trainee had just arrived, and when Gonzales' suspect saw Mendoza, he smiled, and in a very loud voice said, "Hey, can I have that woman cop frisk me? She could even strip search me!" Gonzales leaned close to the suspect so no one would hear him. "Shut-up, Asshole! Not another word out of you." The suspect looked into Gonzales' angry eyes and noticed the size of his arms and said, "Yes sir, you got the power."

Villanueva asked if he and his trainee could handle the paper on the call. "It'll be a good caper for her to write," he said. "No problem," Nolan said. Go ahead and take them. I'll get the assistant manager's information and statement and get it to you right away. Nolan then made contact with the assistant manager.

"There was a flyer out from the F.B.I. about wanted bank robbers. When I saw these guys in here, I noticed they looked very much like the guys in the wanted poster. Besides, they were acting weird," she said. "Well, you did a very nice job," Nolan complimented her. "The one fellow was in the process of writing a robbery note. More than likely, with what you just told me, the F.B.I. has at least one case on these guys.

Coupled with today's activity, they should go away for a while," Nolan said to the lady. "By the way, can I get that flyer from you?" "Sure officer, it's in here," she said, reaching in her drawer. "Thank you, ma'am."

Gonzales had been standing by with Nolan. He wanted to talk to him. "Don't clear just yet, John. I'm gonna go pull my car around to the back. I need to talk to you, man." "Okay Gonz," Nolan replied. Gonzales' real first name was Heriberto, but he preferred to be called Gonzales or "Gonz." When Gonzales pulled up in the parking lot next to him, Nolan asked, "By the way Gonz, what are you doing rolling on calls? Aren't you a detective now?" he teased. "I was on my way back to the station from the D.A.'s office. Heard the call and decided to roll. I needed to talk to you anyway. There's a problem," he said sadly.

"What's up man?" Nolan asked. "It's Meyers. He's all screwed up in the head. He and his wife have been having problems for almost a year now. Two weeks ago Saturday, he came to work as usual on P.M's, but he wasn't feeling very well. After a few hours, he went home sick. He caught his wife in their bed with another dude." "Aw Jeez, I'm sorry to hear that," Nolan responded sadly. "He didn't do anything crazy, did he?" Nolan probed. "He said he almost lost it and that he reached for his gun, but fortunately for him, at the last minute, he regained control of himself and decided that wasn't the right thing to do. Meyer's kids are teenagers, and they were out for the evening. The sad part is they found out what happened. The whole family is screwed up now. Anyway, I'm real

174

worried about him. He moved out of the house, and he's been living in his cab-over camper in the parking lot."

"That explains why I keep seeing that thing in the parking lot. I kept wondering why he was hauling it back and forth. He usually drives his pickup with nothing in the back," Nolan said. "I guess he moves the truck every day so people won't think he's living in it," Gonzales reasoned. "John, he's really humiliated. The kids are pissed off at his wife for cheating on him and they want to be with their father. He's so humiliated that, at this point, he can't face them. Says he's too embarrassed to see them now. I've been talking to him as much as I can. He's really depressed. Working detectives now, I don't have much time during the day. Obviously you're on days too, but if you could help me keep an eye on him, I'd sure appreciate it," Gonzales said with a great deal of concern in his voice.

"No problem Gonz," Nolan said. "I'll call him and talk to him as much as I can. Is he getting counseling or anything?" "He's too damn proud, man. I tried convincing him to go, but he wouldn't have any part of it. We were partners for six years. I know him like a book, and I've never seen him so screwed up before. I'm very concerned," Gonzales added candidly. Nolan thought for a moment, then said, "He should start seeing his kids. It's not their fault. They're suffering too. Anyway Gonz, I've gotta get going, but I'll make it a point to see Meyers at change of watch. Meanwhile, let me know if anything changes or if there's anything else I can do." "Okay, John, thanks."

A couple of hours prior to his end of watch, Nolan drove by the station parking lot to see if Meyers was around. Nolan was disappointed to find that Meyer's truck was not there. As he pulled out of the lot, he received a call to phone the station. He pulled back into the parking lot and went into the station to find out who was trying to reach him. It was Sergeant Rosenthal. Nolan hadn't had the opportunity to work with Sergeant Rosenthal very much over the years, however, on those occasions when he did work with him, Nolan found him to be a very fair and straightforward supervisor.

He had tremendous knowledge, and he was always happy to help. Everyone, including Nolan, respected Sergeant Rosenthal. "Hey Sarge, long time no see. How are you?" "I'm good John, thanks for asking," the sarge replied. "Listen. A guy called in a few minutes ago and asked for you. When the operator tried to take his information for a message, he asked for the watch commander. That's how I ended up with the call."

"Anyway, it turns out the guy is a city employee who works for the Department of Parks and Recreation. He wouldn't give me very much at all. Only that he owed you, and that he had some good dope information. I told him I could take the information from him and pass it to you. He told me he wouldn't give the information to anyone but you. Said his name is Jaime Diaz. Here's his phone number," Sarge said as he handed Nolan a piece of paper. "He'll be in his office until 1700." "Offhand, the name doesn't ring a bell, Sarge," Nolan said. "The guy said he owes you one from about a year ago when you helped his mom." Nolan thought for a moment, trying to recall the incident.

After a few seconds, Nolan said, "Okay, I remember him now. His mom lives by herself in a small house on the East Side. Real nice older lady. Some local hoodlums decided to harass her because of her age and vulnerability. Everyone in the neighborhood knows she's lives alone. The guy is married and doesn't live too close. He asked me if there was anything we could do to help his mom. I made it a point to drive by her house several times per shift. Finally, I caught some little punks messing with her. We had a little attitude adjustment session. They don't bother her anymore. Guess he thought it was a big deal." "Good. Now listen, if this has anything to do with dope sales at any of the local parks, let me know. That's a real pet peeve of mine." "I know Sarge, will do," Nolan replied.

Nolan called the number on the piece of paper the sarge had given him. "Jaime Diaz, please." "Speaking." "Mr. Diaz, this is Officer Nolan. I understand you called for me earlier today." "Yes Officer, thanks for calling me back. I have some narcotics information that might be useful to you. I'm at North Park in the office area. Can you stop by to see me?" "Sure. I can be there within twenty minutes." "Great, see you then."

Nolan left the station and drove directly to the park to see Diaz. "Thanks for coming over," Diaz said as he stood and offered a handshake. "No problem Mr. Diaz." Nolan said as he shook Diaz' hand. "Please, call me Jaime. You know, I'm still very grateful to you for helping my mom," Diaz said. "Part of the job, Jaime. Has she had any more problems?" Nolan asked. "No sir, and we're glad about that," Diaz smiled. "But unfortunately, we do have some problems at the park."

"There is a group of young punks that sells grass almost every afternoon starting at about 3:00 o'clock, when the kids get out of school. They hang out in the northwest corner of the park, and they hide their stash in the bushes. They flash the "mota" (Hispanic slang term for marijuana) sign by holding their fingers together at passing cars. When a car stops, two of the punks approach, negotiate the deal, and take the money from the buyer. Then, they signal their buddy, and he comes up with a dime baggie, or whatever, from the stash in the bushes," Jaime explained. "Do they arrive in a vehicle?" Nolan inquired. "Yes, they do. It's a beat up old Ford Tempo. It's brown with lots of primer on the left side. I know you'll ask me for the license plate number next—I didn't get it, sorry." "That's okay, you've given me plenty. Thank you," Nolan said politely. "Will you guys do something about this?" "You can count on it," Nolan smiled.

It was late in the shift when Nolan arrived back at the station. He made a quick check of the parking lot to see if Meyer's truck was there. It wasn't. I know he works today. I wonder where he is, Nolan thought as he parked his black and white. Nolan caught up to Sergeant Rosenthal just as he was about to leave for the day. "Sarge, got some info for you," Nolan advised him. "Come on in and tell me about it," Sergeant Rosenthal responded.

"I went to see Diaz from Parks and Recreation, and he told me about drug sales at North Park. Just about every day, close to 3:00 o'clock, the sellers arrive. They do their business on the northwest portion of the park, across from the fire station. He says they work in a group of three, and they keep their stash hidden in the nearby bushes. It's the typical set-up, Sarge. They flash the marijuana sign to passing cars announcing they're open for business."

"Well, we're gonna put them out of business," the sergeant smiled. "You've done lots of these capers, haven't you, John?" "Yeah Sarge. You want me to take care of this?" "Yes I do. Tell me what you're gonna need as far as equipment goes and we'll set it up with your crew." "Okay. We'll need one undercover car, two pairs of binoculars and a couple of portable radios with all the tactical frequencies plugged in. We'll also need some buy money." "You'll have it tomorrow. Anybody in particular on your crew you want to make the buy?" Sergeant Rosenthal inquired. "Yes, I'll have Steve Villanueva do it. He's done it before, and he's good at it. He fits right in, talks the talk." "Okay. Let's plan this for tomorrow. To cover calls, I'm going to have a couple of the P.M. guys come in early. Let's figure on starting your operation right at 1500 tomorrow." "Okay, Sarge, we'll be ready."

When Nolan entered the parking lot on his way to work the following morning, his first thought was to check for Meyer's truck. It still wasn't there. In briefing that morning, Sarge told the crew Nolan would be setting up a "buy / bust" operation at North Park. He told them the operation would commence at 1500 hours (3:00 P.M.) that day. He also praised Villanueva, his trainee Mendoza, Nolan and Detective Gonzales for apprehending the two attempted bank robbery suspects a day earlier. "Nice job, folks. The F.B.I. has four cases on them, not counting the attempt from yesterday. Looks like they'll be going bye-bye for a while."

Sarge then served subpoenas to officers being summoned to court and ended briefing by saying, "I talked to the burglary guys upstairs. There is no new information on the burglars who are clobbering us in the strip mall east of the business district. We all know these burgs are occurring at night, however, talk to your street people, interview the hypes, see what you can find out."

As soon as briefing ended, Nolan went upstairs to the detective bureau to talk to Gonzales. "Gonz, I wanted to talk to Meyers yesterday, but he wasn't around. I figured okay, I'll catch him this morning. I got here this morning, looked for his truck and it's not here." "I know. He called in sick yesterday. I don't know where he is, and I'm real worried. I called his house, but his wife Cindy said she has no idea where he might be. I asked her to check with the kids to see if he contacted one or both of them. She hasn't called me back yet." "Well, let me know as soon as you hear something," Nolan said. "Okay John," Gonzales answered nervously.

Nolan loaded up his unit and went out in the field. His first stop was the fire station across from North Park. He needed permission from the Fire Captain to use the fire station so that he could covertly watch the drug activity at the park. Fire Captain Marcus told him he and any other police officers were always welcome at the station. Nolan thanked the captain and told him he'd be there around 1500 hours. He also told him they'd be doing a buy bust with one of the officers as the undercover. "Great," Captain Marcus said. "If there's anything I can do, let me know." "Thanks, Cap," Nolan smiled.

After leaving the fire station, Nolan handled several calls and then got a bite to eat. Later that day, he stopped at an auto repair shop close to the business district. One of the tow truck drivers employed there was an informant of his. Nolan hadn't talked to him for some time, and he wanted to see if he knew anything about the rash of burglaries at the strip mall the sarge had talked about in briefing. This particular ex-con was very "hardcore." A huge man, he spent most of his adult life in and out of prison. He'd been paroled one year earlier on a manslaughter conviction for the beating death of an individual in a bar fight. His large, tattooed arms and body told a tale of a con-wise and experienced ex-con. His moniker, or street name, was "Bomber," because in his younger days when he was a biker, he liked to play around with explosives and ended up serving time for an associated crime. The name Bomber stayed with him.

When Bomber saw Nolan approaching, he turned to him and said, "Haven't seen you in a long time, Officer Nolan." "How've you been, Bomber?" "Just working. Trying to finish out my parole without any more problems," Bomber said candidly. "Looks like you're doing okay," Nolan observed. "Yeah, the boss is good to me. Has a big heart. I don't know what I would have done without him giving me a job." "Does he still let you sleep in his trailer back there?" "Yeah, he lets me stay here and, in return, I watch the place at night." "Bomber, this is more than a social call," Nolan told him. "I figured that by the way you were carrying yourself. What's on your mind?" Bomber asked the veteran street cop.

"You're right, and I'll get to the point," Nolan said. "You know the large strip mall about a mile east of here?" "Sure, what's going on there?"

Bomber asked. "A lot of the businesses have been hit recently. Burgs, lots of them. They either do a roof job or pry the back door. Have you heard anything?" Nolan asked the savvy ex-con. "No, but I'll do some checking around. I'll call you if I come up with anything." "Okay."

"Meanwhile, here's ten bucks. Go get a halfway decent meal," Nolan said while trying to nonchalantly hand Bomber a carefully folded $10.00 bill. "Tell you what, man. Hang on to the ten. If I come up with some good information, how about giving me a twenty?" Bomber asked. "Deal," Nolan said. Guess he's pretty sure he can get something for me or he'd have taken the $10.00 bill and kept his mouth shut, Nolan mused as he drove away from the repair shop.

Oh shit! It's almost three o'clock, Nolan thought as he glanced at his watch. While hustling through traffic to get back to the station, he prepared a mental checklist of items he had to take care of for the caper at the park. When he arrived at the station, several of the officers assigned to participate in the operation were already seated in the briefing room awaiting his arrival. Sergeant Rosenthal entered the briefing room carrying portable radios and car keys. The sarge approached Nolan who was preparing a diagram on the blackboard at the front of the room. Quietly, the sarge asked, "John, you don't mind if I come along, do you? I don't go out in the field very much anymore—too damn old and loaded down with other duties. But, I love working these capers."

"Sergeant Prewitt relieved me as watch commander so I could tag along with you guys." Nolan smiled. "We'd consider it an honor, Sarge." "Great. If you can, use me as one of the troops. Assign me wherever you need me." "Okay Sarge," Nolan said as he finished his diagram, and brushed the chalk off of his hands.

Sergeant Rosenthal took a seat, and Nolan pointed to the blackboard as he addressed the officers. "A citizen informant gave us information that a group of three individuals is involved in marijuana sales at North Park. If you look at the diagram, it shows the area where they're selling. It's in the northwest quadrant of the park, almost across from the fire station. That makes our lives easier. We've got a place to sit and watch. As you can see, Steve Villanueva dressed for the occasion. He's our U/C (undercover) for this operation. He's done this before, and he's comfortable with it, right Steve?" Nolan asked as he looked directly at Steve. "No problema, vato. I buy mota for you," Villanueva smiled smugly. "Like I said, he's real comfortable doing this gig."

"I'm going to read off the assignments, then we'll go over exactly how this caper will go down. You should all have a copy of the operations plan. Everybody got one?" Nolan asked. All in attendance answered in the affirmative and Nolan continued, "Flip to the last page. That's the assignment sheet. Villanueva, you've got the U/C gig. Clark, you'll take Mendoza with you and handle backup, arrests and transportation. That way, if we arrest a female, Mendoza will be right there to search her. Phillips, you'll be a rover in the area in case there's a problem. Dominguez, as you can see, I was going to have you in an undercover car, but instead, you'll be with Williamson. You guys are an extra rover and backup team. Sarge doesn't get to come out and play very often, so let's give him a choice assignment. Pencil him in place of Dominguez as the watchdog in an undercover car. Dominguez, next time we'll have you as the U/C." "Cool, man," Dominguez smiled.

"I'm sorry Dominguez," Sergeant Rosenthal said as he turned towards Dominguez. "No problem, Sarge. We're glad you could come out with us. Everyone knows you have a thing for dope dealers at the parks," Dominguez reassured the older sergeant. "You're right. I don't like drug dealers, but I really despise drug dealers who sell dope to kids, especially at parks. Parks are supposed to be a special place for kids. They should be full of fun, laughter, sports and childhood memories, not lousy dope-selling pieces of shit," the sarge said excitedly. After a momentary pause, Nolan continued, "I'll be in the fire department with binoculars, calling the play by play. Any questions about the assignments?" Nolan asked.

"Since there are no questions, let's move on. Villanueva, limit your activity and movement to the area we discussed. For the rest of you, that's the small parking lot, northwest section of the park. Information is that the suspects keep their stash tucked in the bushes just beyond or east of that small parking lot. When buyers respond to the suspects' signal for dope, they pull their cars into this lot where they are approached by two of the suspects. Once the deal is made and money has changed hands, a signal is given to the suspect guarding the dope. He then reaches in, retrieves the appropriate amount, and delivers it to the buyer in the vehicle."

"Let me say this very clearly… Under no circumstances is Villanueva going to move out of our sight range. He will not be wired. We will have visual on him at all times. If something goes very wrong or the suspects produce a weapon of some sort, Villanueva will extend his arms in the air and act like he's giving up or submitting. Remember, no amount of dope or money in the world is worth compromising the safety of our people. Any questions about Villanueva's role? Steve, any questions from you?" Nolan inquired. "How much dope am I buying?" "Two dime baggies will be plenty for this caper." Sergeant Rosenthal handed Steve a twenty dollar bill.

"Rovers and backup officers, your role is to stay close, but remain out of sight. Pay very close attention to the radio. While we're on the subject of radios, as you can tell by referring to the front page of your ops plans, we'll be operating on channel six. The watch commander, the dope crew and communications have a copy of our ops plan as well. Clark and Mendoza, you guys are the primary arrest team. When you hear the signal to take them down, move in immediately. At that point, you'll be assisted by the rovers who will come in as backup. You guys can sit in one spot as long as you're hidden. Just stay very close.

Sarge, you're the watch dog in an undercover car. Position your car so that you have a nice visual of Steve. Since I'll be in the fire station looking south, why don't you find a sweet spot south of where this will go down so you can have a view to the north. That way, between the two of us, we'll maintain an uninterrupted view of Steve." "You got it, John," the sergeant acknowledged. "Speaking of cars, I left that open on the ops plan because we didn't know what would be available to us." Nolan advised. "Sarge, what did you come up with?" Nolan asked. "I've got a green, primered '74 Monte Carlo for Steve and I'll be in a faded blue

Firebird. The Firebird is a surveillance car so it has a radio in it." "Okay. Steve, you'll have one of the portables and I'll have the other," Nolan announced.

"One more thing. The suspects supposedly arrive at the park in a beat-up Ford Tempo, brown, with lots of primer marks. They probably park it close by, although we don't know that for sure. Alright, I think that covers just about everything. I do want to watch at least one buy go down before I send Villanueva in. We'll need to make a traffic stop on that particular vehicle to either arrest or detain the occupants and to recover the dope they bought."

"I suggest the rovers position themselves so that whatever direction the "buyers" take when they leave the park, one will be in position to quickly locate the vehicle and effect a traffic stop. Make your stop well away from the park. We do not want to spook our salesmen. Sarge has allotted one hour for this operation. More than likely, we'll be done within thirty minutes. Again, any questions?" Nolan asked as he wrapped up the briefing. "Okay, let's go do it. Remember to switch to channel six."

Out on the parking lot, personnel involved in the operation were getting ready to depart. Nolan drove up to Villanueva's car as he was just about to get in. "Steve, same as last time. No bullshit. If it doesn't look or feel right, get the hell out of there." "Thanks, John," Villanueva responded. As Nolan drove to the fire station, he conducted a radio check on channel six to make certain everyone involved in the operation had "come up" on the frequency. Everyone acknowledged they were up.

When he arrived at the fire station, Nolan found himself a great vantage point at a south-facing window and got set up.

He immediately saw three young male Hispanic subjects fitting the description, loitering in the parking lot. He advised the units he had the probable suspects in sight and would be observing them. He gave their descriptions to the units one by one. Scanning the parking lot, he saw an older brown Ford Tempo. He wasn't able to read the license plate so he asked the sarge to do a "drive-by" prior to picking his parking spot. Sarge ran the plate and had communications hold a print out. The vehicle was registered to a female Hispanic somewhere in North Hollywood.

Nolan watched as the suspects played with a frisbee so as to blend in and not be conspicuous. For fifteen minutes, nothing happened. Then, an older Buick pulled in to the parking lot going very slowly. One of the suspects held his thumb and index finger together and raised his hand towards his lips, holding the two fingers there for a moment as if he was taking a puff of a cigarette, or in this case, "a hit off of a joint." The Buick stopped, and two of the suspects approached on the driver's side. The Buick contained two male occupants. Nolan advised the rover units, "Heads up, guys, I think we may soon have a buy in progress."

Nolan continued to watch and saw the driver hand one of the suspects a single bill of U.S. currency. Nolan could not discern the denomination of the bill, but when he saw the suspect turn towards his buddy near the bushes and momentarily hold up two fingers, he figured the guy in the Buick had handed him a twenty dollar bill. Nolan advised the rovers, "Standby, the deal is in progress." Nolan gave the description of the vehicle, including the license number and the fact that there were two male occupants.

Meanwhile, the suspect standing near the bushes reached in and retrieved two small plastic baggies. He walked them over to the driver of the Buick and handed them to him. Then, the Buick slowly pulled out of the parking lot. Nolan advised the rovers, "Okay, the deal went down. The vehicle is exiting the parking lot and is turning southbound. They bought two dime bags."

Williamson and Dominguez came on the air and announced they had the vehicle in sight. They would follow the vehicle and make the stop several blocks from the park. A few minutes later, Williamson announced they had two juveniles in custody, and they had recovered the evidence. Williamson asked Nolan, "How about if you wait just a few (minutes) before sending the U/C. That way, we can transport these guys to the station, drop them off, and scoot back out here. We'll be back in less than ten." "That sounds good, do it. We'll wait for you," Nolan replied. Nolan watched as the suspects resumed playing frisbee. They had displayed the "marijuana for sale sign" at several other passing vehicles, however, there were no other buyers in the time it took Williamson and Dominguez to return.

"Okay, Steve, do your thing," Nolan said. Villanueva acknowledged Nolan's message, at which time Nolan announced, "Units be advised, the U/C is on his way in." Everyone acknowledged receipt of the message. Nolan watched as Villanueva pulled his vehicle into the parking lot. Sarge confirmed he had a visual on the U/C as well. As if it was a rerun of the last transaction, one of the suspects displayed the dope for sale sign and Villanueva stopped his car right where he was supposed to. Perfect position, Steve, Nolan thought as he watched the transaction unfolding through the binoculars. Two suspects approached Villanueva's vehicle as he was exiting. The three men engaged in conversation for a few moments before Villanueva handed over the twenty dollar bill the sergeant had given him.

As in the previous transaction witnessed by Nolan, one of the suspects signaled to his buddy guarding the stash. The fellow responded by retrieving two small baggies. Nolan advised the units, "The transaction with our U/C is almost completed. Arrest and backup units standby." The fellow who retrieved the baggies handed them off to one of the suspects with whom Villanueva had spoken. That suspect, in turn, gave the baggies to Villanueva.

The transaction completed, Villanueva slowly re-entered his vehicle. Nolan advised the arrest and backup units to move in for the arrest. Units intentionally arrived on the scene from different directions, thereby effectively eliminating the possibility of escape and within seconds, all three suspects were arrested, and their stash recovered from the bushes. The stash was packaged in a larger plastic bag that, in turn, contained twenty-two additional "dime" or ten dollar bags.

Sergeant Rosenthal couldn't have been happier. He loved seeing dope peddlers go to jail. The three adult suspects ranged in age from nineteen to twenty-four years old. They were subsequently booked for sales of marijuana and possession for sale of marijuana. A check of their records revealed two of them had recent priors for drug sales.

Before the end of watch, Nolan called Gonzales again to see if he had heard from Meyers. "No John, still no word. But today would have been a regular day off for him. His wife finally called me back. She spoke to the kids and they haven't heard from him either. I know he has a sister who lives somewhere in Arizona. Maybe he just took off over there for awhile. I'm not sure what to think anymore." "Well again Gonz, if you hear anything, let me know right away, Nolan said. Gonzales replied, "I will. I'm also gonna get his sister's phone number and call her to see if he's there or if she's heard from him. But, if he doesn't turn up soon, I may just file a missing persons report. This is so uncharacteristic of him."

When Nolan arrived home that evening, Marie could tell something was weighing heavily on his mind. John was quiet and he seemed somewhat withdrawn. After dinner, he played with the kids and later in the evening, as he did whenever he worked day watch, he helped Marie put them to bed. After everything had settled down and the kids were asleep, Marie asked, "What's wrong, Sweetie?" "Remember I told you Meyers caught his wife in his bed with another man?" "Yes." "Well, he obviously took it very hard. And who wouldn't? Anyway, since then, he's acted strangely, didn't want to see his kids and now, he's missing. No one's heard from him. His kids are frantic. Gonzales is going nuts, and I'm really worried about him too." John admitted. "Maybe he just wanted to get away for awhile and think things through," Marie offered. "I sure hope that's all it is," John replied.

"All I know is that I'm the luckiest guy in the world to have you for my wife. We live by the same code of ethics and honor. We respect and trust each other implicitly and I never worry about your faithfulness or question any of your actions," John said. Marie responded, "That's why our marriage has been and will continue to be so successful. Policemen have the worst reputation for remaining faithful to their wives, but never once have I doubted you."

"I would never betray your trust. I have too much respect for you," John stated candidly. Marie went over to her husband and kissed him a long, lingering kiss. "I love you and I trust you with my life," she said. "I love you too, Baby," he answered. John picked up his bride and carried her to their bedroom where they hungrily, and very passionately, enjoyed each other.

The next morning as Nolan sat in briefing, Sergeant Rosenthal made it a point to thank everyone involved in the buy / bust operation the previous afternoon. "I want you folks to know, I had a great time. The focus was on safety and everything went smoothly. It was a nice, clean operation. The only problem is that by next week, there will be other dope-peddling pieces of crap waiting in the wings to take up where our suspects from yesterday left off. But we won't let that phase us. We'll bust the next ones too," Sergeant Rosenthal said enthusiastically.

The sarge continued, "Now, on to a new subject; I had a conversation with Detective Lieutenant Singer, and he told me that in the very near future, we are going to restore a program we had in place here many years ago. That program is a rotating six-month assignment to detectives. The reason for the program restoration is simple. There isn't very much movement in the detective bureau, and by having a program such as this, many more officers will have an opportunity to gain some precious investigative experience, even if it is for a limited time period."

"The assignment will not be to any specific section, such as burglary or robbery. Instead, the "temporary" detective will work different desks and fill in where needed under the direction of one of the detective sergeants. Senior officers, and officers with five years or more, will be rotated through first, although formal requests for consideration for the position must be made via memorandum."

Sergeant Rosenthal continued, "As I look around the room right now, I can see at least three or four people who should strongly consider applying. In fact, I urge you folks to apply, because, keep in mind ladies and gentlemen, there will be a sergeant's test coming up in about eight or nine months. A little investigative experience sure wouldn't hurt your resume..." That wouldn't be a bad gig, Nolan thought as he listened to the sergeant's words. Besides, I've been "pushing a hack" (driving a black and white) for years. A little break in the action would be nice. I'll talk to Marie tonight.

As Nolan was leaving the briefing room, Gonzales approached him. "John, I wanted to catch you when you got out of briefing to bring you up to date. There's nothing from Meyers yet. I called his sister in Arizona, and she hasn't heard anything. I feel bad about that too, because now she's very worried along with the rest of us. She had no knowledge that her brother and sister-in-law were having marital difficulties or anything," Gonzales said.

"Have you talked to his sergeant about any of this yet?" Nolan asked. "No, I haven't, but you're right, I need to do that. I'm also thinking I should go ahead and file a missing report today." "He's supposed to work today, right Gonz?" "Yeah." "Why don't you wait until this afternoon to see if he shows. If he doesn't show, and we don't hear anything from him, then file the missing right away." "You're right man. That's exactly what I'll do. See you later."

Nolan was checking a shotgun out of the armory, preparing to go out in the field when he was called over the intercom. "Officer Nolan, contact Sergeant Rosenthal." Nolan responded to the call and located the sarge in the watch commander's office. "John, a guy named Bomber called for you. Said he had some information you'd be interested in." "Thanks Sarge. I asked him to find out what he could about the burgs at the strip mall. Maybe he's got something good." "That would be great," the sarge said.

Sergeant Rosenthal paused for a moment and then added, "Listen John, as long as you're already here, I wanted to talk to you about the program I mentioned in briefing this morning. Everyone working here knows how sharp and how talented you are. Your record is exemplary. In my opinion, you need to apply for this and get some investigative experience."

"You'd be great as a detective, and I strongly urge you to put in for it as soon as it's announced." "Thank you, Sarge," Nolan replied humbly. I paid close attention to what you were saying in briefing today. It sounds really good. I was going to talk it over with my wife tonight. "There you go," Sarge said happily. "By the way, you *are* going to take the sergeant's test, aren't you?" "Yes. I've been preparing myself over the past few months. This'll be my first crack at it," Nolan replied. "Very good, son," the old sarge nodded with approval. "I know you'll shine."

Out on the parking lot Nolan was setting up his unit when he was approached by Villanueva. "Wassup, Homie?" Villanueva teased. "What are you doing man?" Nolan replied with a smile. "I forgot to mention this in briefing. I've got two prelims going in court this morning. I know I'll be tied up for a while. Rather than having Mendoza just sit, waiting for me to testify, could you take her out in the field with you till I'm done?" "It's not a problem. Just let the sarge know right away, and have Mendoza bring her gear over here." "Thanks, John. Also, I need to talk to you later about what we discussed the other day." "I'll be ready when you are, Steve," Nolan said to his young friend.

After Mendoza loaded her gear into Nolan's unit, they drove out of the parking lot and Nolan headed straight to the auto repair shop. He was hopeful Bomber would have some good information on those burglaries. "Hey Officer Nolan," Bomber said with a smile as he greeted Nolan. "Got something for me on those burgs?" Nolan asked anxiously. "Yeah, I do. Do you want me to tell you in front of her?" he asked, pointing at Mendoza. "Sure, it's cool," Nolan assured him.

"Okay. I talked to a couple of dudes I know from 'inside' (prison) and one of them knew about the burgs. Problem is, he wants some money for the info." "This better not be a scam, Bomber," Nolan warned. "Nolan, I've known you awhile. I know better than to fu... uh, excuse me, ma'am, I know better than to try to pull one over on you."

"What's the price?" "The dude wants fifty bucks." "That's too much. Set it up so I can talk to him. Call me when you've got it set up," Nolan ordered. "You're pissed at me, aren't you?" Bomber asked. "Yeah, I am. You're better and smarter than any other ex-con I've ever talked to. I believe you when you say you're not trying to scam me, but the dude is scamming you and you're letting him." "I'll see him later. I'll get it straight," Bomber promised.

As they were driving off, Nolan smiled. "What is it, sir? What was that all about?" Mendoza asked. "Bomber is a part-time snitch, an informant. He makes a little extra money by occasionally "ratting" on others. But he hasn't tested me for a long time. "Tested you?" "Yes. Remember the B.S. story he told about some "dude" having the information and wanting money for it? Chances are there is no dude, and old Bomber is trying to make a few extra dollars."

"I'm almost certain he already has the information. He's just trying to squeeze out whatever he can. I had already promised him twenty dollars for the information, and he was overly confident he'd get it for me. This way, I let him know in a roundabout way that I'll pay more money to the "dude," but not fifty bucks. He'll come back and say the dude dropped his price to thirty or whatever. I'll give him twenty for the "dude," and Bomber will be happy to make forty on the deal. Ex-con Scams and Financing 101."

"Are all informants like that?" "Well, there are different types of informants, and it's their motivation that determines their so-called classification. For example, the citizen informant. That's your everyday average good citizen who provides information to the police because he or she knows of some crime or wrongdoing. The motivating factor is simply to do the right thing."

"Another type of "citizen" informant is the angry citizen. Example: A woman catches her boyfriend messing around with another woman and gets pissed. Though she's not involved in his criminal activities, she knows her boyfriend is involved in criminal enterprise. Revenge, not good citizenship, is the motivation here. Even though she had prior knowledge of her boyfriend's criminal activity, she would never have given the information to the police if he hadn't done her wrong," Nolan explained. "I get it," Mendoza said.

"Then there's the criminal trying to work off a 'beef.' Example: You arrest a hype for a residential burglary. He wants to work his beef off by providing information about a drug dealer, a robber or other felon. As the police officer, you always tell him the truth. You make no promises, but advise him if he does give good information, you can inform the D.A. who can, in turn, allow him to plea or make some arrangement other than a straight sentence behind bars. He could receive a shortened sentence and an extended probation. He could get a short sentence and commitment to a drug rehab or counseling program, etc. Deals are struck all the time."

"Next, we have the paid informant. This guy does it for the money. That's his full-time job, if you will. I've been told by several of these types that they actually get a "rush" or a high, because of the obvious inherent danger. Whether you're talking about a D.E.A. informant being paid thousands of dollars for informing on heavy-duty drug dealers, or whether you're paying an ex-con like Bomber forty bucks to get some information on a burglar, the motivating factor is the same. Money is one hell of a motivator. The informant will almost always negotiate to try to get as much money for his information as possible," Nolan said as he finished his mini-lecture on informants for the trainee.

"Thank you, sir, I appreciate the information," Mendoza said humbly. "No problem," Nolan replied, always happy to teach the youngsters. "Sir, can I speak freely?" Mendoza asked. "Sure, go ahead." "Well, I'll probably get in trouble for this, but I just want you to know that Steve, I mean Officer Villanueva, always speaks very highly of you. You are much more to him than just his old training officer," she explained. "Well thanks, but why are you telling me this?" a puzzled Nolan asked.

"I really like Officer Villanueva. He's a handsome, mature and honest man. I'm very attracted to him, and I believe he's equally attracted to me. I know you two had a conversation about all this. He told me about that. We're in an awkward position now because he's my T.O, but I believe we're both professional enough to see this through without compromise. I don't want him to ever cut me any slack, and I will work as hard as I can to be the best police officer I can possibly be. He knows that."

"Also, I don't mean to sound arrogant or conceited, but as far as what you said about the guys coming on to me, I'm sure you were right, they will. But sir, guys always come on to me. Ever since I blossomed into a woman, guys have always tried. In fact, sometimes it gets real old. The academy was no different. I even had to advise one of my D.I.'s to back off and leave me alone. I can assure you, I would not do anything to hurt Steve and though we've only known each other a very short while, I can tell you I've never been so strongly attracted to anyone before." "Wow, I'm at a loss for words," a surprised Nolan said. "I'm sorry, sir, but I just felt you should know." "Did you tell Steve you were going to talk to me?" "No, sir, I didn't know I was going to have the nerve to say anything at all." "Did Steve tell you he was going to talk to me?" "Yes, he said he would talk to you today." "Okay, Alicia, why don't we just leave it at that?" "Again, I'm sorry, sir, I just wanted you to know," Mendoza said apologetically.

Nolan and Mendoza handled a few calls together and Nolan thought she carried herself well for a trainee. In the early afternoon, Nolan received a call to go to the station. Villanueva was done in court and wanted to pick up his trainee. While Mendoza went to the restroom, Villanueva and Nolan took the opportunity to talk. "John, I thought about everything you said and I decided to stay on as her T.O. I can handle this and maintain my objectivity," Villanueva explained. "Can you?" John asked. "She just laid the whole thing out to me, Steve. She told me you let her know what you and I had talked about the other day."

"I'm sorry, John. She should have kept her mouth shut." "Look, you do what you need to do. My opinion hasn't changed, but you've got to live your own life," Nolan said quietly. "Don't be angry with me, John," Villanueva pleaded. "I'm not angry, Steve. We both have our opinions, so let's just let it go at that," Nolan said as he smiled and offered a handshake. "Okay," Villanueva agreed as he shook Nolan's hand.

Nolan went back out in the field and eventually made his way back to the auto repair shop. "Bomber, did you get my information?" "Well, here's what happened. I told the dude that fifty was too much and he said he'd give it up for forty." Nolan was tired of the game. "Bomber, you're full of shit. I know you've got the information and I need it now. No more games. I'll give you twenty-five bucks and that's it." Bomber didn't answer. He just stood there looking at Nolan. Nolan turned and walked back towards his unit. Bomber ran up behind him. "Okay, okay. I'll give you the info. I was just trying to get a little more money," he confessed. "You're screwing with the wrong guy. If you would've just asked me for more money, I'd have given it to you. Instead, you lied and made an ass out of yourself. You destroyed your credibility with me," Nolan retorted.

"Tell you what," Bomber said, trying to make amends, "I'll give you the information. Don't pay me for it unless it turns out good. How's that?" he asked, trying to salvage Nolan's belief in him. "Okay," Nolan said. "Good. Now what I found out was that the guys ripping off the places at the mall are a burg crew that hooked up when they served time together in Chino. The ringleader's name is Maldonado. I don't know his first name. I got an address for you," Bomber said as he handed Nolan a folded piece of paper. "Anything else?" Nolan asked. "No, that's all I got." "Alright, I'll pass this to the burglary dicks. If it works out, I'll be back to pay you," Nolan said. "Okay," Bomber agreed.

Nolan went back to the station. It was close to his end of watch and that meant the P.M. shift would be arriving to work. He was anxious to see if Meyer's truck was there. He searched the entire parking lot, but Meyer's truck was nowhere to be found. He went up to the detective bureau and found Gonzales. "I just checked the parking lot. His truck is not there." "I know. I've already talked to his sergeant. He agrees we should file a missing report, and he will handle the notification to the brass about the situation." "So, no one has heard from him? Not his wife? The kids?" Nolan asked desperately. "No man, nothing," Gonzales replied. "What a horrible feeling. I want to do something and there's nothing I can do," Nolan said. "You're so right. I've been going nuts. My wife even told me I'm a basket case," Gonzales admitted.

"Oh, by the way," Nolan said reaching into his shirt pocket to recover the paper Bomber gave him, "this is supposedly the address of the ringleader of the crew that's doing the burgs at the mall. Guy's name is Maldonado. He and the others did time together at Chino. Will you see to it the burg guys get this, please? They can work him up and maybe do a surveillance on him." "No problem John, and I'll call you if anything breaks with Meyers." "Thanks."

On the way home, Nolan thought about Meyers. That poor son of a bitch, he thought. I'd go nuts if I found out the woman of my dreams had betrayed my trust. He wondered where Meyers was and what he was doing at that very moment. Then, his thoughts shifted to his own family. Nolan knew he was lucky to be Marie's husband. She was always there, always supportive of him. She sensed his moods and always knew the right thing to say. She was truly his partner in life.

That evening, after the kids went to bed, he and Marie discussed what Sergeant Rosenthal had said about the six-month detective program. Marie was excited and agreed wholeheartedly. "John, you're the perfect candidate for it, and you should put in for it as soon as you can," she encouraged him. But as they sat and talked at the kitchen table, Marie could sense how uptight John was about the Meyers situation. She got up and started rubbing his neck and shoulders. "I love you, my husband," she whispered after a few moments. John began to relax, and he could almost feel the stress leaving his body as his beautiful wife continued to lovingly massage his neck and shoulders.

A few days later, Detective Lieutenant Singer sent a memo to all sworn personnel, announcing that the temporary detective position was open. The memo encouraged qualified personnel to apply promptly. As instructed, Nolan made formal request for consideration via memorandum. That same day, Nolan also received a note of thanks from the burglary detectives. They worked up the information he had passed along to them, and they subsequently conducted a surveillance on the ringleader. Maldonado and his cohorts were apprehended while perpetrating yet another burglary of a store at the very same mall. Ever true to his word,

Nolan went and paid Bomber the twenty-five dollars he had promised to pay if the information turned out to be good.

The following day Nolan's worst fears came to pass. Word funneled down from the Chief's office that Meyers had been found dead in the desert in San Bernardino County. Hikers had stumbled across his truck as they trekked through a remote area. His body was found inside of the vehicle. The San Bernardino County Sheriff's Department would be handling the investigation, although it appeared to be a suicide from a self-inflicted gunshot wound to the head.

The San Bernardino County Coroner's Office estimated that Meyer's body had been there for at least two days. Meyers left a long suicide note in which he justified and validated his reasons for ending his life. He apologized profusely to his children and extended that apology to members of the police department, but he made absolutely no mention of his wife. Meyers was a good man. Many tears would be shed for him and he would be sorely missed.

Chapter Ten

Jenny Comes For A Visit

The mid 1980's brought about significant changes for Nolan, both in his personal life, and in his professional one. More than eighteen months had passed since he had submitted his request for consideration for the temporary detective position. He'd been selected almost immediately after putting in for it. Nolan worked very hard to do a good job as a detective, and he enjoyed himself immensely. The six-month period flew by, however, Nolan did not return to patrol.

Instead, his sergeant and lieutenant approached him and asked him to stay on because one of the older detectives was ill and would be out on long term disability for an indefinite period of time. Nolan was told that if he accepted, he would fill that detective's slot, pending his return. His superiors had been very pleased with his performance, and they had great confidence in his ability to get the job done. Nolan accepted the opportunity and the challenge, and he worked an additional nine months in the detective bureau before the older detective was able to return to work.

Nolan was grateful for having had the opportunity to work in the detective bureau. But after fifteen months, he was happy to return to patrol division, and get back into a black and white. The experience and knowledge he had gained from his assignment to detectives had been well worth the effort. His opinion of the temporary detective program was that it was a great success, providing excellent opportunity for growth and experience for the men and women of the department.

During his assignment, he received a letter of commendation for his diligent work on a difficult armed robbery case in which several suspects were eventually identified, arrested and prosecuted. One of those robbery suspects was also wanted for homicide on a case from another jurisdiction. For his yearly employee evaluation during that time period, his superiors gave Nolan an overall rating of "outstanding."

The sergeant's promotional test had been given months earlier, and Nolan did quite well. His study and preparation for the entire examination process helped him achieve a very high score. Were it not for the fact that there was a temporary freeze on promotions due to department budgetary constraints, Nolan would have already been promoted to sergeant. However, command personnel assured Nolan and the other high-scorers the freeze was only a temporary setback, and that they would be promoted as soon as it was lifted.

Nolan also learned that Sergeant Carter had done well on the lieutenant's exam, and that he, too, would be promoted when the freeze was over. Nolan really liked Carter and thought he was a decent man. He had all the attributes of a great leader and a personality to match. He was Nolan's first sergeant and Nolan had nothing but admiration for him. There was no doubt in Nolan's mind that Carter would make a fine lieutenant.

On the home front, Marie had given birth to their third child, a strapping baby boy whom they named David. Nolan couldn't have been happier. He loved his daughters with tremendous intensity, but now he had a son! He couldn't wait to play catch with him or toss the football around with him. Marie would laugh at him and tell him to be patient. "He can't even walk yet and you can't wait to play catch with him," she would tease. As usual, life with Marie was as close to utopia as possible. She was always consistent in her love and commitment to her family, and she lived life to the fullest every day. Marie was the perfect mother, the perfect wife, and the perfect lover. Nolan never faltered in his belief that she was the epitome of womanhood.

Together, they had created three healthy and beautiful children, and they enjoyed a superb family life. Nolan thanked God every day for his beautiful family. Whenever he was depressed or upset with something at work, he would just focus his thoughts on his family. That helped him cope, and it enabled him to handle the often very strange world of "the streets."

Nolan also felt blessed because his mother and father were such wonderful people. And so, too, were his mother-in-law and father-in-law. He could not have asked for better in-laws. The two sets of parents got along well, and looked forward to seeing each other at family functions. This proved very advantageous to John and Marie because, not only did they have help with babysitting, and other issues pertaining to the children, their fathers were both pretty handy. Because of their dads' abilities, John and Marie saved a lot of money when they added on to their house.

Initially, when it became obvious they needed more room, they debated moving, but they liked the area and the neighbors so much, they decided to remodel. They added another bedroom, bathroom, and enlarged the family room. Their fathers did most of the work, from obtaining required permits from the city, to framing and drywall. In fact, they really only used a contractor for the plumbing, electrical, and a portion of the finish work. All in all, the addition came together very nicely, and they were happy with it.

When Nolan returned to patrol, he was reassigned to day watch with Sergeant Rosenthal. Still carried on the books as a training officer, Nolan had hoped to work for a while without a trainee. He needed some time to get himself back into patrol mode. Unfortunately for him, several new trainees were coming aboard, and there weren't enough training officers to go around. "I'm sorry, John," Sergeant Rosenthal told Nolan. "I've got no choice but to assign you a trainee. His name is Humberto Lopez, and he's waiting for you in the briefing room."

"But listen, we've got three officers in F.T.O. School right now. They'll be back in two weeks. At my earliest opportunity, I'll pull Lopez from you and assign him to one of the new training officers. I'll keep you clear after that until you're ready to train again." "Thanks, Sarge. I appreciate that. It's just that I'm not mentally ready to train again just yet," Nolan said. "No problem, John. You've been an excellent T.O., and you've successfully trained plenty of cops. You won't hear any complaints from me," the sergeant offered. "Thanks for understanding," Nolan smiled.

Nolan went to the briefing room to meet his new trainee, but prior to opening the door, he peaked through the small glass window located within the door itself. He could see the interior of the room very clearly. There sat a brand new police officer, obviously anxious and full of nervous enthusiasm. Nolan couldn't help but smile as he recalled how he'd sat in a similar fashion many years earlier waiting to meet his new training officer.

"Hi, you must be Lopez," Nolan said with a welcoming smile and a handshake. "Sir, yes sir," Lopez replied as he jumped to attention. Nolan continued to smile and said, "Lopez, here's your first task. You can only say 'sir' once in any sentence. Is that clear?" he chuckled. "Yes sir," Lopez replied with a sheepish grin on his face. "Good. Then let's go to work," Nolan said as he started towards the parking lot. When they were out in the field, Nolan told Lopez, "For the next couple of days I want you to simply observe. I know you're nervous, but just relax and watch, listen, take notes if you need to and ask questions. I'll start working you hard in a few days. Study your map because you'll need to learn the district as quickly as possible." "Yes sir and thank you. You're right, I am very nervous." "That's okay, I was pretty nervous my first day too. Don't worry, you'll be fine."

As Winters had done with him many years prior and as he had done many times in the past with his brand new trainees, Nolan showed the new officer around the district, pointing out hot spots, trouble areas and potential safety issues. As the day wore on, Nolan continued Lopez' indoctrination into the real world of the streets when he heard a crackle on the radio, "Units be advised, there is a pursuit entering the district westbound on Flower Street from Central. The vehicle is wanted for grand theft auto, hit and run felony and assault on a police officer."

Nolan and Lopez were only a few blocks from the approach path of the pursuit. Nolan drove his trusty black and white into the area, positioning himself to intercept the pursuit. Moments later, he heard the approaching sirens and observed that there was a small imported sports car being pursued by two black and whites. The vehicle was closing at a very high rate of speed, and Nolan watched as the vehicle drove right through a major intersection on a red signal without even slowing down. Because of his wanton disregard for the public safety, Nolan feared the suspect would soon cause a major accident that would likely result in the serious injury or death of an innocent pedestrian or motorist. Nolan noticed that the pursuing units, sirens wailing, were momentarily delayed at the intersection avoiding cross traffic. The suspect vehicle continued to speed away from the pursuing units. Seconds later, the vehicle blew by Nolan's position.

Nolan advised communications he was entering into the pursuit. He turned after the vehicle and began pursuing it. When Nolan checked his rear-view mirror to determine the status of the other two units, he realized they were still far behind. Until the initiating units caught up, Nolan would take over the pursuit or at least keep the suspect vehicle in view. In between advising communications he and his trainee were involved in the pursuit, and giving them a location update, Nolan requested a helicopter, but he was told none were available at that time.

By this time, the suspect vehicle was approaching another major intersection on a red signal. Nolan silently prayed no one would be in harm's way. Fortunately, the vehicle blew through the intersection without hitting anyone or anything, although there was a close call with a man in the crosswalk. Nolan had had just about enough. His fear that before very long this individual would undoubtedly hurt or kill someone grew stronger.

The powerful V-8 engine in his unit roared as Nolan quickly began to close the gap between his vehicle and the suspect's vehicle. Further closing the distance as they entered a less congested industrial area, Nolan witnessed the suspect's stolen vehicle suffer a blown tire in the right front. Seconds later, the suspect lost control of the vehicle and crashed into a vacant commercial building while still westbound on Flower Street. Nolan estimated the vehicle had been traveling about seventy miles per hour when it crashed.

Nolan brought his unit to a screeching stop behind the suspect vehicle. From the force of the impact, he could see that there wasn't much left of the vehicle. It literally looked like a large accordion. Nolan quickly exited his unit and ran towards the suspect vehicle, weapon drawn. When he realized what he was looking at, Nolan re-holstered his weapon. He was looking at what appeared to be the back portion of a disfigured head sitting atop a lifeless body in the driver's seat of the mangled sports car. There was brain matter on the dashboard and pieces of the suspect's skull lay about his body. Blood and more brain matter were everywhere. It wasn't very pretty. As Nolan's young trainee approached the vehicle, he stared in awe at the gruesome sight and promptly threw up the lunch he had enjoyed only thirty minutes prior.

By the time Lopez composed himself, Nolan had made all of the required notifications and the original two pursuing units arrived at the scene. Shortly thereafter, a supervisor, paramedics, tow trucks and the press arrived as well. The officer who initially engaged the suspect in pursuit, Ed Flores, told Nolan the chase started in the harbor area. He also told Nolan that the suspect was known to him and other officers assigned to the harbor district. The fellow's name was Thomas Rickman. His specialties were stealing cars, doing purse snatches and other street robberies.

Flores said that Rickman was just plain mean and evil. Rickman liked punching and kicking his victims as he robbed them. His preferred targets were older women, generally incapable of defending themselves against a strong, young male. Rickman's mother lived in the harbor area, and the local officers had known him from years of contacts. When Rickman was a teenager, he frequently beat his mother. More often than not, she was the one who called police. She was afraid of her own son. Sadly, this is a common refrain from far too many single mothers trying to work to make ends meet while raising their sons without the influence of a decent father or stepfather.

Officer Flores went on to explain that he had first met Rickman a few years earlier, when, as an adult, Rickman stole a high performance model Corvette from a Chevrolet dealership. He drove right through a plate glass window and out onto the street. Several units gave chase but were unable to keep up with the Corvette. Ultimately, they lost him before a helicopter could get on him.

A few days later, the Arizona Highway Patrol went in pursuit of Rickman and since he would not stop, they laid a spike strip in his path, causing all four of the Corvette's tires to go flat. Rickman had no option but to pull over. After a violent physical struggle, Rickman was taken into custody. Several weeks later, he was extradited back to California. Shortly thereafter, he went on trial for stealing the Corvette and other charges related to that particular incident. Officer Flores testified in the trial because he had taken the initial reports from the Chevrolet dealership from which Rickman had stolen the Corvette.

Flores recalled that, on the first day of the trial, immediately following the judge's announcement for the first morning recess, Rickman turned toward the uniformed Flores, made eye contact and sneered at him, telling him he would be back to steal more cars out of his district. After serving just eighteen months of a four-year sentence, Rickman was paroled. He returned and stole a car, just as he said he would.

In the process, he hit a pedestrian and fled the scene, leaving that pedestrian lying in the street. While making his getaway, Rickman spotted a police officer directing traffic in the middle of a major intersection. He purposely steered the vehicle towards the policeman in an obvious attempt to run him over. At the very last moment, the policeman was able to dive out of the way. Shortly thereafter, Officer Flores spotted the vehicle and the chase began.

Hours worth of paperwork completed, Officer Nolan leaned back in his chair and reflected on the day. His first thought was for Lopez, his new trainee. Helluva first day, he mused. Wonder if he's having any second thoughts about being a police officer as the result of seeing Rickman's brains strewn all over the interior of that car. Nolan made a mental note to debrief his young partner and to make sure he was dealing with the ugliness he saw on his first day in the street. Nolan then recalled *his* first night on patrol many years earlier. He thought about the two little girls who died at the hands of a drunk driver, and although it had occurred many years earlier, he remembered the incident in detail, as if it had just happened. Whenever he thought about that incident, it never failed to sadden him.

Nolan's thoughts then turned to Rickman. Nolan had always disliked seeing the useless loss of life, but in this case, he wasn't at all saddened by the outcome. He couldn't help himself. He felt no sadness and no pain over the loss of a fellow member of the human race. For that particular day, the score was: good guys one, bad guys zero. Rickman was now rehabilitated. He'd never steal another car or beat another senior citizen while stealing her handbag. All in all, it had been a pretty good day.

When John arrived home that evening, Marie greeted him with some great news. "I spoke to Jenny today. She told me that her parents just bought a motor home, and that they're finalizing plans for their first trip. Jenny and the kids are going to go with them. They're gonna start off by traveling down the coast. They plan to stop here before moving on to Arizona to see the Grand Canyon. Jenny said she promised to take the kids to Disneyland while they're here. I told her we could take our kids as well. She thought that would be wonderful and she said she can't wait to meet David."

"That's terrific," John said happily. "When is all of this going to happen?" "They haven't set a final date as yet, but they're thinking they'll leave in the next three to four weeks. The kids will be out of school by then. They'll stay down here for two or three days. That should be enough time for them to see Disneyland and have a nice visit with us," Marie added. "It'll be really nice to see Jenny and the kids again. I'm looking forward to it," John said happily.

Later that evening, once the kids were in bed, John and Marie sat at the kitchen table to talk and make plans. But on this particular evening, Marie was very quiet and for a few moments, it seemed she was somewhere far away in deep thought. "What's wrong, Babe?" John asked his wife. "Oh nothing," Marie answered as she refocused her eyes and shook her head slightly. "I was just thinking how nice it would be to have a motor home and have the ability to do some traveling. No big deal," she rationalized. "Don't worry," John said consoling his wife. "We're doing okay. We save a little something every month. That'll pay off years down the road. You'll see. Meanwhile, we can plan little outings or vacations. As long as you and the kids are healthy and happy, life is good."

"I know Sweetie, I'm sorry. Maybe, at some point, I'll be able to work full-time instead of part-time and we'll be able to do more," she reasoned. "Marie, if it was up to me, you wouldn't work at all. Listen, you're a terrific mom with three kids and, in addition to working, you keep this household running very smoothly. Hopefully, my promotion will come soon. That'll mean a halfway decent raise. After that happens, we'll take the kids and go on a nice little vacation. I promise." "No, John, you need to think about a new car for yourself. That old jalopy is falling apart." "No, it's just fine. I only use it to go to work and home. When we go somewhere as a family, we take your car. Besides, I've taken pretty good care of that old buggy. She'll last a lot longer than you think," John smiled.

Marie got close to her husband and hugged him. "You're a good man," she said. John stroked her beautiful hair and said, "As gorgeous as you are, why did you want to go and hook up with a policeman who barely grinds out a living? You could have had your pick of doctors or any other rich guy. You can't even plan a decent vacation." "Don't be silly," she scolded. "I didn't marry you for your money, or your earning potential. I married you because I adore you." Marie took her husband's hand and looked into his eyes. She had a very sexy look on her face. John grinned and said, "You're seducing me, lady." "That was the plan," Marie whispered as she led her husband to their bedroom.

Days later, Sergeant Rosenthal informed Nolan that the officers who had been away for their certification as training officers had returned. He told Nolan he would honor his request and reassign Lopez to one of them. "Thank you, Sarge. Lopez is a good kid. Lots of potential. Please be sure to pick a mature and capable T.O. for him." "Those were my thoughts too, John. You're going to make a fine sergeant. You have compassion and concern for others. Very important traits. Oh, by the way, it's still unofficial, but word has it the promotions will happen very soon. I heard that tidbit of information at the staff meeting the other day. The captain believes the freeze will be lifted sooner than anticipated. If I were you, I'd start getting some uniform shirts ready to go." "Thanks, Sarge," Nolan said, grinning happily.

About thirty minutes into his shift, Nolan received a radio call to phone the station. When he made his call, he found out that Steve Villanueva wanted to meet with him. They picked a café close to the station and met there. When Nolan arrived, Villanueva was already there, in uniform. "Hi, John, thanks for coming," he smiled. "No problem. I heard you'd gone to mid-watch. What's up?" Nolan inquired. "I did go to mid-watch. That's why we hardly run into each other anymore. I'm due in court this morning, but I wanted to take this opportunity to talk to you. The reason I called you over here is because I wanted you to be the first to know...Alicia and I are getting married," Villanueva said proudly.

"Well, congratulations, Steve!" Nolan said excitedly. "I'm very happy for you both. How about your parents? How do they feel about you guys getting married?" "My mom and dad love her. They think we're right for each other. Her dad is gone, died when she was very young. But her mom loves me." "Outstanding," Nolan commented. "It's great when parents put their blessing on their children's marriages. Life is so much easier."

"So when did you guys decide to do it?" Nolan asked. "We've known all along we're right for each other, but we wanted to wait until Alicia's career was on track. She's been doing fine. She's still working PM's, but she applied for detectives a while back, and she finally got picked. She reports next week, and we decided we didn't want to wait any longer." "My congratulations to Alicia for the marriage and for going to detectives. She's a damn good cop. I've never heard anyone say a bad word about her. She's got a terrific reputation. She's got tenacity and determination. That'll help her solve her cases. She'll definitely do well as a detective," Nolan said. "Thanks, John, I know that'll mean a lot to her," Villanueva said candidly.

"You should have brought her with you," Nolan said. "Uh, she was a bit nervous about coming with me," Villanueva admitted. "Nervous? Because of me? What are you talking about? She's never been nervous around me before." The officers momentarily paused in their conversation when the waitress came over, filled their coffee cups and took their breakfast order. As soon as she left, they resumed their conversation right where they'd left off. "Tell me what you meant when you said Alicia would be nervous around me," Nolan said demandingly.

"Okay, it's like I mentioned a moment ago. Her dad is dead. She has one uncle, but he's bedridden and he's slowly dying of cancer. Alicia has a step-dad, but she can't stand him. Doesn't like the way he treats her mother. Apparently, there's no physical abuse, he just talks to her like she's a piece of crap." "Has she told her feelings to her mom?" "Yes, but her mom is from the old school. She wants to hang in there, you know, make it work," Villanueva explained. "I'm really sorry to hear that, Steve, but why are you telling me all this?" Nolan asked.

Villanueva paused momentarily, then humbly said, "Well, Alicia and I would like to know if you would consider giving her away at the wedding." She thinks very highly of you. She always has. Ever since that first morning she rode as a trainee in your car, when I was in court. Remember? Besides, she knows how I feel about you...And that's another thing I need to talk to you about."

"But first, will you do it, I mean, will you give her away?" "Of course I will, I'd be honored," Nolan replied. "She's a very fine woman. You tell Alicia that I said I'm honored she chose me, but also tell her I'm very upset she wasn't here with you. She should have asked me, or at least been here." "You're right, of course, and that's exactly what I told her. But once I tell her you'll do it, she'll call you right away. John, she's had real bad luck with men all her life, starting when her dad died. Don't be upset with her. She was afraid you might say no." "I understand, Steve, but tell her I want to talk to her just the same," Nolan replied. "You got it."

"Now, about you and me, John," Villanueva said as he rubbed his hands together. "What about you and me?" Nolan asked. "Come on, John, we used to be very close. Ever since I failed to make the decision you wanted me to make about Alicia's training, you've been kinda standoffish," Villanueva charged. "I guess I'd have to say you've been cordial, but not close like before," Villanueva added. Nolan thought for a moment before giving his response. "Well, I gotta admit, I was disappointed. I just thought there was too much of a conflict, and that the right thing to do was as I had suggested. But I'm obviously glad it turned

217

out the way it did for the both of you. And as far as me being standoffish, perhaps you're right."

"Steve, I never stopped caring about you as a close friend, it's just that I was momentarily stung by your choice. But if my behavior toward you changed so noticeably, why didn't you come to me to discuss this sooner?" Nolan inquired. "Well, I guess deep down I knew why you were acting the way you did. But, if you don't mind, I'd like to just put all that behind us now," Villanueva said. "I couldn't agree more," Nolan concurred as the two shook hands.

During breakfast, Nolan said, "Steve, as long as we're talking, I'd like to get your opinion on something." "Sure, what is it?" Villanueva inquired. "The other day in briefing, several of us were discussing the "affirmative action" issue. If you looked around the room at that time, there was a smattering of just about every race and ethnicity you could think of. Most of the minority men and women felt as I did. While I'd like to see more minorities and cultural diversity on police and fire departments in Southern California, I question the need for federally mandated hiring quotas. That seems a bit much."

"Anyway, one of the Hispanic guys said he heard that several departments maintain two hiring lists. One for women and minorities and one for white males. I sure hope that's inaccurate information. That just doesn't sound right." "I agree," Villanueva said. "And let me tell you, the affirmative action issue was not only discussed on your watch, it seems to be a topic cops and firefighters everywhere are discussing. Now as I understand it, with respect to the quota system, if a certain percentage or ratio of minorities and women is not hired, tremendous sanctions and penalties can be imposed on the 'offending' departments."

"I'm with you. I believe we need more minorities and women on our department as well, but I don't want this stuff shoved down my throat. To me, that's overreaction. And as a minority, I can tell you, no one lowered or altered the standards for me, back when I got hired. I had to meet or surpass the department standards in order to get hired. That's the way it should be. Equal across the board, no quotas or mandates."

Villanueva continued, "But from what I'm hearing now, in order to meet the quotas, command staff are often forced to bend or lower their department standards and accept minority candidates who would have ordinarily been washed out. If that's true, then for me personally, it seems like they're insulting my race. The hiring process shouldn't be about race or ethnicity. It should be about hiring the most qualified candidates, regardless of their sex or the color of their skin. Are they in effect saying that Hispanics, women and other minorities can't meet male white standards?"

"As far as I'm concerned, they're sending the wrong message and I for one really resent that." "You're not alone," Nolan added. "That really hit home with virtually every one of the minority officers who'd been on the job for a while. They basically echoed most of what you just said. Their collective feeling was, hey, no one lowered any standards for us. Why should standards be compromised now?"

"As far as I'm concerned, we're all correct in our feelings toward this stuff. I don't know, maybe an even stronger recruiting campaign in the local communities would help," Nolan suggested. "Or maybe improved or expanded Police and Fire Explorer programs would help to get youngsters interested in law enforcement or firefighting early in life," Villanueva offered. Nolan added, "Perhaps successful minority professionals like you, Steve, should be called upon to go to the schools and colleges to do recruiting." Villanueva replied, "You know, I'm sure the powers-to-be have thought of most of our suggestions. I just wish there was a better way to hire minorities than by federal mandate. I don't care for the idea of being force-fed. We need to find a way to get the best candidates, minority and white, and not settle for whatever we can get, just to satisfy the numbers quota imposed upon us by politicians and federal judges."

"Well, I was just curious how you felt about the whole thing. It seems this topic has created quite a stir on the department," Nolan said. "Yeah, and you know, I do understand why they're doing it," Villanueva said. "The community as a whole needs to see that some of its own have become law enforcement officers or firefighters...that they're represented on the police and fire departments. You know, when I first got hired, there weren't all that many minorities on the job. If you randomly looked at a large group of officers back then, only a few would be Black, Hispanic, Asian or female. And frankly, too many of the good 'ole white boys seemed to resent us. I know I could feel the resentment from some of them," Villanueva said. "I know, and I wouldn't disagree with you there," Nolan said sadly. "And as a white guy, I can only apologize for that."

Nolan continued, "You know, as unfortunate as it sounds, the fact of the matter is that when you recruit from the human race, you're going to have undesirables slip through the testing process from time to time. It doesn't matter how difficult or seemingly accurate the testing process might appear to be. I'd be the first to admit we still have some guys who, while I wouldn't necessarily classify them as prejudiced, are unmistakably less tolerant of minorities than they are of other whites."

"I even experienced a little taste of that myself a few years ago, when one of those types found out I was married to a Hispanic woman and that my kids were half Mexican. He made some uncalled for, and downright rude remarks to me regarding their ethnicity. In response, I invited the S.O.B. out onto the parking lot after work. We resolved the issue. He never made any comments about my family again." "Well, as you well know, John, in the past, I've had to tune up a few people myself," Villanueva reminded his friend. But I have to admit, things have gotten much better over the last few years." "Agreed."

"Alright, now that we've solved the world's problems, we'd better get our butts back to work," Nolan said jokingly as he reached into his pocket for money to pay the bill. "I'll get it," Villanueva announced as he reached for the bill. "No, Steve, I've got it this time. You get it next time," Nolan responded. "Alright, then I'll leave the tip," Villanueva said as he left money on the table and glanced at his watch. "Jeez, look at the time. I've gotta get to court. Thanks, John and thanks for breakfast too. I'll have Alicia give you a call." "Okay, Steve, take it easy."

When Nolan drove out of the restaurant parking lot, he felt his pager vibrating in his shirt pocket. He'd only had the newfangled device for a few weeks, and it momentarily startled him. He couldn't help but laugh at himself. Marie usually paged him once or twice a day with their agreed upon code for "I love you." This time, however, the pager display simply indicated the home phone number. Nolan wasn't very far from the station so he headed in to call home.

On the way to the station, he drove by one of the larger high schools in the district. He was flagged down by a uniformed school police officer. The school police officer advised Nolan that an indecent exposure suspect had just left the area after exposing himself to two fourteen year-old girls on their way to school. Nolan immediately obtained and then broadcast the suspect information to communications, who in turn re-broadcast it to all the units in the field. Time lapse was less than one minute. The suspect was a male Hispanic in his thirties driving an older white Chevrolet Chevelle with damage to the right rear. His last direction of travel was northbound from the high school. Nolan interviewed the victims.

The suspect perpetrated his crime by first choosing a heavily traveled street adjacent to the high school. This was one of the main pedestrian routes used by the children as they walked to school. Insuring he would have lots of kids to prey on before selecting his victim or victims and performing his perverted act, the suspect parked his vehicle along the curb in the direction the children were walking. There he sat, waiting for his unknowing prey to approach as they innocently walked to their school.

Just as the young victims were about to walk past the rear portion of his vehicle, the suspect called to them through his open passenger window in order to attract their attention. When they looked over at him in his vehicle, they were startled to see that he was masturbating. The girls reacted by screaming and running the remaining two blocks to the school where they found the school police officer and told him what had occurred. When the girls fled after having seen the suspect masturbate, he initially drove after them, scaring them even more. But when they made it to the school grounds, he turned northbound and quickly drove away from the school. The girls were able to provide a good description of the suspect vehicle and the suspect himself, although no license plate information was obtained.

Nolan was finishing his interview with the victims when he was advised by communications that Ricky Watson, one of the motorcycle officers, had a vehicle stopped that matched the description of the suspect vehicle he had given out in his crime broadcast regarding the incident at the high school. Nolan told the victims that a possible suspect had been stopped. He explained that he would need to transport them to the location of the stop so that they could look at the suspect and his vehicle. He also told them that just because the police had stopped a vehicle that looked like the one they had described, that didn't mean it was the right vehicle. He would need them to positively identify the suspect and his vehicle, or state that it was the wrong suspect and vehicle. Both of the girls said they understood.

Having given the required admonition to the victims regarding "field identification," Nolan transported the girls to Watson's location. As Nolan made a slow approach, Watson had his detainee stand up and look straight ahead. In unison, both girls exclaimed, "That's him." Nolan asked, "Are you sure?" "Yes, positive," they both replied with confidence. Nolan then asked, "What about the car?" One of the girls said, "Yes, that's the right car." The second girl immediately confirmed that statement. Nolan informed Watson he had stopped the right vehicle and the suspect was placed under arrest. The girls were driven back to school, after which Nolan went to the station where he met up with Watson.

"John, when I searched his vehicle I found these porno publications under the seat. They're pretty raunchy. They show very young looking girls engaged in all kinds of sick sex acts," Watson said angrily. "That sick bastard," Nolan said, disgusted at what Watson had just told him. "Let's go ahead and book those into evidence and add possession of pornographic materials to his charges. By the way, thanks again, Ricky, you bagged that piece of crap real quick." "Yeah, thanks, but too bad it's only a misdemeanor," Watson said as he started tagging the porno magazines into evidence. "No kidding," Nolan responded. "I'll bet this isn't the first time that pervert's been popped for this kinda stuff. I'll get a rap sheet on him. Maybe he's on parole, and we can get a parole hold on him too," Nolan added hopefully.

Because of the incident at the high school Nolan hadn't had the opportunity to call home. By the time he did, there was no answer. Later that morning, he received another page to call home. This time, he called home right away and spoke to Marie. "Hi. Sorry I couldn't call back right away when you paged me earlier. I got tied up, but I called as soon as I could and there was no answer. What's up?" he asked his wife. "David woke up with a fever this morning. More than likely, it's that flu thing that's going around.

Besides the fever, the little guy was tugging at his ear. I was afraid he might have an ear infection so I called the pediatrician's office, and they had me bring him in as an emergency. I finally got his fever to break and the doctor confirmed my suspicion about the ear infection. I stopped at the pharmacy on the way home and got him some medicine." "Wow. You guys have had quite a morning," he said. "Is the medicine that liquid stuff that you keep in the fridge?" "Yup, that's the stuff," Marie quipped.

"By the way, just before I left to take David to the doctor, Jenny called. She said that she was wrong about when her kids finished school. They're done at the end of this week. Anyway, to make a long story short, they're leaving on their trip next week, which means they'll be here towards the end of the week. We're going to have to do some major shopping and expedite our preparations for their visit." "Okay, no problem. I've got one more day then I'm off for two. We'll get everything done on time, don't worry. In fact, since I've got lots of time on the books, I think I'll see if I can take all or most of next week off." "That's a good idea, John," Marie told her husband. "Alright, give David a kiss for me and tell him I hope he feels better soon. I'll see you guys later." "Okay, bye...love you." "I love you too."

Nolan finished his workweek, and he and Marie busily prepared for their guests the following week. As he had hoped, his request for that entire week off was approved. He was very anxious to see Jenny and the kids again, and he wanted to take full advantage of their stay in California to visit with them. Many years had passed since they moved to Oregon, and there was so much to talk about.

Towards the end of the following week, on a typically warm Southern California afternoon, a brand new, medium-sized motor home pulled up in front of the Nolans' house. The entire Nolan family went out to greet their guests. Jenny was the first to emerge from within the vehicle, and she yelled excitedly as she and Marie rushed towards each other. The two women hugged each other for a moment, cheerfully exchanging pleasantries. Next, Jenny embraced John, and they kissed each other on the cheek. Then, Jenny hugged the two Nolan girls and commented on how beautiful they were. "The last time I saw you two was just before we moved to Oregon. Samantha, you were four or five and Kimberly, you were just an infant. Your mother sends me pictures, and she's kept me informed about you guys over the years, but it's really good to see you in person."

Meanwhile, the three Winters kids piled out of the motor home, and John and Marie fussed over them as well. Linda, the oldest, was already seventeen and preparing to enter her senior year in high school. She was an attractive young lady, and Nolan noticed she had a very strong resemblance to her father. Jason was sixteen, and he had evolved into a fine-looking young man. He was an athlete who excelled in all sports, but favored football. The youngest of the Winters children, Helen, was initially shy with the Nolans, however, before long she relaxed and had a great time. Jenny's mom and dad were the last to get out, and they too were met with hugs and a warm welcome. John and Marie had first met Jenny's parents when they attended Dennis' funeral many years earlier.

After the initial excitement of greeting her old friends, Jenny asked, "Where's David?" "He's sleeping," Marie responded. "Come on, let's go inside. The men can take care of whatever bags you want to bring in later," Marie said as she put her arms around the Winters kids and led them toward the front door. Jenny followed and said, "Let's go wake the little guy up. I can't wait to meet him." As Marie led Jenny into David's room, he began to stir and wake up. "Oh, he's a beautiful baby," Jenny said as she stared at the Nolan boy. "Come here, handsome man," she said to him as she reached into his crib and picked him up.

Marie fixed some food and invited everyone to gather in the family room to eat and socialize. Before long, John got up to put on a fresh pot of coffee. "I was wondering how long it would be before you put more coffee on," Jenny teased her old friend. "You haven't changed a bit. You're still hooked on that stuff," she smiled. "You're right," John returned the smile. "But you know, I don't really have any other vices or bad habits. I mean I don't gamble, cheat on the wife or kick the dog. And I don't drink much alcohol, so I figure I'm allowed to indulge my coffee habit. Marie is always on me about drinking too much of the stuff, and she's actually right—I *do* drink too much coffee." John stayed silent for a moment and then, almost jokingly asked, "By the way, would anyone like some fresh coffee?" Jenny and Marie just smiled at each other and shook their heads. "He's hopeless," Marie said.

Jenny's dad announced he would have a cup and then asked John if Orange County was very far. "Well, from here it's probably about thirty-five miles or so to the county line. But it's a big county. Do you know where, or what city in Orange County?" "Yes, Anaheim," the man said. "Jenny's mom has an old friend there with whom she's kept in touch over the years. We promised to visit her and stay a night or two at her place."

"In fact, if we could, we'd like to use your phone to call her." "Of course. Please consider yourselves at home here. You don't have to ask permission to use the phone," Nolan said. "Thank you, John, that's very kind of you. At any rate, if she's there, Jenny's mom and I will just head down there this evening." "Aren't you guys tired?" John inquired. "I don't feel tired at all. Jenny helped me drive and the motor home is very comfortable. Almost as if you're sitting in your living room," he smiled.

Jenny's mom made the call to her friend. She promised the lady she and her husband would arrive later in the evening to visit and spend the night. John got the map book out and plotted a course for them. When it was time for them to leave, John suggested they take his car instead of driving the motor home on the freeway system in the heavy L.A. and Orange County traffic. Still enamored with their new motor home, Jenny's dad said, "Oh no, we'll take our little home with us, but thank you very much for offering. You folks are very kind." With that, Jenny's parents kissed and hugged their grandchildren and their daughter. They also said goodbye to the Nolans and thanked them yet again for their hospitality. "We'll see you all in a couple of days, but I'll call you tomorrow," Jenny's mom told Jenny as they left.

The kids settled in to talking, playing and watching television in the family room. Jenny, Marie and John moved to the kitchen and sat at the table, fondly reminiscing and talking about old times. Jenny recalled, "I remember that shortly before Dennis was killed you guys had us over for a barbecue. After dinner, we sat around this very table laughing, talking and stuffing our faces with desserts. Life was so good back then," she sighed. Though she tried hard not to show it, John saw that Jenny still had a very heavy heart. She was a beautiful woman, but her face looked tired and there were several premature lines and wrinkles. The death of her husband had had a profound and lingering effect on this wonderful person.

John was concerned about her. "Jenny, earlier you said things were going pretty well and that you were happy. But now that it's just us three, tell us how you're *really* doing?" he insisted. "Leave her alone, John!" Marie snapped at her husband. "No, no, it's okay, Marie. In fact, this is probably good for me," Jenny said as she touched Marie's arm. "I know you guys are concerned. I can see that—it's obviously very genuine, and I'm lucky to have friends like you. To answer your question, it has gotten a little easier. I guess time does eventually heal most wounds, as the saying goes. But for me, it varies. I have good days and bad days. Sometimes I laugh out loud when I think about some of the comical things Dennis used to do. I smile and I get very happy when I remember the romantic times we shared," she said as she smiled.

Then, Jenny got a sad look on her face as she said, "Other times I cry, John. I remember when you took me to the hospital after Dennis had been killed. You pulled the sheet down and I saw my dead husband, the man of my dreams, lying there on the gurney. I can recall every nagging detail. If I close my eyes I can see him lying there with the blood soaked bandages on his head. Sometimes, I even have nightmares about how the shooting occurred. I see it unfolding in slow motion. It really scares the hell out of me. And, to this very day, I still wake up at night reaching for him," she admitted.

Jenny had her hands on the table fidgeting with a tissue Marie had given her. She stared down at the tissue as she nervously rolled it back and forth between her fingers. John and Marie both sensed her frustration and unsettled anger. Then suddenly, Jenny blurted out, "God, I miss him," as she started crying uncontrollably. Marie and John immediately hugged and consoled her.

"Can we talk about something else now?" Marie demanded as she glared at her husband. Jenny sniffled, wiped her tears and said, "No Marie, it's okay. I never talk like this to anyone, not even to my own parents. I just keep it all inside," she admitted, still crying. "But that's the worst thing you can do," John argued. "You know, every now and then, all of us can use a little counseling. But more often than not, a simple chat with someone we trust and with whom we can comfortably vent our emotions without fear of embarrassment or betrayal is all we need to keep our sanity."

"I was fortunate enough to have Marie. If it hadn't been for her, I might have lost it after Dennis died. I had a real rough time of it," John confessed. "I didn't know," Jenny said as she wiped her eyes and stared intensely at John. Marie added, "Jenny, I purposely neglected to mention anything to you about it. John and I figured you had more than your shares of worries and problems." "Well I appreciate that, but you should have told me." "No, Jenny, you had to be strong and function as the only parent to your children while trying to deal with your grief and sorrow. You had more than enough on your plate. It took us a while, but we got through it," Marie said.

"As long as we're talking about your kids, I have to tell you that it's obvious you've done an absolutely fantastic job with them. They're polite, well-mannered, considerate and very confident. It's obvious they are the most important concern in your life. You should be very proud," John complimented her. "Thanks John. They're all doing so well in school too," Jenny said, grinning from ear to ear while still wiping tears from her eyes. "That's good to hear," Marie smiled. John then inquired, "Jenny, it's been over ten years since Dennis died. Have you ever dated or even spent any time with another man?" "Well, I tried dating a couple of times a few years after we settled in Oregon. I guess I just wasn't ready then. It didn't seem to work out too well."

"Since that time I've thought about dating again, but so far, I've haven't gone out with anyone." "Jenny, forgive me for being pushy, but don't you think it's time you enjoyed some male companionship? Is there anyone who's shown interest in you? Or, to turn that around, have you been attracted to anyone?" "Okay, John, that's about enough now," Marie interrupted. "You're not questioning a suspect," she said, upset by her husband's very direct questioning of Jenny.

Jenny looked at Marie and gently touched her arm as if to say it's okay. Then, she took a deep breath and responded to John's questions. "Well, John, there is this gentleman I've talked to at the high school. His name is Jim. He's also a single parent, and he's really very nice. We've talked on a number of occasions when we run into each other at various school functions. He knows my situation. On a couple of occasions, he's hinted at going out to lunch, or for coffee, but I haven't taken him up on it," she said as she looked at John. "Maybe you should," John said. "Try it. You know there will never be another Dennis, and maybe you'll never completely get over losing him, but you have to move on with your life. You have to do what's best for you. I know Dennis would want that for you."

John continued, "You *should* go to lunch with this guy if you like him. Or, just meet him somewhere for coffee and see how it feels. Jenny, you're still a very beautiful woman." "Thank you, John, but I just don't know if I'm ready," she admitted. "You need to stop mourning now, Jenny. You've been a widow for over a decade. You need to get on with your life. You deserve happiness," John said, almost pleading. Jenny hesitated for a moment and then said, "Maybe I will go out with Jim, I don't know yet. I need to think about it." "Okay, enough said. I won't say another word on the subject," John promised. "Come on, Jenny, it's getting late. Let's get all the kids ready for bed. Tomorrow's another day," Marie said, effectively ending the evening's discussion.

The following morning when Marie and John woke up and came out of their bedroom, Jenny ran up to them and gave them each a big hug. "Good morning," she said cheerfully. "All the kids are awake, and I've started cooking breakfast for them. "Thanks," Marie said. "I'll jump in and help you." "Okay," Jenny smiled, "but first, I want to thank you both for being such wonderful, caring friends. The talk we had yesterday really helped my outlook. Maybe you were right. Maybe that's all I needed. I've kept all that frustration and all that anger inside me these past years."

"Thanks for making me talk about it and forcing me to come to terms with it. I know it won't happen overnight for me, but at least I do know I'll be on the right track and I'll start making some headway. Say, have you guys thought about hanging a shingle and going into counseling?" she laughed. "I'm just glad to see you bright-eyed and bushy-tailed. That's the old Jenny I remember," John chuckled happily. Marie responded to Jenny's profound announcement by simply hugging her and saying, "I know you'll be just fine, Jenny."

After breakfast, the adults found themselves engaged once again in deep conversation. "John, having been married to a policeman, I've always been fascinated with hearing opinions on the effectiveness of our legal system from someone who's out there in the streets every day. Dennis used to give me an earful all the time. I enjoyed that immensely and I must admit I have missed it. I read the newspapers and the newsmagazines, searching for the truth. Personally, I believe they sometimes try to bend or sway public opinion in the direction dictated by their board of directors. Also, too often, a story is tainted by an author or reporter's personal opinion. I wish I could just get the facts. I'll formulate my own opinions, thank you very much," Jenny said.

"Well Jenny, not too much has changed over the past few years. As you might imagine, most police officers share the same or similar opinion when it comes to our legal system. Unfortunately, most of us become disenchanted with the system when we learn how it *really* works. Nevertheless, it is still the best system in the world, albeit flawed. Let me go about clarifying all of that."

"First and foremost, I believe we are very fortunate people. We live in the finest country in the world. Our way of life, our freedoms and our democratic system of government are envied by masses the world over. Additionally, ours is arguably the most technologically and scientifically advanced country on the planet. And yet historically, we have the highest crime rate of any civilized democratic country in the world. Why is that?" John asked.

John continued, answering his own question, "Well, for so-called third world countries, or 'developing nations,' as the politicians like to call them, their answers to a criminal justice system are simple. In the case of very serious crimes, the death penalty is often imposed, once the offender is convicted. The sentence is carried out quickly. No muss, no fuss. If a person steals or commits a less serious crime, he will likely spend a very long time in prison. He'll struggle to survive in prison conditions that are often deplorable. He might have to deal with unsanitary conditions, rats and disease just to survive. In some of these nations, if it is determined a person is a thief, they simply chop one of his hands off. Now he has one less hand with which to steal."

"Those are pretty strong deterrents to crime, wouldn't you say?" John asked Jenny, who replied, "Well yes, but we should never treat our criminals that way." "You're right, of course, we don't treat our criminals that way. Nor should we. But obviously, we *are* doing something wrong. Do we, as a people in the greatest nation in the world, have too many civil liberties? Is our society too tolerant of the criminal element?" he asked. Jenny just looked at him as he took a sip of water. "Go on, John, I want to hear what you have to say," she said. "Okay," he answered.

"In advanced nations such as Japan, for example, laws are clearly defined and readily adhered to by the people. There is tremendous respect and consideration for one another in that society. Honor is an issue in everyone's life. Criminals and ne'er-do-wells are simply not tolerated. That doesn't mean they don't have crime. They do. But, what it does mean is that their criminal justice system is set up to deal with it very effectively. Their laws were designed to protect their society, and they are strictly enforced. Japan's people strongly believe in and support their justice system, resulting in a relatively small criminal element."

"Another example of an advanced nation might be Great Britain. For the most part, the English are a very proper people, but obviously, they too have a criminal element. Their laws and their judicial system are among the oldest in the modern world and were the model for many younger nations, including our own. One of the unique things about England is that handguns, and firearms in general, are very strictly regulated."

"With few exceptions, people are simply not allowed to have them. And, as you know, British police officers or Bobbies, don't normally carry weapons. But more importantly, the criminal element as a whole understands that if a firearm is used in the commission of a crime, the consequences are far more severe. An individual convicted of a crime in which he used a firearm knows he's going to be sentenced to the penitentiary for a very long time. Does this have a significant deterrent value? I'd say so."

"What about America, John?" Tell me about us," Jenny said. "Yes, John, let's get back to America," Marie challenged her husband. "Alright, alright," John smiled. "I'm getting there. I was just trying to illustrate a point for contrast with our own country," he explained. "Well to begin with, here in the United States we treat our prison inmates much better than the way most other countries treat theirs. Clearly, there are some differences in the way prison systems are viewed and operated from state to state, but I think it's safe to say that the prison population in this country as a whole, is treated quite well. Inmates stay in relatively clean facilities, they eat reasonably well, and they receive medical treatment when needed."

John continued, "Generally speaking, inmates in most states have the opportunity to participate in reading or educational programs. They are also afforded the opportunity to participate in physical fitness activities ranging from a variety of team sports, to weightlifting and bodybuilding.

Some states provide the opportunity for rehabilitation and assist the inmate with re-introduction into society after he has paid his debt, while other states mandate inmate participation in hard labor. Then, there's California. But before we talk about California's prison system, let me just give you a very brief history and explain why we have so much crime in this state."

"For years, criminals have considered California the 'Santa Clause State.' The reason for that is simple. We, in this state, have had a reputation for being very liberal and for many years now, criminals have known that they can get away with more crime in this state than in most others. They also realize that if they're apprehended perpetrating their crimes, they'll serve considerably less time in this state than in most other states. There are several reasons for this, none the least of which is a previous State Supreme Court that rendered some ridiculously bizarre decisions."

"That ultra-liberal court made it painfully obvious that it cared much more about the criminal, than the law-abiding citizen with proper social values. Some of the case decisions rendered by that particular court were so bad that even diehard liberals reacted with disbelief and disdain. Fortunately, that reign of terror has been over for some time, and we're slowly but steadily, recovering from the damage imposed on the good people of this state."

"But, before we go on with California, let's finish with the country as a whole. Let's briefly discuss the first amendment to our constitution. When that inalienable right was written by our founding fathers, those learned men who carefully sculpted the laws of our great land, did they really intend for it to be carried out to the extremes to which it is carried out today?"

"Look at hate groups for example. Would our founding fathers really have intended to give radical, hateful groups the *absolute* right to advocate violence and spread their evil through public forums via the written and spoken word? I believe civil libertarians would argue that everyone in this country has that right. I don't know, but somehow, I really don't think that's what our founding fathers had in mind for our people. Notwithstanding the meaning and intent of the first amendment, if we know this hatred is something that "shocks the conscience" and is extremely detrimental to the well-being of our society as a whole, shouldn't it be outlawed or banned?"

"One last point. For years the topic of flag burning has been hotly debated. Is it a first amendment right to burn the American flag? Does it actually violate any of our laws? Politicians, lawmakers and civil libertarians continue to adamantly debate this issue. Let me give you my take on this whole matter. It's really very simple. The flag of our beloved United States of America is our nation's symbol. It's *our* flag. It's who we are. It represents us. And, as far as I'm concerned, any American who burns it should be put on trial for treason and, if found guilty, should be punished to the fullest extent of the law. If a foreigner living here or visiting this country participates in flag burning, he should be expelled immediately and banned from ever setting foot on our soil again."

"I'll even take that a step further. If some subversive or radical group in another country burns our flag as a display of hatred for what America stands for, there's not too much we can do about that. However, if through our intelligence sources, we determine that the particular subversive group operates under the auspices of that country's government, we should immediately sanction and, at the very least, economically punish that country for allowing and supporting the burning of our precious flag."

John glanced at his watch, took another sip of water and said, "Okay, I need to get off my soapbox now. You shouldn't have gotten me started," he said. "Can you just finish with California?" Jenny asked. "Yes, Ma'am," John sighed. "I'll make it quick. I've already commented on this state's unfortunate reputation for being soft on crime. Combine that with a highly overcrowded court system, an equally overcrowded prison system and, for good measure, toss in far too much plea-bargaining, and its no wonder we've got problems," he pointed out.

"As a policeman, I can think of several issues that bother me with respect to our prison system in this state. But the main point I wanted to make about California prisons is this. Generally speaking, in our state, if a defendant is found guilty and sentenced to prison, he will only serve about half of his sentence because of the overcrowded system. That fact seems to hold true pretty much across the board. It doesn't really seem to matter whether it's a violent armed robber or a commercial burglar. In some instances, because of severe overpopulation of a particular prison, they'll even release inmates before they've served half of their time. And amazingly, police officers often run across parolees in the field who were paroled after serving little more than one third of their original sentence. Unbelievable, but true. Not much of a deterrent to crime, huh?" John asked.

He continued, "But on the bright side, I believe the pendulum is beginning to swing the other way. People are sick and tired of crime and politicians have been put on notice that public safety must be top priority. We've already seen some laws enhancing sentencing in certain situations. For example, there is now a gun enhancement. If a suspect uses a gun during the commission of crime, that theoretically adds a substantial period of time to his sentence if he is convicted. That's a good thing and hopefully, we'll continue to see improvement over the next few years," John said as he concluded his dissertation.

"Go on, John," Jenny said. "No, no more!" John said as he chuckled. "I don't want to talk anymore. Let's go take the kids somewhere. Or better yet, since we're taking them all to Disneyland tomorrow, maybe we ought to plan our trip and go shopping for any last minute supplies we might need." "Jenny, are your parents going to just meet us at Disneyland in the morning?" Marie asked. "I'm not sure. My mom said she'd call me today. When she does, we'll figure it out. But John's right. We do need to have a plan. Between us, we've got a lot of kids to keep track of. And John, just so you know, I still have a couple of questions for you," Jenny said with a smile. John responded, "Okay, let's get some things done today, and later in the evening, we can relax and talk about anything you want." "Sounds good," Jenny replied.

As he had promised, John answered the rest of Jenny's questions that evening as they sat and chatted. Early the following morning, Jenny's parents did meet them at Disneyland, and the families spent all day enjoying most everything the park had to offer. They stayed well into the evening, and the children continued to marvel at the fantasy world enhanced by thousands of lights. By the time they drove home late that night, all of the children had fallen asleep. Jenny's parents spent the night at her mom's friend's house once again, as she lived in the city of Anaheim, only minutes from Disneyland.

Mid-morning the following day, Jenny's parents arrived in the motor home and after everyone had feasted on an enormous breakfast prepared by Marie and Jenny, it was time to say farewell. The entire group spent several minutes exchanging hugs, well wishes and good-byes. Marie and Jenny cried as they hugged each other tightly and said their good-byes. It had been a great visit. Marie and John were very happy to have seen their good friend Jenny and her family after so long.

As for Jenny, the visit with the Nolans really helped her put things back into perspective. Upon returning home after vacationing with her children and her parents, Jenny took John's advice and went to lunch with Jim, the gentlemen she had told John and Marie about. She had a very pleasant time with him, and though it would be a very slow process, Jenny would finally begin enjoying life again.

Chapter Eleven

The Promotion

Shortly after Jenny's visit in that summer of 1986, Nolan was promoted to Sergeant. Although it is said to be difficult, the transition from police officer to sergeant did not seem to present any major hurdles for him. Nolan had been assigned as an "acting" sergeant or field supervisor countless times over the preceding several years in the absence of a regular sergeant, and he was accustomed to leading. He was respected, trusted and known for his sound decision-making. With his self-imposed high standards, his ability to get along with people and his years of experience, Nolan quickly established himself as an excellent supervisor.

Nolan was comfortable with his new job. He welcomed his new duties and responsibilities. He was responsible and held accountable for activity in the field on his assigned watch. He clearly understood that as a supervisor, he could be deemed vicariously liable for the actions of the officers assigned to his shift. Occasionally, Nolan worked in the station as watch commander, although he much preferred to be in the field.

Since he was a new sergeant, Nolan would have to pay his dues with respect to shift assignments. Consequently, he was assigned to the A.M. watch, also known as the graveyard shift. Some of his ancillary duties included scheduling the men and women on his watch, and overseeing their on-going training. But of course, his favorite role was being there for the officers in the field. In his mind, the most important role of the supervisor was to direct, teach, oversee and act as senior advisor to the officers in the field.

Nolan led by example. He was fair and consistent. Moreover, he demanded professionalism from the men and women with whom he worked. He used the daily briefing periods wisely and regularly left a few minutes at the end of each briefing to provide training and updates on the latest court decisions, officer safety issues, liability issues, and other topics relevant to officers assigned to work in the field. He almost always threw in a few pearls of wisdom, especially directed at the younger officers. "Remember, if you do it clean and do it right, you don't need to be overly concerned about getting beefed," he would tell them. "Just do your job as if the chief of police was there with you," and, "Always keep your mind and your body conditioned so that you're prepared for any situation you might encounter."

Unless he was assigned as the watch commander for a particular evening, Nolan spent the majority of his time in the field. Even though he'd already been a policeman for more than fifteen years, he still enjoyed being out on the street. One night, at about 3:00a.m., while driving through a large parking lot to the rear of the municipal courthouse, Nolan came upon something quite unusual. From a distance, he could see the silhouette of a large man pouring liquid out of what appeared to be a gasoline type canister. The man was hurriedly pouring and sloshing the contents of the can onto the hoods of the clearly marked Marshall's units that were all parked side by side in the lot.

Nolan immediately took action. He requested a back-up unit and drove toward the man. The man looked up and saw Nolan's unit approaching him. He reacted by tossing the gas can to the ground, and removing a cigarette lighter from his pocket. Before Nolan could reach him and bring his unit to a stop, the suspect lit the lighter and momentarily held it against the hood of the Marshall's car he had just finished dousing with the contents of the can. The hood of the unit immediately exploded into flames. The man then attempted to flee on foot.

By the time the arsonist was turning to run away from him, Nolan was getting out of his unit. He sprinted after the suspect and managed to tackle him within about thirty feet of the burning Marshall's unit. The suspect was big and strong, and he fought like a madman. As backup officers David Wong and Armando Calderon were arriving on the scene, they immediately called for the fire department because the unit was fully engulfed in flames. The officers also saw that their sergeant was rolling around on the ground with the suspect. They hurriedly ran to help Nolan subdue the suspect enough to get him handcuffed. The suspect screamed and yelled and exhibited incredible strength. He tossed one of the assisting police officers several feet in the air in an effort to get him off of him. As they were in the process of fighting, and attempting to subdue the suspect, Nolan initially thought he might have been under the influence of PCP.

Finally, after what seemed like a very long time, Nolan and the other two officers managed to get the suspect handcuffed. He continued to yell obscenities at the officers and kicked at them as they picked him up to get him into their unit for transportation to the station. Meanwhile, the fire department arrived and quickly extinguished the fire before it could spread to any of the other vehicles. However, the burned vehicle was obviously a total loss.

Sergeant Nolan and the other two officers were understandably tired. During the fight, each of them suffered an assortment of bruises and contusions. One officer's uniform pants were ripped on the knees as a result of the violent struggle and somehow, Nolan's watch was broken. The suspect had also sustained a number of minor injuries, ranging from a bloody lip to bruises and torn clothing. However, he remained combative even after arriving at the city jail. Because of that, jail personnel had to keep him isolated from everyone else until he was calm enough to be processed.

As part of his investigation, Nolan recovered the gas can and the cigarette lighter the suspect had used to start the unit on fire. He checked the other six units and determined that the suspect had doused four of them in the same manner he had doused the unit that burned. Nolan took detailed pictures of the scene and had the fire department hose down the remaining units to rid them of the gasoline the suspect had poured on the hoods. In addition, he had communications notify Marshall's headquarters of the incident.

There was an apartment building that overlooked the parking lot, however, even with all of the noise and activity that took place, no one came forward as a witness. Nolan returned to the station, and prior to handling the paperwork surrounding the arrest of the violent arsonist,

Nolan tried to talk to him. He had hoped to calm him, advise him of his rights and talk to him about what he had done that night. At the same time, he wanted to determine whether or not he was under the influence of PCP.

Even though the arsonist remained belligerent and uncooperative, Nolan saw no characteristic telltale indicators that would have led him to believe his suspect was under the influence of PCP. He knew that a violent mental patient and an agitated person under the influence of PCP were difficult to tell apart because their demeanor and behavior were very similar. And since there were no objective symptoms indicating the suspect was under the influence, Nolan suspected he was dealing with a troubled individual with serious mental problems.

Fortunately, the suspect had identification on him when he was arrested. His name was Angel Valenzuela. A records check quickly confirmed Nolan's suspicions. Not only did the thirty year-old Valenzuela have a long and violent criminal record, he had also spent years going in and out of mental institutions. Still, the bizarre act of torching Marshall's units seemed very unusual to Nolan.

Nolan was glad when morning came and his shift ended. He was bruised, tired and anxious to get home, take a shower and hit the sack. Marie knew he was exhausted and she let him sleep most of the day. From personal experience, she knew that when working the graveyard shift, sleep becomes a very precious commodity. She took the baby and went to her mom's house for part of the day, and when the girls got home from school, she made it a point to tell them to be very quiet so their dad could get some extra rest.

When he reported to work that evening, Nolan was surprised to learn that there had been quite a bit of attention paid to the arrest of the arsonist. Lieutenant Carter, assigned as the P.M. watch commander, called Nolan into his office to give him a briefing on what had transpired during the course of the day. "John, your arrest of that arsonist last night has drawn quite a bit of attention. It started late this morning with a phone call from the suspect's family. The mother apparently claimed her son is non-violent because he's been taking his medication," Carter briefed Sergeant Nolan.

"Later in the afternoon, the suspect's older brother, Miguel, called me to not only echo what his mother had said, but to also inform me that the family believes that we beat his brother because he's a Mexican." "Oh great," Nolan reacted. "He was angry, but I did manage to calm him down enough to have a half-way decent conversation with him," Carter added. "I asked him why he thought his brother was out and about at three o'clock in the morning and why it appeared he had some sort of vendetta against the Marshall's office. He had no answer for why his brother was out so late, but he did say that about two years ago, Angel was in custody in the lock-up at the courthouse awaiting arraignment on some type of assault charge. He remembered that his brother had complained about the way a deputy Marshall had talked to him. Miguel added that sometimes, little things seem to aggravate Angel, and he really didn't like that particular deputy marshall."

"He said that was two years ago?" Nolan asked. "Yeah." "Did you happen to ask what type of medication he takes and who sees to it that he takes it?" Nolan inquired further. "Yes I did. Angel lives with their mother, and in theory, she's the one who makes sure he takes his medication regularly. Miguel claimed he wasn't sure of the name of the medication."

"I read your report and I explained what happened out there. Miguel didn't believe our version of the story and insisted we'd beaten his brother because he's a Mexican. He told me we would be hearing from the family's attorney. My conversation with him ended shortly thereafter. Anyway, within an hour of my chat with Miguel, an attorney out of Stephen Simon's office called. Pretty interesting, huh?" "Are you talking about that parasitic, cop-hating attorney who makes his money by suing police departments and ripping off his own clients?" Nolan asked Carter. "Yup, that's right. And within two hours, Angel was bailed out." "Wow, Simon must really think there's lawsuit potential here," Nolan remarked. "Oh, I'm sure he sees dollar signs. If he didn't think he could line his pockets, he wouldn't have gotten involved in the case," Carter added.

"Did they make a complaint against me too?" Nolan asked. "Yes, of course they did. They have nothing to lose and everything to gain. In their minds, regardless of the outcome of the personnel complaint, it makes their lawsuit look better if they make a complaint. And as you know, if you're cleared of any wrongdoing, they'll claim there was a cover-up. But, if it's determined that you acted inappropriately, it'll serve to strengthen their lawsuit. So again, they have nothing to lose by filing a complaint. They see it as win - win situation.

Wong and Calderon are named in the complaint, but you did receive top billing," Carter explained. "This is sad," Nolan remarked. "We did absolutely nothing wrong. On the contrary, we did everything right, clean, and by the book." "John, everyone who knows you, knows you did nothing wrong. This is just the system at work. You and I both know the system, and we know it can be very unfair," Carter reassured Nolan. "Anyway, internal affairs will be talking to you pretty soon." "I'm not really worried about this," Nolan said. "Absolutely nothing was done wrong, and we *will* be exonerated. It's just irritating to know that even though we'll be cleared of any wrongdoing, the complaint will stay in each of our personnel files for a very long time."

"You know, I kinda miss the old days when even the crooks had some honor," Nolan sighed. "It seemed like there were far less of these bogus complaints against police officers. The bad guys and their attorneys didn't arbitrarily point the finger at the cops as part of their defense strategy." "Let's not forget lawsuits. We live in a sue-happy society and because of 'deep pockets,' it almost seems like the 'in thing' to sue public entities such as police departments," Carter added. Nolan responded, "Well, I see all of this as part of what I call *the demise of our society*. Take cops for example. I remember when a police officer's word was as good as gold. When the courts showed a specific tendency towards believing or giving the benefit of doubt to police officers. When society in general thought much more favorably of its protectors," Nolan said. "Yeah, I sure remember those days," Carter said as he recalled earlier times.

The lieutenant continued, "There seems to be much less respect in general by our society. Just look at our kids. When I was young and I went over to a friend's house, I always addressed his parents as Mr. or Mrs., and their last name. Nowadays, kids call their friends' parents by their first names!" "You're right," Nolan concurred, "But I don't think I'd label that as a lack of respect. I do think that as a society we've allowed our standards to slip. We've become far too permissive and lackadaisical. We've steadily done away with many of our existing traditions and protocols. As I see it, the main cause is a weakened family structure, combined with less caring and discipline. Many in our society have either failed to learn, or have forgotten the meaning of pride and honor. As a result, our previously high standards as a nation and a society are being eroded. And we're allowing it to happen."

"Look at our work force as an example. What's happened to pride in workmanship? Has it all but disappeared? A contractor builds a house and does a half-ass job, knowingly leaving crooked walls and other flaws. Or perhaps he gets away with using cheaper materials than called for in the specifications. Why? What happened to his integrity? Where is his personal and professional pride? Have we as a society exchanged doing the right and proper thing for getting as much of the almighty dollar as we can? Is this a contributing reason for the demise of our society? And what about the automotive industry? Why is it that we've lost the edge on quality and workmanship? Foreign automakers have all but taken that away from us. It used to be that if you wanted quality, you bought American. That's changing now. Companies like Honda, Toyota and Nissan have steadily chipped away at America's dominance in that arena."

"I'll say," Carter quipped. "Diehard patriots like you and me buy American cars, only to have more reliability problems than our neighbors who purchase Hondas and Toyotas. My American pickup truck is less than three months old. I've already been back to the dealership for several problems. And here's one that adds to your comment about pride in workmanship. I complained about a constant rattle in the driver's door, and I was standing there when the service guy removed the door panel. To my amazement, there was a Coke bottle and a plastic sandwich bag inside the door panel. Unbelievable, huh? The worst part was when the service guy said that was no big deal. He said that sort of thing happens all the time."

"That's exactly what I'm talking about," Nolan said. A lack of professional pride. And while all of these are disturbing issues, consider for a moment the way attorneys have manipulated and exploited this country and her people. Don't get me wrong. We do have many fine, honest lawyers in this state and in this country. And lest we forget, judges are all attorneys too. But I'm talking about the overabundance of attorneys we have, particularly in this state. In my opinion, it seems that too many of these attorneys are of questionable character, to say the least. They focus on finding new ways to exploit the system to make more money. Why do we have so many frivolous lawsuits? Attorneys. Who keeps lining their own pockets? Attorneys. Who has connections, power and strong lobbyists? Attorneys!"

"In California our car insurance prices are ridiculously high. A major reason for that is because insurance companies have to defend themselves against far too many frivolous lawsuits. For example: A motorist gently bumps into the car ahead of him or her. Neither vehicle sustains any damage and it's obvious no one was hurt. The driver of the vehicle that was struck seeks an attorney who in turn files a claim with the striking motorist's insurance company. Because of the plethora of lawsuits with which it must contend, the insurance company is willing to pay what they call a nuisance claim and give the attorney and his client a few thousand dollars to go away. Or, they can deny the claim altogether."

"If they deny the claim, more often than not, the attorneys representing the driver of the vehicle that was struck will sue. They'll claim injuries. 'Soft tissue damage' is what they call it. Of course a doctor or chiropractor aligned with the attorneys has been 'treating' their client for his so-called injuries and has built up a substantial medical bill. Everyone from the uninjured and lying motorist seeking to make a quick buck, to the attorneys representing him, to the so-called doctor or chiropractor treating him, to the judge hearing the case knows it's pure, unadulterated baloney. Yet, this scenario happens hundreds of times virtually every day in California. Our lawmakers know about it, and they allow it."

"The state of New York had the right idea. They passed a "no-fault" insurance law. The number of lawsuits has been drastically reduced. In fact, lawsuits are now considered an anomaly. Moreover, residents of that state are saving millions of dollars in lower insurance premiums. Their system is proven and it works. Why can't we get that done here? Because the attorneys groups and their lobbyists will not allow that to pass in this state and because we have more attorneys per capita in this state than any other state in this country. Pretty sad, wouldn't you say?" Nolan asked.

As he digested what Nolan had said, Carter simply shook his head in agreement. Nolan stood up and moved towards the closed office door. "Well, I guess I needed to vent a little. Thanks for telling me what's going on with this caper and for letting me vent," Nolan said. "No problem, John," Carter replied. "Oh, by the way, expect a commendation from the Marshall's office for your actions in the arrest of the arsonist," Carter said with a big smile. "Catch-22, huh Lieutenant?" Nolan laughed. "In the same caper I get beefed and commended," Nolan joked as he shook his head and left the lieutenant's office.

In the weeks that followed, Internal Affairs conducted their investigation and subsequently determined there was no culpability on the part of Sergeant Nolan or Officers Wong and Calderon. It was further determined that there was no merit to the complaint made by Angel Valenzuela and his attorneys. All three were cleared of any wrongdoing. However, the mere fact that the three lawmen had been the subject of a complaint would require the department to place the complaint and all of the accompanying investigative reports in their respective personnel files where they would be kept for several years.

In the interim, the criminal portion of the case had gone through its first phase, the preliminary hearing. At that hearing, the defendant's attorneys didn't offer much in the way of an affirmative defense as they apparently felt there would be sufficient evidence for their client to be "held to answer." And in fact, Angel Valenzuela was held to answer, his case set for trial in Superior Court a few weeks later.

Several days prior to the trial date, Susan Saldana, the deputy district attorney assigned the case, called the station to ask for a meeting with Nolan. The next day, Nolan met with Saldana in her office to discuss the various aspects of the case. The two knew each other from when Saldana was a D.D.A. in the municipal court. Nolan had had numerous cases with her and thought she was a very capable and thorough prosecutor. Similarly, Saldana liked Nolan because he was honest, professional, and he testified well.

"This is actually a pretty straightforward case, although it certainly would have been nice to have an independent witness," Saldana said. "I know that you and the other officers were beefed. Has all of that been resolved?" she asked. "Yes, all three of us were completely cleared. The whole thing was ridiculous anyway." "Agreed, but that's how Simon plays the game. As you know, he had subpoenaed all three of your personnel files under a 'duces tecum' subpoena to determine if you'd been the prior subject of an investigation or complaint involving allegations of excessive force or other mistreatment of the public. If there was some negative information in your personnel files he may have been able to use that to show a pattern or improper behavior, thus increasing his chances of swaying a jury's decision, or getting a large damage award in the inevitable civil trial."

"Much to his dismay, all three of your personnel files were clean. As I understand it, there were no complaints in your file, none in Calderon's, and Wong had received a written reprimand for some silly incident that occurred a couple of years ago. Nothing with which Simon can attack your reputations. I really enjoyed hearing that," Saldana grinned. "This trial is going to be a war between the good guys and that cop hating attorney representing his guilty client, isn't it?" Nolan asked. "Well, let me put it this way. Simon is a conniving, underhanded, establishment-hating attorney who prides himself on tarnishing peoples' good names. He routinely pushes the envelope and seems to enjoy angering judges. The state bar has suspended his license two or three times for unprofessional conduct, but he's found himself a niche suing police departments. I fully expect a battle out there. I just hope the judge keeps a lid on it because Simon can be very dramatic, and he has the ability to play jurors quite well."

Nolan remarked, "From what I know of him, it seems he generally uses the same M.O. Beef the cops. Hold a press conference and denounce their actions. File a claim with the appropriate city or county and then sue. I've also heard he even accuses police officers of being prejudiced against minorities even when there's no evidence to support that claim." "Yes, he's been known to do that. Remember, he plays jurors quite well and all he has to do is raise just a bit of doubt. If he's successful, his client is found not guilty. And of course, when he does prevail, that increases the likelihood of him winning a handsome money award in the inevitable lawsuit that follows the criminal trial," Saldana added. "Well, all I know is we're the good guys and we'll be telling the truth," Nolan said. "That's all you can do," Saldana replied.

Judge Holmstead seemed to grow impatient as juror selection took almost two full days to complete, but finally, the trial got underway. The prosecutor and the defense attorney each made short, but poignant opening statements to the jury. Then, the actual trial began. Called as the first prosecution witness, Nolan approached the witness stand, and as he had done hundreds of times over the preceding fifteen years, he raised his right hand as he swore the oath, "To tell the truth, the whole truth, and nothing but the truth, so help me God." After he was seated, Deputy District Attorney Susan Saldana, following the usual protocol for a police officer witness, had Nolan state his name, his occupation and his current assignment. Saldana then took him step by step through the entire arson incident, starting from his initial observation of the defendant and ending with the investigation and the gathering of physical evidence at the scene of the arson, following the violent confrontation between suspect and police during the arrest. Her direct examination was thorough and precise.

When she finished her direct examination of Sergeant Nolan, D.D.A. Saldana sat at the prosecution table while lead defense attorney Stephen Simon had the opportunity to cross-examine Sergeant Nolan.

Simon: "Sergeant Nolan, you testified that you first saw Mr. Valenzuela as you entered the parking lot to the rear of the municipal courthouse. Is that correct?"

Nolan: "Yes, that's correct."

Simon:	"You also estimated the distance at which you first observed Mr. Valenzuela as approximately 150 feet. Is that also correct?"
Nolan:	"That is correct, sir."
Simon:	"Were you able to clearly see Mr. Valenzuela's face at that point?"
Nolan:	"No, I wasn't."
Simon:	"Well Sergeant, tell us at what point were you able to clearly see Mr. Valenzuela? Was it when you tackled him and beat him?"
Saldana:	"Objection, Your Honor. Not only is Mr. Simon stating facts not in evidence, he is being confrontational with the witness while trying to suggest to the jury that the police beat the defendant."
Judge:	"Sustained. Mr. Simon, you have quite a reputation for being overly aggressive with law enforcement witnesses. I caution you... conduct yourself appropriately in this court. The jury will disregard Mr. Simon's innuendo alleging this witness beat or otherwise mistreated the defendant. Proceed, Mr. Simon."
Simon:	"Sorry, Your Honor. Sergeant, at what point were you able to clearly see my client's face?"
Nolan:	"I really couldn't see his face clearly until I got very close to him."

Simon: "So you didn't know then and you don't know now that the silhouette or shadow you first observed was Mr. Valenzuela. Isn't that correct?"

Nolan: "No sir, that is not correct. From the time I first noticed Mr. Valenzuela to the time he was handcuffed, I never took my eyes off of him and I never lost sight of him."

Simon: "And how is it that you were able to drive toward him and negotiate the curves and the parking dividers in that parking lot?" Do you expect the jury to believe you didn't look where you were going while you were driving?"

Nolan: "Well sir, I'm very familiar with that particular parking lot, its curves and parking dividers. Using my peripheral vision, I was able to keep driving as I focused on the defendant. I had a clear view of him at all times."

Simon: "You testified you saw a male subject pouring a liquid out of a gasoline type can or container. Is that correct?"

Nolan: "Yes."

Simon: "Do you know what that liquid was?"

Saldana: "Objection. Asked and answered during direct examination."

Judge: "Sustained."

Simon: "Alright then. Let's move ahead. When did you first address my client?"

Nolan: "As I was getting out of my car, he was in the process of turning to run away. We made eye contact for a brief moment.

I yelled for him to stop at least twice as I started to chase after him."

Simon: "Is that when you tackled him Sergeant?"

Nolan: "Yes."

Simon: "Sergeant, did you at any time strike Mr. Valenzuela?"

Nolan: "After I wrestled the defendant to the ground, a very violent struggle took place. During that struggle I talked to him, trying to convince him to stop resisting. I..."

Simon: "Just answer the question, Sergeant."

Nolan: "I was trying to explain, sir."

Simon: "It was a straightforward question. A simple yes or no will do."

Nolan: "Yes."

Simon: "Is that yes you struck him?"

Nolan: "Yes."

Simon: "Please explain why you found it necessary to strike Mr. Valenzuela and while you're at it, tell us about the arrival of the other two officers. Did you see them strike him too?"

Nolan: "When we were down on the ground I tried convincing the defendant to stop resisting. I ordered him to stop fighting several times—to no avail. He is big and strong, and he fought like a madman. Initially, it was a physical struggle. I was trying to get him into handcuffing position, but he was just too strong. Then, before any assistance arrived, he punched me in the chest and it hurt. When he pulled his arm back and clenched his fist to hit me again, I hit him as hard as I could, and I kept hitting him until back up arrived. My blows didn't seem to phase him. That caused me to become very concerned for my safety. Then, when Officers Wong and Calderon arrived, we continued to struggle with the defendant for what seemed like a very long time. He even threw Calderon off of him, not unlike a child tossing a teddy bear. Finally, between the three of us, we were able to overpower him enough to handcuff him."

Simon: "You mean to tell me that three strong police officers couldn't overpower Mr. Valenzuela?"

Nolan: "It took a long time for us to subdue him enough to handcuff him. He's very strong."

Simon: "When did you realize Mr. Valenzuela is Hispanic."

Saldana: "Objection, Your Honor. Mr. Simon is reaching into his bag of tricks again. The fact that the defendant is Hispanic has absolutely no relevancy to this case."

Judge: "Mr. Simon, what is it you are trying to accomplish by posing this question?"

Simon: "Your Honor, my client informed me that at some point during the time he was being manhandled and arrested by police, he heard one of the officers call him a 'stupid Mexican.' That statement infuriated him and caused him to become very upset with the police officers."

Saldana: "Your Honor, that's ridiculous. Mr. Simon is attempting to trigger the emotions of the jurors by making this false accusation."

Judge: "Come forward, both of you."

Judge Holmstead leaned forward from the bench and sternly admonished the two attorneys standing before him regarding appropriate courtroom behavior. As he glared at Mr. Simon, he informed him he would permit him to explore the possibility of a derogatory remark. However, he warned him to proceed with caution. "If you fail to heed my warning, sir, I will find you in contempt of this court. Is that clear?" Simon responded, "Perfectly." The judge then called a brief recess. Nolan stepped down from the witness stand and walked over to Saldana who had returned to the prosecution table. She turned to him and said, "Let's go for a walk—I need to get a cup of coffee."

"You're doing a great job on the stand. Simon recognizes the fact that you're a good witness. But, he did manage to introduce the idea that this poor defendant may have suffered a beating at the hands of police. Since your testimony in that area was strong, he's steered clear of that subject, for now at least." "I'm just telling it exactly the way it happened," Nolan said. "I know and I believe the jury knows it too. You're a very credible witness."

"Having said that, I can assure you Simon is going to launch an all out attack on you for the alleged racist remark." "There *was* no racist remark," Nolan said angrily. "I know. And he knows it too, but he also knows we've done well, and he has a lot of ground to make up. From a tactical point of view he really can't attack Calderon or Wong because they're both minorities. Couple that with the fact that you had the biggest role in this case, and the fact that you're white, he'll definitely reach into his bag of dirty tricks to attack your credibility," Saldana warned.

"Susan, so that you know, I'm married to a Mexican woman and my three kids are half Mexican, but I don't like to bring my family life into the public eye." Saldana thought for a moment and then said, "Well, maybe in this case you should reconsider. I mean, I could let Simon ramble on and on and let him make the attempt at convincing the jury you have something against Mexicans. Then, when he's finished, I'll ask you a simple question, and you can tell the jury what you just told me. More than likely, that will blow him right out of the water," Saldana smiled. "I'm really not very comfortable with that. Please don't bring my family into this unless there are no other options," Nolan asked of the savvy prosecutor. "Okay John, you have my word."

The bailiff announced court was back in session and Sergeant Nolan returned to the witness stand. The judge reminded him he was still under oath. "Yes, Your Honor," he replied.

Simon:	"Sergeant Nolan, how long have you worked in this area?
Nolan:	"Over fifteen years."
Simon:	"And in that time period have the demographics changed?"
Nolan:	"Yes."

Simon:	"Would you agree this area is now predominantly Hispanic and that Hispanics probably make up ninety percent of the population?"
Nolan:	"Yes. That would be a fair statement."
Simon:	"Does that bother you?"
Saldana:	"Objection, Your Honor."
Judge:	"Sustained. Last warning, Mr. Simon. Tread carefully."
Simon:	"Yes, Your Honor. I'll withdraw my last question. Sergeant, during the time of your so-called struggle to subdue Mr. Valenzuela, did you hear anyone call him any names?"
Nolan:	"No."
Simon:	"After the three of you had handcuffed Mr. Valenzuela, did you hear anyone call him any names?"
Nolan:	"No, I did not."
Simon:	"Sergeant, did you call Mr. Valenzuela a stupid Mexican?"
Nolan:	"Absolutely not."
Simon:	"No further questions."
Judge:	"Ms. Saldana, any re-direct?"
Saldana:	"Yes, Your Honor. Sergeant Nolan, would it be fair to say that many of your fellow police officers and other co-workers are Hispanic?"
Nolan:	"Yes, Ma'am."
Saldana:	"Have you ever been involved in any type of racial incident with any of them?"
Nolan:	"No, Ma'am."

Saldana: "In the many years you've worked this area has anyone ever accused you of being racist or otherwise anti-Hispanic or anti-minority?"

Nolan: "No."

Saldana: "Have you ever received any awards or commendations from Hispanic community leaders or Hispanic citizens?"

Nolan: "Yes, I have."

Saldana: "Sergeant, do you speak Spanish?"

Nolan: "Well, I'm not fluent, but I can get along well in the Spanish language."

Saldana: "Sergeant…"

Deputy District Attorney Saldana was just about to ask another question of Sergeant Nolan when court proceedings were interrupted by a loud noise. Saldana reacted by turning toward the source of the noise, and as she did, she saw that an older, well-dressed Hispanic woman had stumbled into the small swinging doors dividing the court audience area from the area enveloping the judge, jury and attorneys. It appeared the woman was attempting to approach the bailiff when one of the legs on her walker had somehow become entangled, causing her to stumble into the doors. The bailiff rushed over to the woman's aide. She whispered in the bailiff's ear. He, in turn, approached the judge.

Saldana was ready to resume her re-direct examination of Sergeant Nolan and was about to pose the question she had started before the loud noise startled her. However, after the bailiff spoke briefly to the judge, the judge asked both attorneys to approach the bench. "The elderly lady who nearly fell a moment ago says she has valuable information for the district attorney on this case. Ms. Saldana, have you ever seen or spoken to this woman before?" "No, your Honor," Saldana replied. "I'll call a short recess. Why don't you talk to her and see if she does in fact have information pertinent to this case." "Yes, your honor. I'll talk to her right away." "Your Honor, this is very unusual, and I'm afraid I'm going to have to object," Simon said angrily. "Mr. Simon, there's no need to be afraid," Judge Holmstead responded sarcastically. "And you can object all you want. The fact is, I've ordered the deputy district attorney to interview this woman, and that is precisely what is going to happen." "Your Honor, I insist..." "Mr. Simon, I've made my ruling," the judge snapped.

The attorneys returned to their respective tables and the judge announced a brief recess. When he stepped down off of the witness stand, Nolan asked Saldana what was going on. "That older lady might have some information on this case. Have you ever seen her before?" "No, never." "Alright. I need to go interview her, but you shouldn't be around when I do so." "No problem," Nolan said. "I'm gonna go get a soda or something cold to drink." "Okay. Just be back here in ten minutes." "I'll be here," he replied.

Saldana introduced herself to the older lady who responded, "My name is Dolores Garcia. I'm very pleased to meet you, young lady. I've been watching you during this trial. You're really very good." "Thank you, Dolores. Can you come with me?" Saldana asked. "I'd like to talk to you about this case. There's an interview room just down the hall."

"Yes, of course, I'll go with you. But please walk slowly. These old bones don't move very fast anymore," Dolores frowned in frustration.

Inside the interview room, Saldana helped Dolores get seated. "Judge Holmstead wanted me to talk to you. He said you may have some information regarding this case." "Yes, that's true. But first of all, I owe you and the police officers an apology for not coming forward sooner." "What do you mean?" the prosecutor asked. "Well, the night this happened I had trouble sleeping...my arthritis again. I had gotten up to take my medicine when I heard a strange noise outside my apartment window. My apartment overlooks the court parking lot where this entire incident occurred. I live on the third floor so I have a pretty good view of the lot. The Marshalls park their cars almost directly beneath my window."

"Until this incident, I felt a sense of security, knowing police cars were close by. I've lived here for over thirty years, and I can tell you this area has changed a great deal. It used to be so nice and pristine here. Unfortunately for me, I'm a widow and a retired schoolteacher on a small fixed income. I simply can't afford to move out of the area," she explained.

"Please go on, Dolores. I have to get back to the courtroom very soon," Saldana said, trying to hurry the charming and articulate senior citizen. "As I said, I heard a noise and I peeked outside my window. There I saw a big man, the defendant, pouring liquid out of a gasoline can, just like Sergeant Nolan said. I was about to call the police when I saw the police car driving up. Meanwhile, the man started one of the cars on fire. Then, Sergeant Nolan got out of his car and yelled for him to stop. The man ran and the sergeant caught up to him and brought him to the ground. They wrestled around, and I could hear the big man calling the sergeant names. He was screaming. The sergeant just kept telling him to stop fighting. Right after that the big man hit the sergeant a couple of times, and the sergeant punched him back."

"Finally, other officers got there and then they all struggled, trying to subdue that big man. The whole incident happened exactly the way Sergeant Nolan said it did. And by the way, my old bones don't move so fast, but when I have my glasses on I see perfectly and my hearing is still excellent." "Did you hear any of the policemen call Mr. Valenzuela a stupid Mexican?" Saldana asked. "I was just coming to that. The answer is no, I never heard any of the policemen say anything like that. My window was open because it was a warm evening. I heard everything. That big man has a very dirty mouth, but the policemen just kept telling him to stop fighting and to put his hands behind his back. They never called him any names whatsoever," Dolores said emphatically.

"What made you decide to come forward?" Saldana asked. "I'm glad you asked. At first, I was afraid to come forward. I was afraid to get involved. But, when I first read about this mess in the newspaper, and then I heard this attorney, Mr. Simon, lie when he talked to the television news reporters, I knew I had to do something. So I came to the trial to watch. I watched until I couldn't stand it anymore. The defendant is a giant piece of garbage, and his lawyer is a plain old liar," she said with authority.

"Dolores, would you be willing to testify in this matter?" "Yes, I'll testify, but I must tell you, I'm scared of what might happen when he gets out of jail," she said nervously. "I understand your concern," Saldana answered. "But listen young lady, you go ahead and put me on the witness stand," Dolores said confidently. "Okay Dolores," Saldana smiled.

The bailiff called the courtroom to order and once again Sergeant Nolan took the witness stand. "Your Honor, I have no further questions of Sergeant Nolan," Saldana announced. The judge looked over at Mr. Simon who replied, "No questions, Your Honor." Nolan was excused from the witness stand and Saldana called Dolores Garcia to testify. Saldana had Dolores explain what she had seen and heard from her apartment that night. Dolores did an excellent job on the witness stand. When it was his turn, Mr. Simon cross-examined her and, when he tried to trip her up, she stuck to her guns and actually ridiculed him. "I may be old, sir, but your tricky questions don't fool me," she said. "Your client burned that car and that's that." The judge looked over at Dolores and half-heartedly advised her to watch her comments while testifying. Nolan looked over at the jury box and saw several of the jurors smiling.

With defense motions and ensuing arguments, the proceeding dragged on for yet another half day, after which Susan Saldana and Stephen Simon delivered their respective and emotionally charged closing arguments. When it was all said and done, it took the jury only two hours to find Mr.

Valenzuela guilty as charged. In addition, the judge ordered him to pay restitution for the officers' torn uniforms and for replacement of Sergeant Nolan's broken watch. Nolan felt vindicated. He shook Saldana's hand and thanked her for doing an outstanding job. Then, he approached Dolores and graciously thanked her for making the decision to come forward.

In the fall of that year, Marie announced she was pregnant once again. Both she and John were jubilant, but they also agreed this would be their last child. The following year, Marie gave birth to a beautiful baby boy. They named him Joseph. John was elated about the newest addition to the family. He was a wonderful father whose greatest joy was being involved with the children. Their two daughters, Samantha and Kimberly, were active in dance classes and soccer. David, now a toddler, was quite a handful himself. With the newborn on board, John and Marie were busier than ever. The girls were old enough to lend a helping hand with their brothers, and their grandparents made regular appearances. Their help was greatly appreciated. It provided the opportunity for a bit of parental relaxation, especially for Marie.

Unfortunately, John's father died of a heart attack that year. As to be expected, John was distraught over his death. He and his father had always been close. Worse yet, after forty years of marriage, John's mom just couldn't deal with the loss of her beloved partner. Even though everyone in the family recognized this and made it a point to call her and spend time with her, John's mom withdrew more and more until finally, less than a year after her husband's death, Mrs. Nolan died of heart failure as well.

Once again, John was devastated for he and his mom were as close as a mother and son could be. John felt that once her husband passed away, his mom just didn't want to go on anymore. He would tell Marie, "It's as if she reached down inside of herself and turned herself off. Her spirit was broken. I believe she gave up on life and simply didn't want to live anymore."

As usual, Marie stood by her man. She helped him cope with the loss of both his parents in less than a year. She purposely engaged him in conversations in which they would reminisce about the fond memories and good times they had had with his mom and dad. John just seemed to feel better when they talked about them. He and Marie shared the belief that even though a loved one may be gone, if you think about them and talk about them, their spirit will live on.

The next few years passed rather quickly. Nolan took a two year assignment as a narcotics supervisor and oversaw the operation of a street crew. He and his crew specifically targeted "street" drug dealers. It didn't matter whether it was rock cocaine, heroin, methamphetamine, marijuana or any other illicit drug. If information was received or developed that indicated drugs were being peddled in the neighborhoods, the team went to work. They used informants, worked surveillance, made undercover buys and wrote a myriad of search warrants. They all put in long hours and worked very hard, but they also enjoyed great success. And, it was always gratifying to put a drug dealer in jail.

At the end of his commitment to narcotics, Sergeant Nolan was asked to remain for another two years. But alas, he declined the offer, opting instead to return to patrol. Working narcotics had been rewarding and fun, but because of the long hours, Nolan was forced to sacrifice much of his precious family time, and that caused him to have feelings of uneasiness and guilt. He lived for his family and preferred to have a more structured schedule. Besides, as had happened during other assignments that temporarily took him from the uniform division over the years, Nolan simply missed being out on the street in a black and white.

The start of the new decade found Nolan pondering the future. He was rapidly approaching the twenty year mark on the job and virtually all of his education, training and experience revolved around law enforcement. Though retirement was still several years off, Nolan felt compelled to at least think about what he would like to do after leaving police work. Marie consistently offered what she felt was a viable suggestion. "John, you enjoy teaching young people so much. For years, I've been telling you to go back to school. Why don't you go back now and finish up? You're less than a semester away from getting your bachelor's degree! While you're at it, get your teaching credential. That way, after you retire, you can teach at the college and university level."

Marie was right, of course. Her suggestion was practical and made complete sense. The fact is, Nolan really did enjoy teaching young people. So, already into his forties, Nolan made the decision to return to school. Within a relatively short period of time, he completed his

271

bachelor's degree and obtained a teaching credential. He even started working towards his master's degree.

As the twenty year mark in his career came and went, Nolan decided it was time to put his teaching credential to work. He wanted to be certain he would be happy as a teacher after retirement, and he also felt it would be advantageous to have some formal teaching experience prior to leaving law enforcement. He started teaching criminal law and patrol procedures two nights a week at a local junior college known for its first-rate administration of justice program. As the semester progressed, Nolan found that he not only received satisfaction from teaching, he actually looked forward to the evenings he taught classes. He was pleased that his level of enthusiasm for teaching remained high.

Nolan had reached a previously unequalled level of fulfillment in his life. First and foremost, his family life provided him with the greatest pleasure. As far as he was concerned, his beloved Marie was the quintessential matriarch. His opinion of her had never faltered, and he still thought of her as the epitome of womanhood. She was an absolutely superb wife, lover and companion. Moreover, she was the perfect mother to their four children, who were all very healthy and happy.

As for his professional life, Nolan was quite content. He felt that being a sergeant was the best job in the world. He was assigned to the uniform division supervising a fine group of police officers, and he loved being on the street with them. He also enjoyed flexibility in his work schedule, allowing him to continue teaching college classes a couple of nights per week. Because of his contentment, he disappointed some of his superiors when he chose not to attempt further promotion.

That didn't matter to Nolan. He knew he had between five and seven years left to go before retirement, and he wanted to finish his career on *his* terms doing what *he* loved most. But neither Nolan nor his colleagues could have known that a very dark and ominous cloud would soon engulf the city of Los Angeles and its surrounding communities. That cloud would prove to be the precursor to a catastrophic event.

Chapter Twelve

The Light At The End Of The Tunnel

The whole world came to know the name Rodney King. He was an ex-convict, paroled after having served a shortened sentence for robbery. One evening, while King was driving a motor vehicle, officers of the Los Angeles Police Department attempted to pull him over. King refused to stop, and a vehicular pursuit ensued. When the pursuit finally terminated, King, a big and strong man, failed to follow the instructions of police officers attempting to control the situation. By his strange behavior, it appeared to the officers that King was probably under the influence of alcohol or some type of drug.

As the situation intensified, the officers perceived that King's behavior was becoming more resistant and more aggressive. In response to this perceived threat, officers used a taser gun in an attempt to take the fight out of him. Used by police, a taser is a non-lethal weapon that utilizes electrical energy to temporarily incapacitate a violent or menacing individual. However, according to the officers' accounts of the incident, even after sustaining a taser shock, King continued to resist their efforts to arrest him. Then, they used their batons and forced him to comply. Ultimately, he was subdued and taken into custody.

From a nearby apartment window, a tenant used his video camera to record most of the incident as it unfolded. Later, he sold his recording to one of the local Los Angeles television stations. The station in turn broadcast the disturbing videotape and supplied all of the other news agencies with copies of it. In the resulting media frenzy, the videotape was aired repeatedly, and before very long, the entire country had seen the footage. Eventually, the tape was viewed all over the world.

Because of the video footage of the incident, the officers involved in this case were relieved of duty. Eventually, they stood trial for criminal charges stemming from their actions that night. The defense asked for and was granted a change of venue. The highly publicized case was moved to a Simi Valley (Ventura County, California) court. The jury found the three officers not guilty, and some in the African-American community saw this as white officers getting away with a criminal act of racism against Rodney King, an African-American.

The April 29, 1992 acquittal date of the three officers would prove to be one of the ugliest days in the history of the city of Los Angeles. Hours after the verdict, rioting began at the now infamous intersection of Florence and Normandie. Small groups of young African-American males vented their anger and frustration by attacking Hispanic and Caucasian people who happened to be in the area. These innocent victims were assaulted, beaten, and their property or cars vandalized.

Reginald Denny, a white truck driver, had the dubious distinction of becoming one of the first to be beaten. He was simply in the wrong place at the wrong time. He was physically pulled from his truck and viciously attacked. He nearly died as the result of the severity of his injuries.

Buildings and businesses also fell victim to the chaos. Rioters smashed windows, looted, burned, or otherwise destroyed whatever they chose as a target. Responding firefighters were met with violence to the extent that fire personnel had to have police escorts in order to respond to fire scenes with some degree of protection and personal safety. The skyline was filled with smoke and flames. There were so many fires that fire departments simply could not keep up with the demand for service. The entire city was in an uproar. The governor activated the National Guard, and the president ordered the U.S. Army to Los Angeles to assist in the restoration of order. The rest of this country, as well as the rest of the world, watched the rioting and looting on television. It was a very sad time for the city of Los Angeles and for many of the surrounding cities within Los Angeles County.

After what seemed like an eternity, but in reality was only a few days, order was restored, and people began to go about their daily lives once again. Army and National Guard elements were systematically withdrawn and an uncanny calm seemed to fall over the city for weeks thereafter. Notwithstanding the tragic and needless deaths that occurred during the rioting, thousands of lives were adversely affected. Millions of dollars in property were lost to looting, arson and other acts of vandalism. People were injured, lost their businesses, their jobs and their way of life. The devastation caused by this disastrous event was simply staggering.

Sergeant Nolan was saddened by the needless loss of life, the turmoil and the destruction that resulted from the two to three days of rioting. He believed that many social implications were brought to light as the result of the riot. Nolan also felt that some in the African-American community would reaffirm their belief that non-African-American police officers care little for them, their heritage or their culture, and that this event would further distance the community from the police officers sworn to protect it.

Ever the optimist, however, Nolan was convinced that the overwhelming majority of African-Americans realized that while relations were severely strained, the relationship between the police department and the community it serves is of paramount importance to both. He hoped that leaders of this segment of the community and all members of the police department would embrace the opportunity to restore, and in some cases, create a strong bond based on trust, understanding and mutual respect.

Nolan also knew the truth about the rioters and the looters. Many of them were not African-Americans. They were just plain criminal opportunists who took advantage of a tragic situation. They looted, destroyed and committed numerous other criminal acts. They could care less about Rodney King, the African-American community, or the police. Theirs was not an emotionally charged civil demonstration gone tragically wrong. They simply saw an opportunity to steal, act out of control and destroy without much fear of apprehension or punishment. In fact, a good number of the looters arrested by police were not even from the Los Angeles area. They had driven in from other parts of Southern California just for the opportunity to loot and pillage!

During the riot and its aftermath, the police department had gone to an emergency schedule. That meant that all vacations and all days off were cancelled, and the entire department rotated to a pre-arranged twelve-hour on, twelve-hour off shift. Because of that schedule, Nolan had been unable to teach his classes at the community college until regular scheduling was resumed. He missed teaching his students.

His return to the classroom was welcomed, and as to be expected, his students immediately pummeled him with scores of questions about the riot. Nolan was pleased that his young students realized the tremendous social impact of that horrible event. It remained the number one topic on everyone's mind for a long time. Nolan answered as many questions as he could and announced the class would have ample time to discuss the issue even further during future class sessions. But the idealistic students were most disheartened when they learned that a substantial number of individuals involved in the riot and looting had absolutely no loyalty to the apparent underlying cause of the upheaval.

Nolan told them about the criminal opportunists and other individuals who reportedly got caught up in the frenzy of the moment and decided it was okay to steal and destroy. He informed them that a number of the looters were interviewed, and it seemed that the majority of them echoed the same theme—"Everyone else was doing it, so I did it too!" Some psychologists would have you believe this is a form of "mob rule" mentality, wherein participants temporarily lose their own identity and follow the "mob," or in this case, the violent leaders, vandals and looters. Nolan told his students he didn't buy into that theory because decent people don't loot, steal or vandalize and responsible people don't do irresponsible things.

That statement brought about an argumentative response from one of his criminal law students, Miriam Hernandez. Miriam was an outspoken, self-proclaimed liberal whose goal was to become an attorney. At the start of the semester, Nolan had asked everyone to stand, introduce themselves and state their reason for taking the class. Most of the students enrolled in Nolan's criminal law class as well as other administration of justice classes because they planned on a career in law enforcement.

But when it was Miriam's turn, she boldly stated her reason for taking the class was to have the opportunity to challenge the laws of the land via the police officer instructor. This was understandable, as she made it known she aspired to become a famous defense attorney. Initially, she thought that Sergeant Nolan would be taken aback by her candor and aggressiveness.

She was wrong. Nolan welcomed her and taught her that it's okay to disagree, as long as one does so tactfully and respectfully. She knew the ground rules and adhered to them. She knew Nolan would not tolerate distasteful outbursts or class disruptions. He demanded that all of his students show respect and consideration for one another. He also mandated the use of a civil tongue while class was in session. Miriam frequently challenged her teacher on issues of law. Nolan enjoyed her challenges and felt the class learned more by being exposed to fruitful discussions of our laws.

In turn, Nolan challenged *all* of his students to think and reason. He sometimes strayed from the text and class syllabus by asking questions of his students such as, "Why do some in society succumb to perpetrating criminal acts?" He knew that over the years, psychologists and criminologists had written reams of paperwork on the subject, but he wanted his students to broaden, and yet at the same time, simplify their views. After all, crime analysis encompasses a plethora of subjects, and it is certainly not limited to an esoteric understanding by a chosen few holding PhD's and doctorates in the field.

Nolan had the pleasure of moderating some very interesting debates on the questions he posed to the class. After the students explored a topic, Nolan would give a simplified and broad-based answer to help them understand. On the topic of why some in society succumb to crime, he started by telling the students, "With very few exceptions, parental influence and a child's environment will decide how that child evolves into adulthood and fits into society. It is important to note that aside from those unfortunate souls who are mentally disturbed, there are some people born into this world who are just plain mean and evil. Luckily, their numbers are few."

"Therefore, for the purpose of this discussion, let's focus on the majority. As a general rule, when loving and caring parents devote themselves to raising their children by providing lots of love and a healthy, structured environment, their children are usually confident and well adjusted. Parents must also be role models who consistently teach their children the right and proper way to live life. Core values must be constantly reaffirmed. When children are raised in this manner, they usually evolve into decent, hardworking adults with all of the right character traits, values and morals bequeathed upon them by their parents."

Nolan paused for a moment and then asked for comments. Naturally, Miriam was the first to respond. "Does that mean you're saying that someone raised by a single or divorced parent, or someone who is poor and doesn't have the greatest of environments won't turn out right?" "No Miriam. That's not at all what I'm saying. There are untold numbers of individuals raised by one parent, or a grandparent or other relative who turn out just fine. And certainly, I can vouch for the 'poor' portion of your question. My family was very poor. But we did well. My parents always taught me the right way. So being poor and being raised by a single parent makes no difference. The bottom line is a child's learning process. Exposure to consistent and structured teaching flavored with lots of love, caring and strong core values. That's what makes good people happen."

Most in the class participated in that discussion and the general consensus seemed to be that without a loving and healthy environment, a child might be more apt to grow up and follow the wrong path. Nolan said, "Okay, now that we're pretty much in agreement on that point, I will tell you that when the child who *has* had the right upbringing becomes an adult, he or she can much more easily resist any temptation to deviate from doing the right and proper thing. It's the strong core values that keep them doing it right," Nolan emphasized.

Nolan ended that particular session by reminding the class, "Keep in mind that the purpose of this entire discussion was to focus on the family unit. The family is the single most influential aspect in a person's life. It sets the tone for a child's evolution into adulthood. When the family unit fails, more often than not, its individual members run the increased risk of failure as well. And many times when they fail, they turn to a life of crime and contribute further to the decay our society."

In addition to his criminal law class, Sergeant Nolan also taught a patrol procedures class at the college. He had taught the two classes every semester for a few years and he felt very comfortable in that role. The patrol procedures class was almost always made up exclusively of students who had their hearts set on a career in law enforcement. As with the criminal law class, Nolan was careful to fulfill the requirements of the course by adhering to the class syllabus, but he also enjoyed involving his students in group discussions of current events related to police work.

Such was the case in 1994, shortly after police pursued O.J. Simpson in his white Ford Bronco. Nolan asked the class for their reactions to the pursuit and the arrest. One student was surprised that there was so much media coverage. Another student couldn't believe so many people were waving Simpson on as if they were paying tribute to some type of hero! Yet another said she had difficulty dealing with the circus atmosphere surrounding the entire matter. But most of the students candidly admitted that whenever they had the opportunity to watch *any* pursuit that was being broadcast live on television, they did so and remained riveted to their seats, waiting for the inevitable ending... When the good guys to catch the bad guys.

Nolan decided to enhance the group discussion by offering some factual information. "Only in the last decade or so has there been so much media attention paid to vehicular pursuits. The fact is the high-speed pursuit has been an area of concern for police departments for decades. In the old days, when life seemed simpler, if someone decided to run, you chased him until you caught him—no matter what. Good must triumph over evil, and the police will chase the bad guy until they catch him, right?" Nolan asked. "Right!" several of the students exclaimed in unison.

"But tragically, many innocent people were being killed or maimed by fleeing suspects attempting to outrun the police officers hot on their trail," Nolan told his class. "Police departments across the nation began rewriting their pursuit policies with the intent of minimizing the likelihood of injury to innocent civilians, as well as police officers. Every police officer wants to protect lives and property in his or her community. The last thing any police officer wants to see is an innocent person being hurt or killed. So choices had to be made. When to chase and when not to chase," Nolan said.

"Our state legislature should follow through with serious mandatory prison sentences, not county jail time, for those convicted of evading arrest and driving with wanton disregard for public safety. The media would need to be a partner in getting the message out to the public, especially to those individuals who would contemplate running from the police to enjoy their twisted moment of glory. That might help to put a dent in the amount of carnage these people cause."

"And speaking of the media, it's the media that has brought about attention and sensationalism to pursuits in the past ten or so years. Starting in the mid 1980's, more and more television stations in the Los Angeles area began contracting for helicopter services. Some stations even purchased or leased their own helicopters and hired their own pilots to fly them. Always looking for a story, these reporters in the sky focused their attention on the activities of police and fire air operations. In the constant war over ratings, station management saw this as a way to not only maintain ratings, but to significantly bolster them as well."

"By using scanners and other information sources, airborne reporters almost always knew when a police helicopter was being requested to assist ground units in a pursuit. Getting airborne quickly and flying well above the police helicopters, these "TV birds" were able to provide excellent live footage of the drama unfolding hundreds and sometimes thousands of feet below them. After all, they were equipped with the finest on-board camera equipment money could buy. The feedback received by television station managers and news directors was that the public loved this stuff."

"But what really reaffirmed and solidified the airborne news reporter's gig was the recent coverage of the O.J. Simpson pursuit. A new media phenomenon has been born. The televised, live action, high-speed pursuit. This television phenomenon will only continue, because as humans, we get caught up in the intrigue and the excitement of the chase. We can't help it. We know we're watching live, true-life drama taking place before our very eyes. We're rooting for our side and we want to see the ultimate conclusion." Nolan told them. "Television station managers know the viewing public craves this type of reporting, and because of that, many stations will provide full coverage of a pursuit and interrupt, or pre-empt other shows just to keep their live-action cameras on the vehicle being pursued," Nolan told his students as he concluded that particular class session.

Nolan derived pleasure out of seeing his students' faces light up as they learned. He viewed his role as a teacher as much more than just a part-time job. He saw it as an opportunity to help students grow. He was helpful and provided guidance to them when it was appropriate. Marie had been right. He did like to teach young people, and he took pride in having a positive impact on their lives.

Reflecting on his own children, Nolan always felt he and Marie had been blessed. All four of their children were healthy, wonderful people, each with their own distinct personality traits. But they all shared the same strong core values and morals he and Marie had instilled in them. Samantha, the oldest, was a very beautiful, but quiet young woman. She lived at home, attended college and worked as a teller in a local bank. She wanted to obtain her bachelor's degree and continue with the bank in a management program. Her long-term goal was to earn her master's degree and then move on to a more lucrative job.

Kimberly was in high school and was quickly evolving into a stunning, blue-eyed beauty. She was into gymnastics, dance classes and borrowing her parents' cars. She loved to laugh and was the practical joker of the family. Both girls were kind and considerate and helped out around the house, easing Marie's burden. They were very close to their mom, and quite often, the three of them shopped together at the mall. John and Marie were very proud of their girls.

David and Joseph attended school and both did very well academically. Each of them was in an advanced reading curriculum for his grade. Both boys liked school, and they were just plain happy, well-adjusted kids. They played all kinds of team sports including soccer, baseball and basketball. But their greatest enjoyment was martial arts. They were in classes together and practiced at home together.

The boys particularly liked double-teaming their father in mach sparring matches. Nolan loved spending time with them, laughing and playing as if he were a kid himself. Marie liked to watch the three of them cavort and play around. She would smile and tell John, "The girls seem to keep adding to your gray hair, while the boys are keeping you young at heart."

Marie decided to return to work part-time after a hiatus that lasted too many years. The girls were grown and the boys were in school all day. Aside from that, they were at an age where they didn't need constant attention. Besides, between John, the girls and Marie's parents, there was always someone to pick them up from school and look after them until either she or John got home from work. She missed her job as a surgical nurse and she was happy to return to her chosen field, if only part-time.

As for Nolan, he still enjoyed his job, but he also admitted he was looking forward to retirement, which for him was right around the corner. All of the "old-timers" he had spent years working with were retired and gone. He did, however, stay in touch with Sergeant Rosenthal, Lieutenant Carter, "Gonz" and a few others. While one or two confessed they missed the job from time to time, most agreed retirement was a good thing, as long as there was something to keep you occupied after a lifetime of carrying a badge.

Steve Villanueva, Nolan's friend and former trainee, had recently made sergeant, and Nolan was very happy for him. Steve and Alicia had also just celebrated the birth of their second child. They had asked Nolan to be Godfather to this one too. Though Alicia was on maternity leave, she remained assigned to detectives as she had been for several years. Steve worked alongside Nolan in patrol several times per month. They like working with one another and they had shared some great memories over the years.

But Villanueva was in a bit of a quandary. He faced a set of circumstances similar to what Nolan had experienced years earlier. Villanueva turned to his old teacher and asked, "Hey John, I need to talk to you about dope," he smiled. Nolan grinned and responded, "About being a dope, or working dope?" he asked sarcastically. Villanueva laughed, "No, old man, I'm talking about working dope. I was offered the opportunity to supervise a street crew like you did years ago. What do you think?" he asked. "Are you asking about the assignment itself or the home life that goes along with it?" Nolan inquired. "Both." "Well, I'll tell you. I had a great time working dope. I had a good crew, we all hustled, and it was fun putting dope dealers in jail. I really enjoyed the work."

"On the other hand, my home life suffered because of that assignment. More often than not, there was too much overtime. It was either another case, an assignment to help out another team, a surveillance operation, or some other pressing assignment that kept me from getting off of work on time. I didn't see enough of my family for the two years I worked dope. And that part got real old, Steve," he told his friend.

"Yeah, I thought about all that, but I'm still excited about it, and I really want to do it. Alicia said she'd go along with whatever I decide." "It's a great gig, but it has to come at a time in your life when you *and* your family can deal with it," Nolan advised. "I'm probably gonna go ahead and do it," Villanueva smiled. "Good for you, man. I know you'll do a great job."

As he had decided years earlier, Sergeant Nolan was content to finish out his time working patrol. He was a "short-timer" now, but as far as he was concerned, he still had the best job in the world. He checked in with the retirement board and verified the benefits he had worked so hard to earn over the years. When he calculated his future pension income and added his salary for his part-time teaching job at the college, Nolan felt satisfied there would be enough to continue to properly care for his family. And, in order to build up their savings, Marie had expressed a desire to transition to a full forty-hour schedule for a few years after John retired.

Even though daughters Samantha and Kimberly lived at home, they were working adults who bought their own clothes and personal items. What concerned John and Marie was the fact that their two boys were rapidly approaching the expensive teen years, which would then be followed by the even more expensive college years.

But as 1998 rolled around, John and Marie finalized their decision for him to "pull the pin" and retire. He was fifty years old and he had long since reached the pinnacle of his law enforcement career. More importantly, John felt comfortable with the timing. He was content and looked forward to his retirement. While making personal reflections on his career, he felt pride and satisfaction for having had the privilege of serving as one of society's protectors for more than two and a half decades.

As they had traditionally done for countless retirees before him, the police officer's association planned a retirement party for Sergeant Nolan. It was a gala event that took place in the ballroom of one of the more prestigious hotels in the area. Nolan was honored by the number of people who attended, and the well wishes they bestowed upon him.

A few of the senior police department officials even took turns addressing the audience for the purpose of recapping some of Nolan's many accomplishments during the course of his distinguished career. But Nolan's biggest joy came when a number of the people he had supervised over the years paid tribute to him regarding his integrity, his honor and his ability to lead and get the job done professionally.

The retirement party proved to be a wonderful celebration and a memory Nolan would cherish as long as he lived. And so it was that John Nolan completed his career in law enforcement. Contrary to many Hollywood versions of police work, he didn't go out in a blazing gun battle. Instead, he served honorably for two and a half decades and retired with a sold gold reputation.

But never one to rest on his laurels, Nolan acquired another teaching assignment within a month of his retirement, bringing the number of administration of justice classes he taught each week to three. Though he had been teaching regularly for a number of years, he still found it exciting to play a role in the education of young people. He also took pleasure in facilitating and moderating classroom discussions regarding important current issues that related to law enforcement. He liked the spontaneity of the impromptu, and sometimes heated debates.

When the news surrounding Rafael Perez first broke, the allegation was that by using trickery and deceit, he had managed to check out and then steal several kilos of cocaine from a police department evidence locker. Subsequently, in August of 1998, the one-time police officer was arrested for the theft of the drugs, and after a second trial, he was found guilty. As if that wasn't enough to collectively tarnish every local police officer's badge, Perez soon struck a deal with senior officials of the police department and the district attorney's office to supply detailed information about alleged horrific wrongdoing at the LAPD's Rampart Division. Perez would provide this information in exchange for a lighter sentence, as well as immunity from prosecution for his involvement in the alleged criminal acts he was about to disclose.

Naturally, the news media stayed on top of this widening investigation day after day and week after week. By this time, the media had also come up with a name for the nightmarish and seemingly endless story. It came to be known as the "LAPD Corruption Scandal," the worst scandal in the history of the department. As one might imagine, an honorably retired police officer like Nolan was absolutely appalled regarding the entire ordeal. His young students, most of them aspiring to become police officers, were astounded and disgusted as well. The investigation and its far-reaching ramifications were discussed at virtually every class session Nolan taught.

At one such class session, Nolan initiated the conversation and stimulated the students by making a profound statement. "My biggest concern is for the people of Los Angeles and its surrounding communities. As this investigation continues to unfold, it will be the citizens who suffer the most. A police department is supposed to instill confidence, trust and professionalism in the community it serves. How can people believe and trust their police department when it appears the police are not worthy of that trust?"

Michael, one of the students, raised his hand immediately, and when Nolan acknowledged him he commented, "But it's not the entire police department. There are only a few who have done wrong," he argued. Next, Marilyn raised her hand and said, "The news media keeps attacking the police department because of the shameful actions of a few officers. Why isn't the media talking about all the good things police officers do on a daily basis?"

Nolan replied, "Well, both of you have made excellent points. First, the media issue with respect to the news. Television stations, both network and independents, giant newspaper conglomerates, as well as radio stations, have to "sell" their product, in this case, the news. Ratings, public opinion, readership and advertising dollars keep these businesses alive and thriving. And television is probably the number one source of news information for most people. Celebrity status reporters, dramatic reporting, sensationalism, and detailed coverage of controversial issues help to keep ratings high. There are a few channels, and a few news reporters who are very pro-police, however, as we all know, when police are accused of some wrongdoing, or they allegedly make a mistake, it's huge news and lots of airtime is devoted to developing the story."

"But when a policeman is hurt or killed, or saves a life, not nearly as much attention is given that story. And that really is a shame, because it's the media that tends to influence the way we all think. Whether we realize it or not, their selection of stories to be covered, and their method of reporting definitely influences our beliefs and opinions. A reporter can essentially put whatever twist he or she wants to put on a story by omitting certain facts, by interviewing only individuals with certain pre-determined opinions, or by adding his or her own perceptions or opinions themselves, as they sum up the story. But I'm with you, Marilyn. I, too, would like to see more positive reporting about all the great things police officers do day in, and day out."

"As to your comment, Michael, you were right on. But let's explore that concept a bit further. It would seem that through his attorneys, Rafael Perez has made a significant deal with high-ranking police officials and their counterparts at the district attorney's office. 'Quid Pro Quo' is the legal term. It simply means something in exchange for something. In this case, the convicted drug thief negotiated successfully and substantially reduced the amount of time he'll spend behind bars by trading important information for that reduced sentence."

"But Perez lost all of his credibility when he stole, when he lied, and when he cheated. And in my book, there isn't too much worse than a dirty cop. Here's a guy who swore an oath to serve and protect the community, a fellow who was supposed to have strong morals and strong values. He was entrusted with authority and discretionary power, and he flagrantly and deliberately abused that power. The fact that he's serving a very short sentence for his crimes is an insult to every honest, hard-working police officer."

"And that brings me to my next point. In a perfect world, no undesirables would ever make it through the testing procedure to become police officers. However, as long as we have to recruit from the human race, occasionally an undesirable will slip through the cracks. But, if we have a system of checks and balances in place, we can deal with questionable individuals who make it through the hiring procedure and get hired as police officers. That's why there is such a long probationary period. It's currently eighteen months, including academy time. During that time, training officers, supervisors and managers can examine and evaluate an individual's performance over an extended period of time. If an undesirable makes it through the process and successfully passes the probationary period, the next line of defense against the potential undesirable officer is the supervisor, or sergeant."

"Take Perez as an example. It's difficult for me to understand how his supervisors apparently failed to recognize a problem with him. But if one or more supervisors did recognize a potential problem and failed to deal with it, shame on them. If a sergeant somewhere along the line knew of inappropriate behavior by Perez and failed to take immediate corrective action, that sergeant sent the wrong message."

"In effect, that sergeant essentially condoned Perez' behavior as well as his deeds. On Perez' next jaunt to the other side, he may have upped the ante and strayed further from department policy and the laws of our state. And again, if his supervisors turned the other cheek, thereby condoning and approving his behavior, an individual such as Perez may have eventually felt invincible or untouchable. That would only bolster his ego and encourage additional unlawful or inappropriate behavior."

"Perez has supplied dates and incidents and has alleged illegal and immoral behavior that included other officers as well as himself. Of course, any information he supplied should have been looked upon very carefully since Perez has proven himself to be a liar and a cheat. But even if all of the accusatory allegations Rafael Perez directed at prior fellow officers with whom he worked were corroborated and proven accurate, the number is very small."

"The fact is, it's probably less than one percent of the entire police department. Obviously, that is still unacceptable. No police officer should ever engage in wrongdoing. However, the media and the public tend to stereotype and paint others with a wide brush. It's time for all of us to speak up for the more than ninety-nine percent of hardworking, honest, decent cops who have dedicated their lives to making our society a better place. They are truly society's protectors, and they deserve our thanks and recognition. This scandal, as it has come to be known, has severely damaged the trust that the community had for the department."

"And with respect to the damage done to the reputation of the Los Angeles Police Department, the 1992 Los Angeles riot pales by comparison to this nightmare. But when it's all said and done, the remedy is the same. Each and every officer will have to work very hard to restore that trust and faith. I believe they can do it and it has to be done. The community will also have to do its share to restore a strong bond. Time moves on and, eventually, time will heal the wound," Nolan said as he concluded his lecture.

And of course, time moves on for all of us. John and Marie planned to work hard and save for a few more years before finally and completely retiring. All four of their children were doing very well, and as always, they provided happiness and fulfillment for their parents. The love affair between John and Marie had never waned, and they looked forward to growing old together.

Despite the fact that many years had passed since Marie said anything about it, John remembered she had expressed a strong desire to one day do some traveling in her very own motor home. John never forgot that. He found an exceptional deal on a near new motor home and surprised Marie by buying it for her. She loved it and immediately set about planning a family vacation.

Shortly thereafter, John and Marie took the entire family, including their dogs, on a three-week tour of the western portion of their beloved United States. Aside from visiting many of the usual tourist spots, they also stopped in Oregon to visit with Jenny Winters and her family. They were happy to find that the Winters family was getting along just fine.

Though she never remarried, Jenny was still involved in a long-term relationship with the man she had told the Nolans about years earlier during her visit. She seemed happy, but the Nolans knew that Jenny never really recovered from the violent and untimely death of her husband.

Back on the road, after their visit with Jenny, Marie and John had a long conversation in which they reminisced about the old days. Their children listened intently as their parents described life in the early days of their relationship. Though they had heard most all of the stories numerous times over the years, the Nolan children seemed to enjoy hearing them again as much as their parents enjoyed talking about them.

That's when Marie came up with an idea for John. "Why don't you write a book that chronicles your life and experiences both as a policeman and as a family man?" she suggested. "What? Me write a book?" he asked in amazement. The children strongly agreed with their mom and encouraged him to listen to her. John offered no immediate response. Instead, he drove in silence for several minutes, pondering Marie's suggestion. Finally, with an almost sheepish grin on his face he quipped, "You know, maybe you guys are right. Maybe I will write a book …"

Epilogue

Twenty-one months later ...

The Los Angeles Police Department was on the road to recovery. All of the investigations surrounding the worst scandal in the LAPD's history had finally been completed. New policies and directives were in place, written in compliance with federal mandates. Morale was improving and once again, police officers began to feel pride in the department. Similarly, the community as a whole commenced the renewal of faith and trust in their police department.

Nolan wrote his book and told the stories of many of his street experiences. He explored the age-old question of why certain individuals in society turn to a life of crime. He examined the myths as well as some of the statistical data surrounding that issue. Nolan readily admitted there was no clear-cut answer. He explained that while criminals may share similarities in their evolution as criminal types, even the most learned criminologists cannot offer a definitive and all-encompassing answer as to the reasons an individual chooses a life of crime. There are simply too many variables.

Nolan enjoyed his writing experience and went on to write another novel about police work. His goal was twofold. He wanted to satiate his readers' quest for exciting "police action," but more importantly, he felt compelled to remind readers of the importance of the law enforcement officer's role in our society.   Throughout history, virtually every successful society or culture had "protectors" of one form or another. Nolan wanted his readers to realize that in these often tumultuous times, as our society leaps ahead into the 21st century, we must recognize that the urgency of our protectors' mission is greater and more demanding than *ever* before.

About the Author

"Jonathan Nerlinger is a retired twenty-five year veteran police officer from the Los Angeles area. Having risen through the ranks and achieved the rank of lieutenant, Nerlinger understands, and has experienced, most aspects of police work. He feels privileged to have enjoyed a number of exciting and rewarding assignments during his career. Prior to his promotions, some of those assignments included; Patrol, Training Officer, K-9 Handler and Detective in the Robbery / Homicide unit.

After his promotion to sergeant, and as an experienced helicopter pilot, Nerlinger was assigned to a multi-jurisdictional narcotics task force as a surveillance helicopter pilot and supervisor of air operations. The task force included officers and agents from municipal, state and federal agencies. Several years later, Nerlinger was promoted to lieutenant, and he was responsible for a plethora of managerial duties. He worked as a "watch commander," managed and coordinated an element of a multi-agency gang task force, managed the helicopter section and oversaw numerous other administrative functions vital to the police department.

During his career, Nerlinger received many awards and commendations, including a commendation from the F.B.I. for the apprehension of bank robbers wanted in connection with a string of robberies, and a commendation from the Chief of Police for his role in solving a difficult homicide with very few leads.

The United States Army commended him for his role in assisting them in the 1992 Los Angeles riot, and at his retirement celebration, the Chief of Police presented Lieutenant Nerlinger with the Medal of Distinction. The accompanying citation praised him for his dedication and his numerous accomplishments for both the police department as well as for the community.

In addition, then California Governor Pete Wilson and State Attorney General Dan Lungren sent their praise and thanks in personal letters to Lieutenant Nerlinger for his contributions to law enforcement and the communities he served throughout his career.

Mr. Nerlinger feels compelled to write and share his experience about the subject he knows best …police work. Although 'True Blue—A Policeman's Story' is written as fiction, every reference to law, police procedure and protocol is precise and accurate."

Printed in the United States
2303

9 780759 659834